Song of the Fallen

Keith McArdle

ISBN-13: 978-0-9925657-7-0

Cover design by Pen Astridge.
Edited by Amanda J. Spedding.

Connect with Keith online:
Facebook: https://www.facebook.com/KeithAuthor
Twitter: https://twitter.com/KeithAuthor
Website:http://www.keithmcardle.com

A catalogue record for this book is available from the National Library of Australia

NATIONAL LIBRARY OF AUSTRALIA

For Jorge

"Rise up, warriors, take your stand at one another's sides, our feet set wide and rooted like oaks in the ground…learn to love death's ink-black shadow as much as you love the light of dawn." - **Tyrtaeus**

Trigger Warning: This novel contains graphic violence, memories of rape and attempted rape.

I

Late morning – fourth day of the siege

Tork urged Might into a walk, and the thousand King's Own followed. The Huronian Cavalry might not carry flintlock weapons but their numbers combined with the open field of battle were their greatest assets. Yet if Tork made even a small mistake in the placement or formation of his unit, the enemy would exploit it with devastating effect. He nudged the destrier into a trot. Might snorted and accelerated. To his left came the soft creak of leather as a soldier adjusted himself in the saddle. A warrior cleared his throat behind Tork and all around him was the faint aroma of horse sweat. The soft rumble behind him told Tork his warriors had accelerated with him.

He raised his visor and leaned across in his saddle. "Roland!"

The bugler looked across at him.

"We're going to flank them with a steep hook left."

"Understood, sir."

A deep staccato of mortar fire roared to life. The huge balls of shot streaked through the sky, arching high over Tork's head with powerful crackles. They were bound for Lisfort but he returned his attention to the matters at hand.

It'd been at least a year since Tork had issued the command for the manoeuvre, and even then, it was during training. The last time he'd used the tactic on the field of battle was as a young officer. Squeezing his thighs, he encouraged Might into a canter straight towards the enemy cavalry, which numbered at least five thousand. They galloped towards the King's Own, closing the gap with blistering speed.

He slammed the visor down over his field of vision and raised his arm high, and with a tap to Might's flank, the horse leapt into a gallop as Tork brought his arm down. The King's Own accelerated into a charge, the soft rumble of hooves now akin to thunder.

Might stretched out with each stride, the ground sliding by beneath them. The enemy force filled his entire vision. Where moments before they had been nothing more than a brown smudge advancing towards Tork, individual horses and riders were now clearly visible. The soldiers were shouting and screaming, but the noise of hooves and his own rasping breath inside the enclosed helmet drowned most of it out.

Another twenty seconds...

He turned to Roland. "At the canter!"

The bugle pierced the storm of noise, and the King's Own slowed.

"At the trot!"

They continued to slow their advance.

"Face left!"

The left flank became the front, and the small force moved sideways to their oncoming enemy.

"At the gallop!"

Even as the bugle blast faded away, the thunder of hooves stifled all else out. Tork flicked his visor up for a clearer view. The Huronian Cavalry had slowed, unsure of how to proceed. A small group of some five hundred strong broke away from the main force and diverted towards Tork.

Good.

"Face right!"

Roland lifted the bugle to his lips and gave the command. The King's Own complied, but slower than when changing direction at the speed of a trot. The small Huronian force chasing them was now headed towards Tork's right flank.

"Face right! Arrowhead! Muskets!"

The Huronians wielded spears, advancing at a full charge. Tork gripped the cold barrel of his musket and dragged it clear of the leather holster forward of his right knee. Tork clenched his thighs against Might's body, released the reins, and pulled the musket's buttstock into his shoulder.

"Fire!"

The musket bucked against his shoulder a moment before the bugle blast cut across the field of battle. A thousand muskets crackled, creating a smoke screen in front of the charging King's Own formation. The acrid blanket of burned gun powder was soon behind them while ahead, hundreds of enemy cavalry were down – dead or dying.

"Blunderbuss!"

Tork dropped his musket in the holster, withdrew his blunderbuss and pulled it into his shoulder. Only fleeting seconds passed before the other soldiers under Tork's command had their blunderbusses aimed and ready. The vacant area of ground separating the two forces diminished with each hoof beat.

"Fire!"

The weapon punched against his shoulder. A deafening disgorge exploded, screaming from the maws of a thousand blunderbusses. The remaining group of Huronian Cavalry who'd split from the main charge were wiped out. Men and horses alike left bleeding upon the dirt.

"Spears!"

Tork holstered his blunderbuss and took up his spear. He could only look on as the right flank of the King's Own arrow formation battered through the enemy remnants. None of the Huronian charge were left alive in front of him, and soon none were left alive at all.

"Halt!"

The King's Own charge decelerated. Sweat glistened from the flanks of the horses, they snorted and stamped the ground. The main Huronian charge now faced them and were approaching in the distance. Tork estimated his force had another few minutes at their disposal.

"Reload!"

The warriors of the King's Own moved with fluid, confident precision. Both muskets and blunderbusses were reloaded in rapid succession then reholstered. Tork leaned down and patted Might's neck. "Good lad," he muttered.

Another volley of mortar fire spoke. The crackling rounds cut the sky in his peripheral vision, but Tork did not watch their fall of shot. He was certain, though, that one round flew in the opposite direction to the others.

He straightened in his saddle and clenched the reins. The Huronian Cavalry charge were closing the distance, their powerful war horses chewing through the ground separating the two units in breathtaking fashion.

Tork stretched his back. "Right flank, break right! Left flank, break left! Join at rear!"

The bugle rang out, Roland blasting each command with careful practice. Tork swung Might to the left and nudged the powerful animal into a gallop; Roland followed closely. The arrow formation split asunder, spearing left and right. He allowed Might his head. Tork Cast a glance over his shoulder he took in the enemy charge. They were slowing, again unsure of how to proceed now their adversary had dispersed before them like smoke.

Slotting Might in at the rear of the column hammering along the flank of the Huronian blob, Tork noticed for the first time the bright blue flash painted onto the rump of the animals.

They're not Huronian Cavalry. They're mercenaries!

Cavalry mounts were unmarked aside from a brand on their neck depicting their year of birth and from which stud they hailed.

When the front of Tork's column passed the far flank of their enemy, they turned in a gentle wheel to their right.

"Come on, Might, have at it, lad!"

Tork nudged the destrier on and the powerful animal stretched out, streaking down the inside of the column towards the front. What had once been the opposing flank of the arrowhead formation were advancing towards him from the opposite direction.

"Arrowhead formation!"

Roland's bugle sang and the two columns turned in toward one another, once more forming the arrowhead, this time facing the rear of their enemy. The throng of mercenary cavalry were still arrayed in confusion. Some of them turned to face the threat at their back, while many others were still unaware of what was taking place.

"Canter!"

Tired horses pushed on into a canter and the few mounted enemy aware of the oncoming King's Own force urged their horses to walk backwards until they had nowhere else to go. Others kicked their mounts and fled the field of battle.

"Charge!"

The destriers gathered their strength and entered the gallop once more, hooves thudding upon the soft ground.

"Muskets!"

Tork's hand closed upon the still warm barrel of his musket and dragged the weapon clear. His master eye staring down the sights. Another fifty yards and they would plough through the ranks of their enemy. He clenched his index finger upon the trigger.

"Fire!"

The weapon bucked in his shoulder and a cloud of bitter, burnt gunpowder surrounded him for a split second. Then Might was beyond it, barrelling straight for a wide-eyed mercenary trying to force his way deeper into the ranks of his comrades and away from the closing King's Own.

"Blunderbuss!"

He exchanged musket for blunderbuss, and squeezed the trigger. At this distance, aiming was not required.

"Fire!"

The kick of the weapon pushed him back in the saddle, his arse sliding along the leather a few inches.

"Battle at will!"

After a musket and blunderbuss volley, Tork estimated perhaps one thousand of their enemy and many horses were down. Some never to rise again. Others lay screaming upon the cold dirt, their life blood pooling beneath them.

He dropped the blunderbuss and retrieved his spear. Many of his soldiers did likewise, although some chose to reverse their blunderbusses and use the butt stock as a club.

"OBRAGARDA!"

The lad with eyes the size of saucepans had survived both volleys, although he clutched one shoulder, blood leaking between his fingers.

You won't survive this I'm afraid, son.

The cool, smooth wood of the weapon's haft felt good in his hand. Might barged into the horse of the frightened lad, sending the mercenary out of the saddle. The boy hit the ground and disappeared beneath Might's hooves. Holding the weapon halfway along the haft to increase his control, Tork gritted his teeth and stabbed his spear. The sharp, glinting head rammed deep into the throat of one man. He pulled the weapon out of the terrible wound before the haft could be ripped free of his grasp. Might bit the face of one horse, the animal rearing, sending its rider to the ground.

His spear embedded deep into the leather chest plate of another mercenary. Had the man been wearing steel armour or even chain mail, Tork's spear would have remained lodged in place.

Might rammed between two horses, ploughing on at a persistent canter. Tork saw the sword stroke coming, a horizontal sweep that could well cleave his head from his shoulders. He leaned back in the saddle, the blade striking his helmet and snapping his head back with a loud *clang* that reverberated in his ears. Straightening, Tork realised he was blind. The sword had caught in the slit of his visor, bending the metal so far out of shape it blocked off his field of view.

Another blade bounced from the helmet protecting his temple almost unhorsing him. The high-pitched ringing was deafening. Tork clenched a grip of his damaged visor and attempted to flip it up. The warped metal moved a little screeching in protest.

Damn it! If I can't see, I'm as good as dead!

He pushed the metal with all his strength but it didn't

budge.

Nothing for it.

Tork changed the grip on his spear and sent it sailing out in front of him, hoping it would strike home into an enemy. With both hands free he unbuckled his chinstrap and lifted the helmet clear. Fresh air teased the sweat-soaked hair plastering his head, cooling his skin as Might continued on. Keeping a grip on the helmet, Tork drew back his arm and brought it forward with a roar, the heavy steel smashing against the face of a nearby mercenary. Blood exploded from his nose and he dropped his sword, both hands nursing the wound. Then Might had battered past the wounded man. Another sword swept straight for Tork's head with the speed of a musket bullet.

Leaning back in the saddle, Tork's back touched the horse's rump. The enemy's blade, inches from his nose, cut the air with a dull hiss. A thin cascade of dark-red blood followed in the wake of the razor-sharp metal. Several tiny globules landed upon his cheek, cold and wet upon his skin. Then Might surged past the sword-wielding mercenary. Tork sat up in his saddle and brought his helmet down in an overhand blow that connected with a forehead, sending a splatter of blood in all directions. The metal, now slick with both sweat and fresh blood was difficult to hold. Tork threw it in front of him with an overhead toss and reached for his blunderbuss. The weapon, much shorter than the musket, was easier to wield as a club.

He reversed it, clenched the cold barrel with both hands and swept the butt stock in a vicious cut. The wood, hard as rock, smashed into a man's jaw. Tork heard the bone break. Blots of claret and yellowed teeth exploded from the mouth of the mercenary. The man's cries of pain were lost amongst the deafening raucous of war. Might barged through, then bit down hard on the nose of a Huronian horse. The animal darted away in pain and shock, sending its rider from the saddle to the ground to be trampled upon by one of the King's Own destriers.

Tork swung his weapon again, the polished wood of the butt stock connecting and unhorsing another mercenary. Then Tork was through the throng of enemy. Might picked up speed with an open field before him, and the warriors of the King's Own unit at his back exploded into view, retaining their arrowhead formation. Turning in the saddle, Tork placed a hand on Might's rump to steady himself and observed the damage left behind. His charge had cut a bloody swath straight through the centre of the enemy formation. He estimated about one thousand Huronian mercenaries remained in the saddle and uninjured. As for his soldiers, perhaps two hundred saddles were empty and a further fifty warriors nursed injuries but were still willing to fight.

"How fair you, sir?" Roland shouted.

He found the bugler on the other side of him. The man, wearing an open-faced helm paraded a deep cut running from one eye to his chin. His face was painted red with congealed blood. Although he still clutched his spear. Small clumps of flesh stuck to the red stained metal tip.

Tork pointed at Roland. "You need stitches."

The bugler grinned, part of the wound cracking open allowing fresh blood to ooze free. "I thought as much!"

The mortars, refusing to be ignored, roared their message again, and another volley of shot sizzled high into the air towards Lisfort.

He gestured at the mass of enemy cavalry left in their wake. "Let us get this done first."

"Aye, sir."

"Call the halt!"

The bugle's piercing scream rent the air and the King's Own charge slowed to a stop. Winded horses took in deep breaths of fresh air.

"About turn!"

Soldiers urged their horses to pivot where they stood so they were once more facing the Huronian mercenaries.

"Reload at the walk!"

He placed the blunderbuss's butt stock between his

thigh and Might's flank, the weapon's dark maw pointing skyward. Opening the small leather pouch at his hip, Tork withdrew a packet, placed one corner between his teeth and tore it open. He pinched the paper so as to allow the powder to pour from the packet, but so the numerous balls of shot remained in place. Once all powder had drained, he unclenched his index finger and the small, lead balls fell free disappearing down the muzzle of the blunderbuss.

He placed the weapon away, took up his musket and reloaded that, too. The rate of Might's breaths slowed, although his flank was still sleek with sweat. Shouts of concern pervaded the rabble that was the remnants of the mercenary force. Some had already fled the field of battle in small groups. Those who'd chosen to remain turned from the King's Own unit.

"At the trot!"

Roland placed the instrument against his lips and the bugle sang its piercing battle cry. The horses increased their pace.

The yelling issuing from the mercenaries increased. Those in the rear rank cast nervous glances over their shoulder at Tork's troop, urging those in front to make haste. Some tried to force their way closer into the middle of the throng and away from the rear rank.

Tork stood in the stirrups and lifted his hand above his head. "Canter!"

Screams of panic took the place of concerned voices and the Huronian force broke into a gallop, heading towards the main Huronian army in the hope of protection.

"Muskets!"

The bugle called the command. Tork was able to pull the musket clear of the leather holster forward of his right knee. "Charge!"

The war horses broke into the gallop.

"Obragarda!"

Muskets were pulled into shoulders and grim eyes stared down metal sights, searching for a target at which to shoot. Screams became shrieks and the mercenaries broke rank and fled in all directions.

"Halt!"

The arrow-head formation slowed and then stopped. Tired horses took in deep breaths.

"Holster!"

Muskets were placed away. The warriors of the King's Own sat in silence, the cries of their Huronian adversary growing fainter with each moment. There was an incessant wailing in the distance, that for all the world reminded him of the Highland bagpipes. Refusing to be distracted, he maintained his focus on the retreating enemy. An enormous black cloud erupted from the centre of the Huronian Army arrayed in the distance. The pall soon blotted them from view, consumed the remnants of the fleeing mercenaries and rushed towards Tork, sweeping the ground like a wave. An earth-shattering *boom* shook the ground. Might lost his footing and Tork slipped from the saddle. He attempted to regain his balance but the dirt met his back like a hammer and air rushed from his lungs.

Other horses reared in fear and several soldiers were unhorsed. One man rolled out of the way to avoid the hooves of a nearby destrier. Only a moment too soon as well. Hooves the size of dinner plates thudded onto the ground where the man's face had been seconds before.

Tork gathered his feet beneath him and stood. He ignored the incessant ringing piercing his ears. Movement caught his eye and he looked up at Roland. The bugler's mouth was moving, but aside from a muffled rumble, his words didn't make Tork's ears.

"What?"

Roland spoke again, this time with more hesitance, each word clearly pronounced. Tork still couldn't hear him, but he understood the question. "I'm fine, Roland." He swung into the saddle and ignored the dull pain in his ribs. Tork ran a trained eye over the leather holster ensuring all his weapons were accounted for.

Nudging Might closer to Roland's war horse, he slapped the man's arm and grinned. "Truly, I'm fine. I don't know what that was!" he jerked a thumb at the fast-approaching cloud of smoke. "And I'm not about to find out."

Roland stole a sidelong glance at the advancing pall. "Aye sir, I like your thinking."

"About turn!"

The bugler lifted the instrument to his lips and sounded the command.

Even as the bugle's blast cut the sky, the dark cloud consumed the formation of King's Own. Tork tasted gun powder and coughed. Visibility retreated until only the first two rows of soldiers closest him could be seen. Most of them had obeyed and were facing Lisfort awaiting further commands. But several were still regaining their feet.

"Hurry up!" he shouted.

They swung into their saddles and turned the powerful animals to face the same direction as their comrades.

"At the trot!"

Tork squinted against the gun smoke, ignoring the sting in his eyes as some of the fine particles made it past his eyelashes. He breathed through his nose to avoid a fit of coughing. From the sounds of it, other soldiers had opted not to do likewise.

"Canter!"

The bugle blasted to life and the pace increased so they were at least moving at the same speed as the thick cloud surrounding them.

"Gallop!"

A horse snorted nearby, another coughed on the far side of him, and the formation accelerated into a gallop. The smoke haze thinned. Breathing was easier. Hell, seeing was easier. Tork blinked the sting from his eyes. With each hoof fall, his vision increased until the thick cloud of gun powder was behind them and the arrowhead formation was streaking across the plain towards the city of Lisfort.

Sergeant Graff's good humour didn't last. Fresh clashes of steel on steel and renewed shouts echoed up and down the wall. But it was half-hearted compared to what the fighting had been like half an hour ago. He took one last look at the Highland Army, then turned away. "What in hells is happening now?"

He jogged back the way he'd come, the small group of soldiers who'd accompanied him following. In minutes the thick cloud of gun smoke, which had issued from the Huronian Army after the enormous explosion, came into view. It'd hidden all from sight, but there was movement from within the front section of black fog. Graff's eyelids drew closer together. *A formation of mounted soldiers. Has to be. Either King's Own or the Huronians.* The first powerful warhorse burst from the cloud, the mist behind the helmetless rider drifting in eddies.

"King's Own. Thank the gods," he muttered.

Then appeared the bugler, easy to pick because of his open-faced helm. The full force of the arrow-head formation appeared a moment later. The unit was riding at a gallop, straight towards Lisfort.

He pushed past a group of soldiers, nodded at another sergeant and made his way back to his post and the group of warriors under his command. Only a couple of ladders remained leaned against the battlements. The few enemy who'd gained a foothold on the wall were easily dealt with. Some were sent over the edge to their waiting comrades beneath, or pushed from the rampart to meet a grisly doom against the cobbled street far below.

Even during the lulls of combat, the dull burr of meaningless noise produced from the huge throng of enemy at the base of the wall never stopped. But that deep growl consisting of shouted orders, cries of wounded, yelling and howling seemed to increase in volume. Graff continued to limp to his section of the wall. He frowned and cast a glance towards what remained of the merlons. The Wendurlund soldiers closest the wall also seemed restless. The burble of an enemy army morphed into a dull roar.

"Here they come again!" a soldier shouted. "They're all coming up this time. This is our last stand, lads!"

Fear prickled the skin of Graff's arms and legs. *What in hell's is going on down there?* He broke into a run, ignoring the stabbing pain in his leg. "Make way!" he barged through a section of tired, wounded warriors. Some wore bandages on their arms, one man's eye was covered with a blood-soaked dressing.

"Sorry, Sarge."

Ladders loomed into the sky, reached their zenith, then fell towards the wall of Lisfort. They landed with deep *thuds*. He reached his soldiers, lungs burning and muscles aching. One of the enemy ladders was leaning against a smashed merlon. Graff pushed his way to the edge of the wall and leaned out staring down at the mob of enemy milling about beneath him.

The soldier wasn't wrong—both general infantry and Mortals were streaming up the ladders. Some of them cast glances over their shoulders. Graff took in the King's Own spear head. They were still advancing at a gallop, putting ground between themselves and the thick cloud of gunpowder in their wake.

Gods! The Huronians think the King's Own caused the explosion and have destroyed their entire army.

The soldiers clambering up the ladder were not fighting to take the wall, but to get away from the King's Own charge. In their minds, the Huronians believed the King's Own were coming to kill the rest of them. They'd rather fight the Wendurlund Army on the ramparts than face the elite force closing on their rear.

The first few reached the top of the wall and died. But those following streamed into view like ants. Graff blocked a sword stroke, kicked a man's knee out from under him, his blade finding a home in the Huronian's chest. Withdrawing his weapon, he sent an overhead swing that cleaved through a leather skull cap and the skull beneath. The man was dead before he hit the ground. Levering the sword free, he was almost too slow to block a stab that would have gutted him.

He dispatched his adversary, stepped forward and slipped on the blood slicked stones. His back met the rampart, his head striking the ground. Stars flashed behind his closed eyelids. Groaning, he sat up and realised he'd lost his sword but couldn't see it through the throng of jostling legs and feet. A screaming man struck the ground beside him, blood leaking from a terrible wound to his neck.

Get up fool, or you're done for!

Graff scuttled backward on his arse until he could get his legs under him. Even though he'd retreated from the coal-face of the battle, there were still Huronians who'd fought their way into the centre of the Wendurlund defence. Cursing, Graff ducked beneath a whistling cut that would have left him without a head. The Huronian soldier yelled his charge, intending to shoulder barge him. Graff stepped back, turned to one side at the last moment and allowed the man to run past, assisting him with a sharp shove in the back. The soldier ran out into thin air, arms and legs flailing, his weapon dropping from his grasp.

Graff pried a sword from a dead hand and immediately felt less naked. The blade was chipped in a few places, but it was better than nothing. His warriors were accounting for themselves well, but the enemy were unperturbed. They continued streaming over the lip of the ladders and jumping down to engage in combat. Graff pushed his way through the mass towards the front. One giant of a man was isolated from his comrades, driving Wendurlund soldiers back with massive sweeps of his double-headed battle axe. Pushing them back gave the Huronians time to advance over the ladder onto the wall. By the time he fell beneath a storm of swords, the enemy had established a defensive position at the section of wall beside the ladder, allowing more of their warriors to join their rank.

King's Own warriors pushed forward and fired their blunderbusses from the hip at point blank range. The enemy position was decimated. The King's Own war cry was almost inaudible over the rage of battle and the few elite soldiers stormed in amongst the surviving Huronians, employing their spears with lethal effect. Cheers and jeers filled the air, but on the enemy came, pouring over the ladder to meet sharp steel.

Graff shouldered through his soldiers towards the front. "Make way!"

The men under his command ignored him. Their blood was up, so he shoved his way through the ranks. He stumbled on a blood-covered body and was close to losing his footing, until he slammed a hand into the back of the warrior before him, regaining his balance. He advanced beyond the man and broke into the front rank. The small force of King's Own were exceptional. They were as skilled on the ground as they were on horseback. If the wall was to hold, it would be, in no small part, as a result of the tiny units of King's Own warriors dotted up and down the ramparts.

A distant thunder of blunderbusses further down the wall dulled the noise of battle for a moment. Graff stopped beside the closest King's Own soldier who stood almost directly beneath the ladder. A Huronian scuttled into view up the rungs and prepared to leap onto the wall. Graff lunged and skewered him in the groin. He fell from view, the next man to appear blocking a spear with his soft guts. He too disappeared, taking the spear with him. The elite warrior attempted to wrestle the weapon free but failed. Without hesitation, he withdrew a musket from the holster on his back, took aim and fired into the face of the next enemy.

Reversing the weapon, he used it as a club. Graff brushed past him and leapt up on the edge of the wall. Heights had never bothered him too much. He glared down and his heart sank. Still panicking over the charging King's Own who they believed had recently destroyed their entire army, the Huronian soldiers showed no sign of slowing. They were streaming up the ladders, willing to pit their luck against the Wendurlund Army than the elite warriors who were intent on finishing them all.

"You!"

Graff looked around to find the voice's owner. A fierce looking King's Own warrior holding a blunderbuss.

"Catch!"

The soldier threw the weapon. He caught it with his left hand.

"It's loaded." He gestured out at the abyss at Graff's feet. "Just point and shoot."

Graff sheathed his sword, pulled the polished wooden stock into his shoulder and pulled the trigger. *Boom!* The weapon bucked in his shoulder. his feet left the ground and the high-pitched scream in his ears drowned out the battle. He sailed through the air, cognisant to maintain a tight grip on the blunderbuss. He met the rampart on his side, pain exploding down his leg and up into his left shoulder.

An enemy appeared on the lip of the ladder, leapt onto the rampart and fell with a sword buried in his neck. He crumpled to his knees at Graff's feet. Ignoring the pain, he pushed himself to his feet.

"You can bloody have that back!" he shouted, tossing the blunderbuss at the King's Own warrior.

The man grinned and caught the weapon with deft skill. "She's got a bit of a kick."

He pulled free his sword and rolled his shoulders. The Huronian Army came on, pushing onto the rampart, more terrified of the free roaming mounted King's Own below than the soldiers who defended Lisfort. A Mortal ran into view up the ladder, launched himself onto the rampart and blocked a spear stab with his forearm. He grasped a hold of the haft, pulled the King's Own warrior to him and rammed a short sword through the soldier's midriff. Another Mortal appeared, backing up his comrade. Within a few minutes a group of red-cloaked Mortals had forced a clear space away from the ladder, allowing more Huronians to pour in behind them.

"On me!" roared Graff, striding forward.

His soldiers rallied behind him. On the left flank the King's Own had formed a wall, some firing muskets or blunderbusses. Others stabbing spears deep into the enemy formation. Once the flintlock weapons were used, there was no longer time to reload.

Graff met the enemy on his front foot, his sword clashing with a helmet and bouncing off, leaving a diagonal dent in the metal. The dazed man lost his footing and he stabbed his sword into the Huronian's gut. His fellow soldiers pushed in either side of him until he was standing shoulder to shoulder with the men under his command. Still more Huronians flooded in over the ladder to reinforce their foothold on the wall.

"Hold your position!"

He blocked a sword, his arm numb with the impact. A distant King's Own bugle rent the air further down the wall closely followed by the thunder of blunderbusses. The noise drew his attention. He cast a glance in that direction and noticed the Huronian Army had gained a foothold all the way down the wall. Even with the King's Own present, a fierce force multiplier in their own right, the army of Wendurlund were being ground down.

This is our last stand.

II

The bagpipes continued to belt out tunes of days gone by. The Great Highland Army remained still, watching the battle. The King's Own were closing with a smaller formation that had broken away from the Huronian Cavalry. The bugle blasted a signal and the mounted warriors, at the gallop, pulled what looked like muskets into their shoulders. The weapons crackled to life.

Then another command was issued and blunderbusses replaced the muskets and the elite Wendurlund charge disappeared for a fleeting second behind a cloud of gun smoke. They reappeared on the far side of the cloud. The rolling thunder of the shot washed over the Highlanders.

Another piercing shriek from the bugle and spears appeared in the hands of the King's Own. The elite unit disappeared into the ranks of the Huronian Cavalry, skewering straight through their centre. Within five minutes the small Huronian force were defeated and the King's Own turned to face the larger enemy force. Unperturbed by the size of their adversary, the elite warriors charged straight for them and once more joined battle.

"Like watching lions amongst sheep," muttered Henry nearby.

One by one the bagpipes stopped until the Highland Army were silent, watching the obliteration of the Huronian Cavalry. They tried to withstand the assault of the King's Own. Attempted to counter-attack, but failure met them head on. Not long after the battle had been joined, the Huronians were in full retreat.

A bright flash swept the land, stealing Vyder's sight for a few seconds. When his vision recovered, a dark pall of gun smoke hid the rest of the Huronian Army from view. The explosion that followed thundered through the earth and broke the sky asunder. Storm's front hooves left the ground and Vyder struggled to remain in the saddle.

Strange how when at a distance, the noise of an

explosion was slower than the smoke and destruction it caused. The further away one was, the greater the time between the gun smoke appearing and the noise of the blast. It was a phenomenon Vyder still did not understand.

Storm's hooves slammed back onto the ground and he calmed her with a soft voice and a few pats. He turned in his saddle to the Highland Army at his back. Some had been unhorsed, one beast galloping clear, the woman on its back somehow remaining in the saddle. She attempted to calm the panicked animal with little effect. The explosion, even at this distance, had been colossal. The hair on the back of his neck stood on end and his hands were numb, heavy. That alone told him Gorgoroth was present. His right arm raised of its own accord, open palm pointing towards the fleeing animal.

Fear not, my son. Gorgoroth's voice was a whisper in Vyder's mind. *You are safe.*

The animal slowed to a walk.

Come back to me, you are safe here with us.

The Highland woman stroked the horse's neck. It turned back to the Highland Army and broke into a trot, making a beeline for Vyder. The animal stopped beside him, sniffing his outstretched hand. He brushed the soft nose with the back of his hand and then stroked the patch of fur between its eyes.

"Are you hurt?" he asked the woman.

The beast's ears flicked forward at his voice.

"I'm well, lord."

"That's good."

The horse snorted and relaxed.

The Highlander smiled and patted her mount's neck. "I think she feels better now."

"You're right." Vyder straightened in his saddle. The animal took a step forward to close the distance even further with Vyder, but the Highlander turned her away.

"Thank you, lord," she said over her shoulder.

And what was that, little brother?

Even Gorgoroth's voice carried a note of concern.

"What in hells was that?" he asked, ignoring the nature spirit.

Henry, having gained control of his mount straightened in his saddle. "My guess? Sounded like one or several of their powder barrels went up. It's happened before in Lisfort. A naked flame or even a spark near a barrel is enough to ignite the gunpowder."

Ahitika remained silent, although she rubbed her ears, muttering something under her breath. A deep drumming resounded from within the expanding cloud that was already halfway to the walls of Lisfort. The formation of King's Own appeared from within the depths and galloped straight for the wall.

"Time to move." Vyder nudged Storm forward, lifted his arm high above his head and swept it down in the direction of the Wendurlund capital. Storm accelerated into a brisk walk. Gradually the Highland Army followed suit. The bagpipes burst into life again.

The ringing in Vyder's ears dissipated with each passing minute. A dull burr of voices overtook the piercing shrill echoing in his skull. The Huronian Army teaming at the base of Lisfort's wall had taken on a new lease of life. They lifted the massive ladders into place and then streamed up them as if their lives depended upon it.

From this distance it was difficult to see what was taking place at the top of the wall, but it seemed clear that the enemy assault was being repelled. That did not detract from the Huronians efforts. They continued to push with renewed vigour. Fear did not seem to find a place in their midst. Vyder's brow furrowed.

Hyglak cantered up beside Vyder. "The Great Highland Army is causing them terror, lord!"

"We're scaring them straight up the ladders!" another voice called.

The high-pitched shriek was almost non-existent. Vyder's hearing had returned and with it the thunder of hooves had increased in volume. The King's Own were still proceeding at a gallop, closing ground with the Huronian soldiers on the ground with incredible speed.

"It's not us," Vyder said. He pointed at the elite unit streaking across the ground in an arrowhead formation, muskets pulled into their shoulders. "It's them."

He grinned. The Huronians were running scared, testament to the fearsome reputation the King's Own carried. Frightened as they were, their persistence was paying off. More of them seemed to have gained purchase upon the wall. Occasionally there came a distant bugle blast, *crackle* or *boom* of muskets and blunderbusses, but for the most part only the song of steel rang out over the muted bur of shouts and screams.

Vyder's grin disappeared, his concerned eyes focused upon the ramparts high above the advancing Highlanders. The Huronians were winning the wall! Or at least that is how it appeared from the ground.

"Gods," Henry said. "We're losing this fight."

Vyder held his hand up and reined Storm in. Ahitika and Henry stopped beside him. Behind him, the Highland Army ground to a halt, although the mournful song of the bagpipes continued. If they put too much pressure upon the Huronians laying siege to Lisfort, it would place no other option upon their enemy but to take the city's wall to ensure their survival. The Huronians weren't fighting to carry out any order given by their mad king. They were fighting to get away from the King's Own.

"Stop!" Vyder roared at the King's Own in the near distance. But they didn't hear him, else they ignored him. He urged Storm after them. "Halt!"

Fast as the powerful animal was, she was not swift enough to catch the charge of the elite force. He reigned Storm in and sat still, silent, watching the wall of Lisfort fall to the enemy.

Graff brought the sword down in a savage overhand

cut which sliced straight through his opponent's shoulder and lodged in the enemy's breastbone. He stepped back and kicked the mortally wounded man from his blade in time to block a sweeping blow which would have cleaved the portion of skull above the bridge of his nose from his face. Graff rammed his sword into the Huronian's guts and ripped it clear, the soldier's agonised scream adding to the already deafening cacophony of war sweeping the wall of Lisfort. His soldiers had conducted a fighting withdrawal from the ladder under which now stood a solid force of Huronian soldiers. They were being organised into a formidable fighting unit by a few of the red cloaks.

They'd lost the initiative and their momentum had long come to a halt. It was now only a matter of survival. Graff blocked another blow and his sword shattered. He dropped the useless hilt to the ground and took a backward step. His adversary grinned and lunged. Graff blocked the thrust with his forearm and guided the weapon away from him. Latching a grip onto the Huronian's wrists, he twisted until he felt a snap. The warrior screamed and released the grip of his weapon. Graff caught the pommel mid-air, reversed the blade and rammed it through the throat of his enemy. Ignoring the blood leaking from his injured forearm, he slashed through an arm, cut free a head, pierced a groin, kicked a soldier back who'd been pushing towards him and fell to his knees with a spear in his stomach.

Graff coughed blood, grabbed a hold of the haft belonging to the spear head embedded in his body and ripped it free of the grasp of the wide-eyed Huronian soldier. Skewering the boy with a stab, he lost his grip on the sword's hilt.

"Sarge!" someone called from behind. "Shit! Sarge!"

The barrel of a blunderbuss appeared above his head, pointing at the wall of enemy pushing forward. "Eat this," growled a voice and the weapon spoke with an ear-shattering *boom* casting a cloud of gunpowder over Graff. Three King's Own soldiers brushed past him closely followed by a group of the young warriors under his command. They fought well. Fatigue gripped him and the cold stones of the rampart rose to meet his face. He groaned. Warm liquid oozed from his mouth and nose. It tasted like iron.

"Fall back lads!" he shouted. Or at least he attempted to. He coughed, winced. Tried to stand and managed to move one leg a little. The rest of his body felt heavy, weighted down by some unseen force. He coughed again. The battle before him was ferocious, the combined force of Wendurlund soldiers and King's Own fighting magnificently. They were pushing the enemy back!

Fresh screams, shouts and clashes of steel came from behind him. Move as he might try, he remained frozen in place, unable to see what was taking place at his back. The shouts and war cries rolled closer. A stab of fear spread down his spine. All of the voices were shouting in the Huronian language.

Has the rest of the wall fallen?

His unspoken question was answered when a thick crowd of Huronian soldiers swept around him. Some of them stepped on him in their desperate bid to close with the last remnants of their Wendurlund adversary. He cried out, fresh agony piercing his belly. The few warriors still battling to defend the city of Lisfort were surrounded.

Graff's blood-stained lips peeled back in a snarl and he pushed his arms beneath him, but he had no strength. The cold rampart once more met his cheek and he was forced to watch the last few moments his soldiers would ever live. The last man on his feet, a King's Own soldier, discharged his musket, reversed the weapon and shattered a skull with the butt stock. Dropping it, he withdrew his spear and skewered the chest of the closest enemy. The haft was ripped clear of his hand by the weight of the dying man. A sword plunged into his guts. The mortally wounded warrior grasped a fistful of chain mail belonging to the man who'd stabbed him and dragged him into a headbutt. The Huronian soldier released the sword and held hands to his destroyed nose. A spear smashed through the King's Own back and exited his chest. Still the man remained on his feet. With a snarl he ripped clear the sword from his own midriff and cut the head from the closest enemy.

He roared the King's Own war cry, but his voice was drowned out by the Huronians surrounding him. Graff lay mesmerised in paralysed pain. The warrior blocked two attacks, dispatched another enemy with an underhand cut and fell to his knees with another spear through his stomach. His eyes met Graff's and he nodded once. Then a tall man standing behind cut off the soldier's head. Graff's eyelids touched for the last time and Lisfort's wall disappeared from view. The roar of uncountable enemy voices, once deafening, was now a muffled burble.

I'm so cold.

Then the voices faded to be replaced by a blustering, freezing wind roaring in his ears. Sleet raked the skin of his face.

So cold.

"Fools!" Vyder shouted at the distant King's Own charge.

Henry reined in beside him. "The wall has fallen. Lisfort is on her own, now."

"Bloody fools!" Vyder snarled.

Ahitika stopped close by. "Keep your mind, crazy one."

Vyder flicked a look in her direction. He returned his attention to the King's Own engaging in combat with the remnants of the Huronian Army desperate to climb the ladders.

"She means no offence, Vyder."

He saw in his peripheral vision the warning look Henry gave her. The line of mounted warriors disappeared in a cloud of gun powder, the thunderous *boom* of blunderbusses washing over Vyder a moment later.

"She's right." He took a deep breath and forced himself to relax. "The fight has only started." He turned Storm to face Henry. "What kind of defences do they have inside the city walls?"

The prince took a deep breath, his eyes wandering to the clouds. "Depends on who was manning the wall. If it was all of our army, then only The Watch remains. I heard some musket and blunderbuss shot during the fighting, so it's fair to say the King's Own were on the wall as well." His eyes fell from the sky and drilled into Vyder. "And if that's the case then they, too, have more than likely fallen. That leaves The Watch, artillery and the palace guards and, of course, the civilians of Lisfort, although I doubt they'll offer much resistance against a professional army."

Ahitika leaned in her saddle and spat. She straightened and glowered at the prince. "Do not mistake a motivated people."

A distant, high-pitched bugle blast rent the air followed almost immediately by a crackle of muskets. The King's Own were making short work of the remaining soldiers. Many of them were on the ladder, climbing for their lives. Those unlucky to still be on the ground attempted to form some kind of defence against the onslaught. They locked shields and crouched, waiting as hell bore down upon them. But it was no use. The galloping horses struck them like a war hammer, shattering their ranks. Razor sharp spears rose and fell, hooves staved in skulls.

The Huronians were whittled away to nothing. Some tried to break and run clear, but they were ridden down. The King's Own morphed into a neat formation and cantered away from the wall, ignoring the jeers of the warriors who'd taken the wall.

"I don't think they'd be so boisterous were they standing down here, somehow."

Vyder grunted, staring up at the dark smear of Huronian soldiers staining the rampart. "Now we must put to siege the very city we came to aid."

The last men climbed clear of the massive ladders and one by one, the giant wooden structures were pushed clear of the wall, gaining speed as they fell. Each met the ground with a *thump* that vibrated beneath the earth upon which Storm stood. The horse flinched. Vyder leaned forward and brushed an open hand against her soft neck. "You are safe, lass."

I hope Miriam still has that blunderbuss.

The growing rumble of hooves broke his reverie. The King's Own approached, the commander leading them, a well-built man of middling age who rode without a helmet, stood in his stirrups and signalled for the formation to halt. He and the bugler approached Vyder. He noticed the bugler wore a savage cut down his cheek, half his face painted with dry blood.

The King's Own officer offered a wave. "Ho! Highlander!" His eyes flickered to Henry and he bowed his head. "Sire." When the man raised his eyes, he broke into a grin. "I thought I'd never see you alive again, my lord!"

"It's been a long time since that day on the hill, Commander Tork."

So not any officer then, this one is the overall chief of the King's Own.

Vyder did not miss the smile which faded from Tork's face or the glint of reflection replace the mirth in his eyes.

"That was a tough fight, my lord."

"We survived, though Tork." Henry chuckled.

The commander nodded but didn't share the same good humour. "Most of us did, my lord."

This one is a good man, little brother. I've met him before. Gorgoroth's deep voice pierced his mind.

Vyder nodded and cleared his throat. "Enough talk," he said. He looked over Tork's shoulder at the walls of Lisfort where the remnants of the Huronian Army remained in place jeering at them. "We are still in a fight."

Tork held Vyder's eyes. "And you are?"

Henry cast a hand in Vyder's direction. "This is Vyder Ironstone, Warlord of the Great Highland Army."

Tork nudged his horse forward a few paces and offered a hand. "Commander Tork."

They shook.

"And, of course, you are correct, Vyder Ironstone."

The rank and file of the King's Own behind Tork remained silent, although stern eyes, the only part of their faces visible behind the slit of their visors, swept across the Highland Army. Not a hand remained relaxed, noticed Vyder. They clenched spears, muskets or blunderbusses. Not one warrior remained complacent. A single command from Tork and battle would be joined between the elite force and the Highlanders. Although he was cognisant to know the commander would never issue such an order.

Vyder shifted in his saddle. "We need to get back into Lisfort."

I have an idea, little brother.

"We don't have the numbers to storm the ramparts with the ladders the Huronians have left behind," Henry said.

Tork shrugged. "We may need to hold off for now. Difficult as it might be to bear, we need to wait until the enemy loses interest in us and moves deeper into Lisfort and away from the wall." He turned to look back at the distant enemy continuing to hurl down indistinguishable abuse at them. "It might take hours, perhaps days. Then we lift a ladder into place and send up a small team to open the gate." Tork faced them once more, his piercing glare fixed upon Henry. "Then we storm the city." His eyes shifted to bore into Vyder. "I mean you no offence, Vyder Ironstone, but I think it prudent that the small team come from the ranks of my soldiers."

Little brother?

Vyder nodded. "So be it. Your soldiers know the city better than us, anyway. It makes no difference to us. Once we breach the city you will be surprised how the Highland clans carry themselves in battle."

The commander nodded but did not reply. His focus drifted over Vyder's shoulder at something. "I think we may have need of your clans sooner than we thought."

Continue to ignore me, little brother, I care not. I know a solution.

Vyder twisted in the saddle to follow Tork's line of focus. Amongst the fading cloud of gun smoke walked a mass of Huronian Cavalry. Far more than Tork's force had faced recently.

"Reload!" roared Tork. The bugler blasted the command. He coaxed his horse backward and nodded at the Highlander. "Nice to have met you, Vyder Ironstone."

Those few King's Own who had neglected to reload their weapons moved with rapid, practised movements. Within twenty seconds they'd finished and waited in silence, grim eyes boring into the enemy menace bearing down on them with methodical lack of speed.

"You too, Commander." Vyder swung Storm away and cantered back to the Highland Army, Henry and Ahitika at his heels.

He cupped his hands around his mouth. "Hyglak! Form squares!"

Hyglak clasped the war horn and brought it to his lips, the deep, powerful blasts cut through the drone of bagpipes. Shouts rippled across the Highlanders and the bagpipes fell silent one by one. The Highlanders jostled into place forming five huge squares. Shields were lifted into place and faces disappeared behind a veritable fort. It needed practice. Far more practice, but it'd do for now.

He brought Storm to a stop beside Hyglak. "About turn."

The war horn spoke and the squares shimmered with movement.

"Original idea!" a voice shouted.

He cast a glance over his shoulder and saw Tork grinning in the near distance. He chuckled. "I've heard it being used before. It seems to work well."

Tork touched his chest with a fist and nodded. "Hold your formations and advance behind us!"

"Aye!"

I leave you now, little brother. I am near, worry not. I shall return.

A freezing shard skewered his body. It passed almost as fast as it'd appeared.

"Gorgoroth?" he muttered under his breath.

But silence was his only reply. Gorgoroth was gone.

The dull *thump, thump* filled Harton's head. He stumbled, lost his balance and fell to the ground. The shouts, screams and cries of those running past was a soft, muffled bur. Some of those who ran past were injured. One of them had lost an arm in the explosion, a gout of bright red blood pumping from the terrible wound. The man made it a few paces beyond Harton and collapsed. One of his legs kicked and then he was still. Harton groaned, gathered his feet beneath him and walked on. The *thump, thump* recommenced, coinciding with each foot striking the earth. He could only see a few paces in front of him. The thick cloud of acrid gun powder worked its way unbidden into his nose, mouth and throat. He coughed and spat. Stopping at the man who'd lost his arm, Harton stooped and tore off a section of his cloak.

"You won't need that anymore," he muttered.

He held the material over his nose and mouth, ignoring the smell of old dirt and mud imbued into the material. It helped a little, although the mist of spent black powder continued to work beyond his eyelids and settled on his eyes. Tears streamed down his cheeks. He wiped his eyes with the back of one sleeve, but it did little good in assuaging the painful sting that resided there. He blinked and stumbled on, ignoring the muffled shouting around him that competed with the high-pitched scream bouncing around his skull. The ground rumbled beneath him and a horse galloped past, an officer yelling something through a cupped hand. Then the animal disappeared into the dark cloud.

Garx was dead, killed in the explosion. Guilt clenched

Harton's guts. *It should have been my job to ignite the barrel.* He snarled and held the material closer over his mouth. "Damn you, Garx!" he growled. He closed his eyes and fresh tears streaked the stained skin of his face.

"Fight hard, boy!" Garx's voice echoed in his memory.

The acrid cloud settled around him, and Harton tripped on a body lying face down but managed to keep his feet before the ground could make his acquaintance once more. He dodged a tree that loomed out of the smoke, ducked under a low hanging branch and ignored another group of disoriented Huronian soldiers blundering past.

Focus! He blinked. *Find the others.* The tiny group that had once been Huronian Cavalry had been positioned with the mortars at the front. They'd been much farther away from the blast than Harton. So, they should be alive. However, the explosion had cast shrapnel in all directions. He'd already come across deceased soldiers who'd also been further from the detonation than he. Distance wasn't any measure of safety. A dark, motionless blob on the ground came into focus amongst the cloud and he slowed. A rider crushed beneath his dead horse. Harton knelt and retrieved the soldier's spear. The smooth, cool haft felt good in his hand.

His other hand still clamped the material over his nose and mouth when a huddle of soldiers appeared. They were talking amongst themselves, but Harton's damaged hearing wasn't able to pick out their topic of conversation. Nor was he particularly interested. They ignored him, which suited Harton.

Again, the earth rumbled and a few horses galloped past. He caught a glimpse of a red flash of paint on their saddle bags before they advanced into the thick mist. *Messengers.* They'd be carrying orders to areas of the army or discovering information to carry back to their officers. The Army was still in disarray, attempting to find out what had happened, why, and then reorganising. It wouldn't take them long. Harton increased his pace, leapt over a man writhing on the ground, and pushed on through the acrid pall surrounding him. He ignored the persistent sting in his eyes. *Where the hell is the mortar line?*

Mingled with the din screaming in his ears, there were muffled shouts from amongst the fog all around him. Orders, yells of panic, the cries of the wounded. None appeared to be curtailing any time soon. A ragged formation of troops marched past him in the direction of the original explosion.

"You there!" a mounted soldier shouted. He was probably an officer. "Fall in!"

Harton ignored the man and strode through the bitter mist assaulting every pore.

"You man! Don't ignore me, I'll have you bloody whipped. Fall in. Now!"

He walked on and negotiated around an overturned wagon. Harton blinked through the thick smoke, scowling to gain focus. Aside from some boxes of supplies, the wagon was empty. The traces had been cut, freeing the horse which had once pulled the vehicle.

"If I find out who you are, you'll hang!" the officer's shouted words pierced the cloud.

He threw a glance over his shoulder. The formation of soldiers, along with the mounted officer commanding them had been swallowed by the shroud of spent gun powder.

"You won't get the chance," he muttered into the piece of torn cloak. Harton rested the spear on a shoulder, tip facing the sky.

A dark smudge loomed from within the murk. Its shape was squat and round. A mortar!

Bloody finally!

A mortar round almost caused him to lose his balance. He cursed and stepped over the abandoned large ball of lead.

"Cavalrymen!" he shouted.

"Here!" a familiar voice replied.

To the right. He turned in that direction and advanced. Another mortar appeared amongst the fog. He walked past it, this time aware of any rounds that may have been left strewn upon the ground. A third mortar formed as he progressed further down the line. A blob of soldiers came into view, their definition sharpening with each boot fall. Some stood, leaning against a mortar, others sat, one of the seated men coughing into a hand.

"How's that for too much bloody powder, sir?" one of them shouted, a grin splitting his beard. It was Ortus.

Harton gave a half-hearted chuckle.

"Where's Garx, Harton?" the smile faded.

Guilt flared in his guts again and he blinked tears from his eyes. The sting of burnt powder was causing irritation in the eyes of almost everyone, so at least he was not the only one with tears cutting the skin of cheeks. "He died in the explosion."

Ortus pushed off the mortar barrel upon which he'd been resting and approached.

Now the insults begin. Coward! Craven! You left him to die!

He held Ortus's glare. The big man cursed. "I didn't think the bastard could die."

You did *leave him to die though. Didn't you?*

"There's nothing you could have done, lad. Good work, Harton!" Ortus slapped him on the shoulder. "We came here to do what we set out to do. Let's get outta here before they find us and stretch our necks."

Harton let the piece of cloak drop away from his mouth. "I shouldn't have left him."

"I know Garx well enough to know he'd have sent you away. One man wandering by himself towards the powder wagons would have drawn attention. You were there to make it look less suspicious. You did nothing wrong, Harton." Ortus looked at the ground. "Truth be known, I was glad you accompanied him. You're braver than me."

He nodded and wiped his cheeks with the piece of fabric. "Time we moved. They'll have reorganised themselves shortly."

"You heard the man!" bellowed Ortus.

Harton organised them into two files and positioned himself to one side, separate from them to give the illusion he was the commander of the formation.

"Forward march!" he hissed.

The group advanced, keeping in step. Harton rested the spear on his left shoulder. They headed back the way he'd come, towards the point of explosion, looting weapons as they went.

An officer galloped past, nodded at Harton's salute and disappeared into the mist behind them. The group moved around the toppled wagon, several of them running clear to clamber in and delve through the boxes. Harton marched alongside the remnants of the formation which blocked up to fill in the gaps of those who'd departed to investigate for potential weapons and equipment. A small group of soldiers marched past them in the opposite direction, none the wiser. Then those who'd left re-joined the group.

Another few bodies appeared among the smudge of gun smoke and were descended upon by several cavalrymen. One of them came away with a sword belt, complete with a sheathed weapon. Another tucked a knife into his belt. The thunder of hooves neared and another mounted officer appeared in the gloom. He slowed when he neared the small formation of troops.

"Halt!"

Thump. A dozen feet slammed against the ground and the group stopped marching. Harton saluted.

The officer, no more than perhaps twenty-five summers in age returned a lazy salute. "And where are you off to?"

"Captain Garx asked us to check on the source of the explosion, sir," said Harton.

"Powder barrel blew up. A simple accident. Return to your mortars and pass the message onto your captain."

"With all due respect, sir, we've been asked to personally investigate by our officer commanding. We are to render assistance if required."

The young officer's eyes narrowed and his jaw bulged. "You listen to me, boy, return to your post right this instant or else I'll see you punished!"

Boy? I'm at least a few years older than this upstart idiot.

"Sir, Captain Garx—"

"I care nothing for this Captain *Garx!*" spat the officer.

The tension emanating from the formation of soldiers behind him was palpable. "We do, sir."

"Fight hard, boy!" the memory of Garx's voice whispered.

"Return to your posts. Return to your posts, now! If you do not—"

Harton's spear rammed through the man's throat, the tip exiting the base of his skull. The man fell from the saddle and slammed to the dirt. Blood soaked into the ground around his head. One of the soldiers darted forward, grasped the horse's reins and stroked its face, offering soft words of comfort. Harton placed a boot onto the forehead of the dead officer and ripped the spearhead free.

Ortus grinned and snapped off a salute. "Looks like you just got yourself a field promotion, Harton."

III
Night – fourth day of the siege

Flames leapt and danced beneath the fresh log, casting vibrant orange flickers of light upon the cave walls. A wisp of grey smoke rose from the fire, ascending in lazy curls towards the stone ceiling far above. Endessa cleared her throat, spat and stared into the coals. The glob of phlegm hissed and bubbled upon the burning log.

The dull, distant thunder had ceased earlier that morning. For the past few nights she had sat at the cave mouth and watched the intermittent flashes of light illuminate the horizon, closely followed by what sounded like a rolling thunder. But it was no light show promising rain. The cacophony had been issuing from the city of Lisfort. No doubt under siege by the Huronian Army. There'd been a sky splitting *boom* much louder than she'd ever heard followed by nothing. Not even the insects of the forest buzzed or chirped.

It was a reprieve when silence reined once more, although she was glad when the insects, one by one, recommenced their symphony. But the distant quiet did not bode well for Wendurlund's capital city. Either the city had fallen, or they'd managed to fight off the threat. She treated the second possibility with a healthy dose of doubt. Had the Wendurlund Army not been weakened by the assault of spiders, wolves and eagles, they might have stood some kind of chance against the mad Huronian bastard of a king.

She sighed. "Damn you, Gorgoroth." The log shifted on the fire sending a flurry of sparks whirling towards the ceiling hidden in darkness.

It's only a matter of time before they burn this forest to the ground.

"They teach their children about the Waning Wood and what lies within," she muttered with a dry chuckle. Endessa flicked a small piece of nearby bark onto the fire. Her eyes were drawn to the flames feasting with ferocious crackles upon the log she'd thrown on some minutes before. "Some of the stories are true. Many are not, though. But that won't stop them, or the madman who leads them."

Her laugh was quiet and held no humour. "And what will they do with you, Endessa?" she muttered to herself, staring up into the darkness. *Will they rape and kill me, I wonder? Torture?*

She swore and climbed to her feet, holding a groan at bay. "It matters not. One way or another I shall return to the earth to feed the beetles and worms."

Endessa stretched her back and walked to the mouth of the cave, stepping out onto the narrow track leading away from her home. Her feet crunched on the small stones as she made her way to Geldrim, the mighty Oak standing guard over her cave. She placed a hand upon the trunk, closed her eyes, and breathed deep of the cool, fresh air.

Fear sizzled onto her palm and swept up her arm causing the small hairs to stand on end. "Yes, we are in danger, Great One," she whispered. "But we will fight if it comes to it. We'll send them to whatever hell they believe in."

Anger's warmth replaced fear, the tiny hairs on her arm falling back in place, making the skin itch. Endessa stared into the darkness down the path that eventually led to the western gate of Lisfort. Nothing moved, and aside from the insect life, the forest slept. Her hand slipped free of Geldrim and hit her thigh with a soft slap.

"We all must die one day," she whispered into the stillness.

Cool night air caressed her skin, soaked into her clothes. She shivered and rubbed her hands together. Casting one last glance at Geldrim, she returned to her cave and sat by the fire, allowing the warmth to imbue her being. *The Huronians may never venture this far west. My fear for the safety of the Waning Wood might be misplaced.*

She leaned forward and prodded the fire. "You can never be too sure, though."

A soft clicking attracted her attention. It was growing

louder with each passing minute and issuing from beyond the cave mouth. When the noise echoed around the cave, she stood, aware whatever was causing the noise was not far away. Her fingers curled around the bone hilt of her knife jutting from the small wood scabbard hanging from her belt.

Several black spindly legs appeared, their shadows massive against the far wall. More legs skittered into view and then the spider itself. It wasn't an adult, not yet anyway, but it wasn't far off. Perhaps another three or four years would see it reach adulthood. The arachnid's abdomen was half the height of Endessa, its head about the size of her chest. Various creatures of the Waning Wood had been known to come into her cave from time to time. It happened. She managed to herd most of them out without too much trouble. Although one wolf, terrified and confused had charged at her, snapping and snarling. She'd dropped to the ground, the huge animal leaping over her and sprinting out of the cave.

Not many spiders did, though. She could think of only a few occasions when young hatchlings had accidentally happened into her home. At that age, she could pick them up in one hand. But this was different. A spider this size had never mistaken its whereabouts. By that age, they usually had taken ownership over their small section of the woods, there to remain into old age. Her fingers tightened on the hilt and she withdrew the weapon, the sharp steel glinting orange in the firelight.

"And what is it you want?" Endessa held the knife before her, the fingers of her other hand opening a pouch at her belt and delving inside. The spider turned towards her and stopped, the light glistening against multiple dark eyes arrayed upon its head. It raised a leg and the tiny segment closest the ground rose up and down, almost as if it was asking Endessa to place down the knife.

The creature took another few paces forward and she noticed of all the gleaming eyes arrayed on the head, one was a bright blue.

"Is it you, Gorgoroth?"

It stretched its front legs out and bent its head low to the ground. She sheathed the knife and beckoned it closer to her fire. "Come and sit." She paused. "Or lie down, whatever is more comfortable."

The spider chattered, as if it was laughing. It clicked towards her and then flopped to the ground. It seemed to stare into the flames. She allowed the silence to grow, her attention on the glowing coals at the base of the blaze. The arachnid made that chattering sound again. She looked up and focused on the black creature. The multiple eyes were boring into her, particularly that blue one.

"And did you manage to save the prince?"

The thing appeared to give a tiny nod.

"But war came to Wendurlund, anyway." She sighed. "Can Lisfort hold?"

Gorgoroth grasped a small piece of wood from nearby with two long legs and lifted it into an upright position. Then he released it and the wood fell to the ground, bouncing once and then lying still.

"It has *already* fallen?"

A small nod.

"Gods." She rubbed her face. "Oh Gorgoroth, what have you done? Had you not weakened the Wendurlund Army…" she sighed and left the sentence unfinished.

The arachnid lowered its head to the ground and chattered softly.

Endessa leaned forward and threw another log onto the fire. "The Waning Wood might be safe for a time, at least."

Gorgoroth held out a leg, pointing it at the blaze and then pivoting to gesture with the same appendage at the blackness beyond the cave mouth.

"But we will eventually burn. Yes, I agree." She stared at the new log and the fresh flames consuming it. "But what to do?" she whispered.

Gorgoroth used the front pair of legs to reach around

and encompass the entire cave and then point back out at the darkness in the direction of Lisfort. She frowned, shifted her position upon the ground and stared at the arachnid. He made the same gesture, but she still didn't understand his meaning.

The spider pointed at itself and then indicated a vacant patch of floor beside it and then another empty section of ground on the opposite side. Her eyes widened. "You mean to bring an army of spiders to the fight?"

The creature raised its head and nodded. It chattered a loud burst of sound and pointed at her.

"I must come?"

A tiny movement of the head up and down.

"And what of Barbaron? Will she accompany this... army?"

Gorgoroth's response to her question made her stomach rise into her throat. Barbaron frightened her. The arachnid, thought to be the mother of all spiders in the Waning Wood was so large she'd be unable to fit inside Endessa's cave.

The arachnid gained her attention with a small wave of a leg. It motioned towards its chelicera and made that chattering noise, then pointed towards her. "Ah, now I understand Gorgoroth. You want me to be the voice of your army."

They reached Rone by dawn. Or at least where Rone should have been. The horses were grazing or stood dozing in the large makeshift paddock within the forest. But of the King's Own officer there was no sign. The men walked to their horses, approaching the animals and talking in hushed tones. Splinters of deep orange speared through the canopy, moving or disappearing with the gentle sway of the boughs. Harton caught movement out the corner of an eye and turned. Rone crouched on the far side of a nearby bush, blunderbuss pulled into a shoulder, one cold eye staring down the sights. He paused, his brow relaxing, a small smile teasing a corner of his mouth. He lowered the weapon and stood.

Harton made his way to the King's Own soldier. "No trouble?"

The man's brow furrowed again, lending a menace to his piercing stare.

Idiot, Harton. He doesn't understand the Huronian language.

Rone ignored his question and swept his gaze around at the others. Some of them had already slung saddles onto their mounts, they tightened girth straps, talking quietly amongst themselves.

"Garx," he said in a strong accent.

Harton shook his head. "He died, my friend."

"Dead?"

He nodded, trying to ignore the lump developing in his throat. The last glimpse of Garx was burned into his mind, the officer stood over the powder barrel readying to plunge the hot poker down into the barrel.

"Fight hard, boy."

Harton swallowed and met Rone's eyes.

Rone grunted, his eyes flint-hard. He stepped forward, slapped a hand onto Harton's shoulder. "Good," he licked his lips and looked unsure. His eyes flicked up to the canopy, then returned to bore into Harton. "Soldier." The King's Own officer nodded. "Good soldier."

Harton cleared his throat. "He was."

Rone nodded and allowed his hand to slide clear. "We ride," he gestured at the Huronian cavalrymen around them, many now watching the conversation. "We kill."

"I agree, Rone. Let's kill them all."

The officer who was once an enemy drew a circle in the air and grinned. "Kill," he said.

Harton frowned. Rone repeated the movement.

A roar of laughter exploded behind him, immediately silenced by hisses of, "shut the fuck up, half-wit!" or, "quiet!"

Ortus offered a chuckled apology and led his horse closer to the two men. He gestured towards Rone. "I think he means we should surround the Huronian Army and kill them all."

"Surround!" Rone said, grinning. "Surround." He punched a fist into the flat of his hand. "Kill."

Harton nodded and smiled. "Sounds like a plan."

Ortus jerked a thumb in Rone's direction. "I like this lad."

"Let's move," Harton said, striding towards his horse. He spotted his saddle nearby and lifted it onto the animal's back. With confident, well-practised movements he soon had the girth strap tightened and the bridle in place. He stepped into a stirrup and swung up into the saddle.

Rone's warhorse was saddled and the officer was already mounted, his array of weapons placed in the leather holster forward of his right knee. Harton led the small column out of the forest in a northerly direction so as to avoid tangling with any Huronian troops. Ortus trotted up alongside him. He pointed towards the left flank. "The enemy's that way."

"I know that. I want to avoid them for the time being so we can formulate a plan. Watch them from a distance, see how they recover from the explosion and then hit them where they least expect it."

Ortus's eyes widened and he held up his hands. "That's why you're out front. You're a thinker." Ortus lowered his arms and took up the reins again. "I'm just spoilin' for a fight. Probably end up getting us all killed if I was in charge."

You'd definitely *get us all killed.*

The thick, dark pall of gun smoke still pervaded the area where the main Huronian Army had been positioned. Although he still heard distant shouts and cries for help, it wasn't immediately clear to Harton how soon the Huronians would be in a position to reignite their siege upon Lisfort. He nudged the animal into a trot and then urged it into a canter. The cavalrymen behind him matched the pace.

"Kill?" Rone spoke from behind loud enough for

Harton to hear.

He glanced over his shoulder at the King's Own warrior and tapped his temple. "Plan first, then kill."

He wasn't sure the foreign soldier understood the words he spoke, but he was confident he understood the gesture. Within ten minutes they'd left the scene of destruction behind and were far enough away they could dismount and watch their enemy's recovery and decide how best to strike. Harton swung out of the saddle, and signalled the others to do the same.

The grasslands were varying in length anywhere from brushing knee height all the way to large clumps that towered much taller than any man. It was to one of these giant clumps that a few cavalrymen led the horses where both riders and animals were swallowed by the depths of the grass.

Harton ducked low and moved with care until he reached an area where he could gain a good look at the Huronian encampment while remaining well camouflaged. A soft *crunch* told him Ortus had arrived. The man moved slow and smooth, kneeling beside Harton.

"What's the plan?" he whispered.

Ortus's clear blue eyes glared through the grass at the dark cloud hugging vast areas of ground in the distance. His brow drew together, mouth shrinking into a tight line. *He's angry.*

Harton returned his attention to the field of battle. "I don't know yet. I want to see how we—" he caught himself and was not oblivious to the look Ortus snapped in his direction. "How *they*, the Huronian Army respond. Then I'll have an idea."

"Not my fuckin' people," Ortus spoke through clenched teeth.

A hand touched his shoulder and he jumped, heart thundering in his chest. Rone was on the other side of him. He'd approached without making a sound. The Wendurlund soldier grinned and removed his hand from Harton's shoulder, offering his palm in silent apology. He gestured at

Harton and mimicked his look of surprise. *He's mocking me!* But the King's Own soldier repeated the look of shock. Then he punched his palm. "Fast. Hit hard."

"I think he's saying to hit them in a fast, surprise attack. Hit 'em fast and get out before they can respond."

Harton nodded. "I think you're right. It's a damn fine idea as well."

The trio sat in silence. Watching. Waiting. An ache worked its way into the muscles of his leg, forcing Harton to shift position.

"Are you ready to die?" Ortus whispered.

Harton shrugged. *Hadn't thought about it. I was ready to die not so long ago when Garx and I walked into the hornet's nest.* That image of Garx stood over the barrel, the hot poker grasped in both hands pervaded his mind.

"Fight hard, boy," Garx's last words continued to haunt.

Harton closed his eyes, but it didn't help. If anything, it caused the image of the last moments of his commander's life to come into even sharper focus in his mind. Harton drew in a deep breath and the plain came back into view, albeit a little blurred. He blinked a few times to rid his eyes of excess fluid, hoping it didn't spill down his cheeks.

"Yes," he replied. "You?"

Ortus's mouth widened in a smile that was all teeth. "Not really. Not much I can do about it, though. What about that one?" he pointed past Harton at Rone.

The King's Own warrior was ignoring their hushed conversation, glaring instead at the area of ground still hidden within the dark cloud. His brow was creased, his mouth pulled into a half-snarl.

Harton chuckled. "I don't believe he thinks death is even an option."

Ortus refrained from laughing. "I'd say you're right."

Harton shifted again to alleviate a burn developing in one thigh. Rone stared at him and held an index finger to his lips.

The gun smoke was dissipating although not enough

to see what was happening. The faint shouts and yells hadn't eased, in fact they'd increased in fervour. *Something's going on.* He squinted. That didn't help. It was simply a matter of waiting for the smoke to thin out even more.

Ortus sat and reached into a pocket, pulling clear a square shape wrapped in several wide leaves. He picked clear the leaves revealing a piece of cake which had broken into many smaller sections. Some of them looked sodden, probably from the man's sweat. He offered a piece to Harton. His belly growled. He took it and shoved it in his mouth. It was sweet and chewy. The soldier reached beyond Harton and tapped the foreign trooper, then offered a piece to the man as well.

Within a minute all three were sitting in silence, chewing on old, soggy cake. *Better than nothing, though.* Ortus pushed another piece his way. He didn't complain. Harton ceased chewing and frowned then carefully pushed aside the blades of grass. Kneeling higher he glared at a section of the black smoke. *I swear I saw movement.* Aside from the shouts of command or yelling of confused soldiers, there was nothing to see. *Must have imagined it.* He finished the cake and wiped his hands on his trousers.

Then he saw them, walking through the dark mist was a huge formation of Huronian Cavalry. One rank after another cleared the smoke, advancing in good order towards Lisfort.

"Kill," whispered Rone.

Harton grunted. "Just hold your horses there, lad. Let's see what's what first."

He felt a sharp tap on his arm and turned to Rone. The warrior pointed closer to Lisfort. "Kill." Then he gestured back at the Huronian Cavalry. They were closing with the remnants of the King's Own and a large standing army. Unless his vision betrayed him, they looked to be Highlanders, although it was difficult to see from this distance.

Realisation dawned on Harton. "He's saying the

cavalry intend to kill what's left of the Death Riders."

"I don't think he is," hissed Ortus. "I'm quite certain he believes it to be quite the opposite."

For some minutes the cavalry continued to appear from the mist. Rank after rank. They seemed endless. Wedged in the centre was a particularly thick square formation at the centre of which would be seated King Fillip.

The Death Riders had already responded, moving to form a tight formation and advancing towards their enemy. He had to respect their courage. Even grossly outnumbered retreat did not seem to be an option they'd entertained. The last rank of Huronian Cavalry appeared from the dark cloud. *That's the lot of them. The full force of cavalry.*

The drones of the Highlanders' instruments blared to life in the distance and the army commenced marching a good distance behind the Death Riders.

"Sounds like a bunch of cats being strangled," chuckled Ortus.

Harton moved into a half crouch and winced when one of his legs threatened to cramp. He stretched the muscle and turned away from the coming battle. "Let's mount up." He prodded Rone and pointed back the way they'd come. The King's Own soldier nodded, cast one last look at his comrades then followed.

He came across the few other cavalrymen sat in a tight circle talking in hushed tones. He crouched amongst them and explained what he'd seen. "We're going to harass their rear. Mount up and ready yourselves."

"You'd like that Ortus," one man hissed flashing a grin. "You've always liked harassing the rear."

"I can't argue with that," Ortus replied with a quiet laugh.

"I think you're crazy, Harton," spoke one. "That's the full force of the Huronian Cavalry out there." He swept an arm to encompass their small force. "What are we supposed to do against them? We fought with them once, as well you know. They're the best mounted troops in the world."

He jerked a thumb in Rone's direction. "I think he'd have something to say about that assumption. As for the rest, we're not attacking the cavalry. We're riding back into the camp. We know the infantry and The Mortals are either inside Lisfort." He cast a glance towards the city. "Or dead. Now we know where the cavalry is, too. Who're left?"

Ortus sat on his haunches, took up a sliver of grass and placed it between his teeth. "Artillery." He chewed a small section off and spat it out. "Cooks, clerks, suppliers, powder monkeys, although they'd all be ash by now I'd say."

"Fuckers who can't put up a fight," another finished.

Harton nodded, a smile playing at the edge of his lips. "Exactly." He returned his attention to the doubter. "So, a fast-moving cavalry force can do a lot of damage against the likes of those. The cloud will hide us as well."

Rone stood and tapped his chest, his face took on a look of fury. "Garx," he said.

"For Garx," Harton agreed.

Within five minutes the small troop had mounted and made ready for battle. Gone were the jokes and easy-going attitudes. Their faces were grim, white-knuckled hands clutching weapons as they stared out at the distant plain which would soon become a field of battle. Harton nudged the animal and took the lead. Back the way they'd come. Back towards the area from which they'd fled. Battles weren't often won by idle soldiers.

He steered the small group parallel to the Huronian Cavalry, ensuring they were moving in the opposite direction to the mammoth unit. When they were behind the cavalry and he was sure they'd not been spotted, Harton changed direction straight towards the still thick, dark pall and nudged his mount into a canter. Then a gallop. Movement in the side of his vision gained his attention. Rone was keeping pace, the warrior having unslung a blunderbuss. He held the weapon one-handed, the barrel resting on the mane of his horse.

The cloud of gunpowder swallowed them and he reduced the pace until the minuscule force were advancing at a walking pace. An itch worked its way into the back of his throat. He coughed into the crook of his elbow and rubbed at the sting assaulting his eyes. Rone halted beside a corpse and leapt clear of the saddle. He ripped clear the cloak and wrapped it around his face in such a way that all that could be seen were his eyes.

"The lad has a brain at least," said Ortus through a series of soft coughs.

Harton twisted in his saddle so as to look back at the others. "Cloaks, lads! Find 'em and bind your faces."

They continued on until they found another few dead bodies. Several of the Huronian men dismounted and tore free or untied the cloaks then wrapped their faces to protect themselves from the acrid gun smoke which pervaded every pore.

One of the men dry retched and pulled clear the material, hurling it to the ground. He wiped his down-turned mouth with the back of his hand. "I think he shit himself!" He kicked the body.

"Thought you would have liked that," teased Ortus.

They pushed further into the cloud, some cursing as they rubbed watering eyes. One man descended into a coughing fit until Ortus slammed an open palm onto his back and told him to shut up. A dark blob appeared at the edge of the thick cloud and loomed into focus the farther they advanced. It was an overturned wagon. A team of men were working together to push the vehicle upright, with marginal success. Rone brought his blunderbuss to bear and fired a shot. The roar of the weapon stole away any vestiges of silence, leaving only a high-pitched din ringing in Harton's ears.

"Obragarda!"

Forward the King's Own warrior rode, his weapon now reversed, the heavy wooden butt stock connecting with a soldier's jaw. Slivers of blood and small pearl-coloured chunks exploded free of his mouth. Harton shook free his hesitance and kicked his horse into a trot. He grasped the spear's haft with both hands and drove the weapon deep into a neck. Ripping it free, he stabbed down again, this time the crimson-stained tip finding residence in a chest cavity. A third strike brought death and a fourth stab was blocked, the enemy taking a hold of the weapon. Harton kept a firm grip on the spear and so did his adversary. His stomach lurched into his throat as he lost his balance. He slid clear of the saddle, one foot wedging in a stirrup and arresting his fall.

"Bastard!" the Huronian warrior shouted and attempted to pull the weapon clear.

Harton refused to release the haft. The horse continued onward and his foot slipped clear of the stirrup. He slammed to the ground, pain erupting from his hip. His opponent released the spear and loomed over him, a knife now in his hand.

The man snarled. "You traitorous piece of shit! Artilleryman turned dog, eh? They'll hang you for your insurrection. But hanging's too good for the likes of you!"

The man lunged, and Harton propelled himself backwards on his arse.

"Where you goin', traitor?"

Harton kicked out, boot connecting with a knee cap. His would-be killer winced, and Harton kicked out again, this time his boot finding solace in the man's groin. A shriek, and the soldier clamped a hand to the soft flesh beneath his pants and dropped to his knees.

"Fight hard, boy." The words echoed in his mind.

Harton grabbed his spear as he jumped to his feet and thrust, the sharp metal tip biting deep in his adversary's guts. Placing a boot on the soldier's chest he ripped clear the weapon and stabbed it again, this time it sunk into the man's throat, stopping its advance when it ground against his spine. The corpse toppled backward and came to rest upon the ground with a soft *thunk*.

He attempted to lever the weapon free, but it was embedded in bone. Movement on his periphery, and he turned to find an enemy bearing down on him at a jog, sword raised above his head ready for a savage overhand cut that would split his skull if it landed. Harton tugged on the haft one last time, but the spear would not come free. He released it then, faced the new threat and stumbled backward. The cold infection of fear laced fingers from his chest into the depths of his intestines.

The snarling warrior closed the distance, increasing his pace into a headlong sprint and shouted incoherent words or noises, Harton couldn't tell which. Five paces and he'd be without half his skull. Four paces. An incessant thunder drove up through the ground, vibrating through his boots and growing in power with each moment. Three. He lost his balance on a dead body but righted his footing and continued on his desperate backward journey. Two paces. The enemy soldier brought the sword down, the sharp metal biting through the air with a soft whistle. One. The flank of a horse barged past his shoulder, the rider's shoe barely missed his face. He felt the wind of something which narrowly avoided the top of his head and the butt stock of a blunderbuss appeared in front of his vision. The rock-hard wood battered into the face of the man intent on killing Harton and caved in half his face. The sword went sailing through the air, end over end. Sunlight glinted from the beautiful steel. Harton couldn't help but be mesmerised by the weapon's flight. It plunged into the ground nearby. As for the enemy, he held one hand to his destroyed cheek and staggered, blood streaming from his chin and soaking into his shirt.

Rone brought the blunderbuss down again, the polished wood slamming into the top of the man's head. Blood and slivers of bone sprayed from the wound and the man dropped to the ground without a further sound. The war horse galloped on, chunks of dirt and grass thrown up by its hooves. Where tendrils of dread had seeped into his innards and curled around his spine, now warm relief washed away fear's unbearable grip.

He took a deep breath and looked around to take in the whole scene. For that brief moment it had simply been him and his enemy, nothing else existed in the world. Now that the corpse at his feet oozed claret and chunks of brain matter onto the grass, the rest of the world suddenly hove into view. All the enemy soldiers were dead. The Huronian men delved amongst the deceased, tearing clear cloaks and looting anything of use.

The sword came free of earth's hold easily, and he held the blade up for inspection. The balance was near perfect and it was sharper than sin. He stared down the length of the edge. Straight as a die. Harton knelt by the newly dead warrior, ripped clear his cloak and then unbuckled his sword belt.

"You won't be needing this anymore."

He sheathed the blade, wrapped his head and face with the cloak and re-mounted his horse. Time to cause more trouble.

IV

Miriam sat at the table, her hands resting upon the beautiful, polished timber. The distant, muffled booms of cannon fire had shattered the quiet burble of Lisfort for the past few days. Some return fire had been close. One heavy, round ball crackled through the sky nearby and smashed through a neighbour's roof.

She'd run out onto the street to see if they needed help, but noticed it was the man who'd been so remiss to help her when Vyder had been badly wounded and dying. She'd made sure that his fear-filled eyes had locked onto her steady gaze before she turned and walked back into Vyder's home. If he came calling later accusing her of ignoring her duty as a slave, she'd give him the business end of Vyder's blunderbuss.

What will they do? Hang me for murder? Her soft chuckle broke the silence of the kitchen. *Better than what the Huronians will do to me if they breach the walls.*

Images unbidden flickered through her mind. Her hands being bound, clothes torn from her body. That bastard on top of her, his stink filling her nose, his unwelcome fingers pushing into her. The material being forced between her lips and deep into her mouth, rending her silent. She squeezed tight her eyes, but it did no good. The memory played in full. Only this time her previous master wore the uniform of a Huronian soldier.

Her hand clamped upon the blunderbuss, her fingers curling around the cold wood of the butt stock. The weight of the rapist vanished and she relived the memory of her master sailing through the air, blood following in a thick stream, his head all but cloven free of his shoulders. A tear escaped.

"It's all right lass, it's all right." The deep, thick, Highland voice echoed in the vaults of bygone years. *"You're safe now."*

The thick gag, a sock, was pulled free of her mouth

and her hands cut free.

"My name's Vyder, and your master's dead."

She smiled at the memory. Her eyelids parted and the room swirled in blurry colours. She blinked the tears free and wiped her nose with the back of her hand. Her vision sharpened. She'd kept her former master's sock as a memory of his violent demise and her liberation from a truly hellish existence. It was light blue, stained all over with fading blood. Miriam had never washed it. The blood-stained sock sat on the table in front of her. But it was not alone. She'd placed a small army of socks in rows upon the table. Socks. Who would've thought socks could be used as a lethal weapon?

Not me.

She sniffed and rubbed her eyes. When Vyder had shown her how to shoot and reload the blunderbuss, she'd noticed how slow and cumbersome it'd been to make ready between shots. For weeks she'd wracked her brain to work out a faster way to reload the weapon. A method that would negate the reason to use a powder horn, place it away and then delve into a pouch for lead balls to drop down the muzzle.

The answer? Socks. The measured quantity of black powder was poured into the sock followed by the small lead balls. She'd then twisted it several times to ensure the fabric held the rounds firmly against the powder. Hopefully this would negate the need to ram the shot. She'd then tied a knot in the sock just above the bulge where the powder and rounds sat. Cutting the excess material on the far side of the knot, she'd cast it in the bin. The knot helped to keep the bullets from moving around too much. Vyder had explained how important it was the rounds remained on top of the powder.

The next problem she'd faced was that the fabric created a barrier between the powder and flash pan, meaning when she pulled the trigger, the spark caused by the hammer could not ignite the charge and send the rounds scudding towards her target. She pulled free her hair pin and placed it beside the old blood-stained material. After brief thought, she'd worked out holding the bulging sock over the weapon's maw and piercing the underside with her hairpin would hopefully release a trickle of the explosive black substance. A few seconds later she'd drop the sock down the muzzle. Even a small amount of unhindered powder would, she hoped, be enough to ignite the entire charge. The small hole in the fabric allowed a path for the explosion to follow. She'd not had the opportunity to test her theory, but it seemed logical.

And what if it doesn't work? A deep breath filled her lungs and she took hold of a charged sock. Miriam held it up before her. She'd once asked Vyder why the Wendurlund Army, particularly the King's Own, practised endlessly. Running drills over and over. She'd once been awoken from slumber early one morning by a horn blast indicating a training drill. A few minutes later, as she was drifting back to sleep, the thunder of many hooves stole any vestiges of slumber. The horses sounded like they'd passed metres from the front door galloping towards Lisfort's wall. Another few minutes later and several horn blasts followed by the crackle of distant muskets had sheered through the night's silence. The next morning she'd queried Vyder about it.

"Better to train from the safety of peace to know that something works, then to find out it doesn't in the thick of battle," his voice told her from the depths of her memory.

Her eyebrows rose. "Best I try this out, then."

She pushed the chair back, the thick wooden legs scraping upon the floor, and stood. Her hand curled around the barrel of the blunderbuss, the other clutching the charged sock. "Time to test this."

She chose Vyder's bedroom door as her target. It was thick, sturdy, and should absorb the lead balls. Standing well back, she placed the butt stock of the weapon on the floor, the dark maw staring at her. She clutched the barrel between her thighs, pierced the sock, allowed a small trickle of the volatile powder to cascade into the darkness and then dropped the small bulging piece of material in afterwards.

Lifting the weapon, the butt stock nestled snug into her shoulder. The polished wood cold against her cheek. Miriam placed her left foot forward and touched the trigger with her index finger. Squeezing shut her eyes, she pulled the trigger. The hammer slammed forward with a dull *clunk* and a hint of gun smoke teased her nose. Proof the flintlock had done its job and scattered a spark down into the breach. *It hasn't worked.* She relaxed. *BOOM!* The weapon slammed into her shoulder forcing her back. Miriam lost her footing and fell onto her arse. Her hand still clutched the smoking blunderbuss. What sounded like an incessant screaming bell attacked her hearing.

A tickle embedded deep in her nose and throat, forcing her to sneeze and cough simultaneously. Rolling onto her knees, she put the butt stock on the ground, maintained a grip on the warm barrel and used it to aid her to her feet. Gun smoke filled the room, stinging her eyes and assaulting her nose. She waved her hands to ward it away and strode to the door. The rounds had passed clean through the thick wood. The spray of bullets had struck the target in a rough circle about the width of a man's chest.

She patted the weapon in her hand and smiled. "I like you after all."

Departing the room brought fresh air and reprieve from the dark, acrid cloud which would no doubt settle upon the floor in time. Miriam's brow creased. She paused at the kitchen table, one hand resting upon the surface. *Must have been my imagination.* The piercing din in her ears continued although it had receded a little. The series of knocks came again, this time much more forceful. No mistaking it this time. Someone was at the door.

Fear and anger swept through her. She clutched a second sock, bulging with powder and bullets and reloaded the blunderbuss as before. Lifting a third charged sack, she shoved it in a pocket. Last but not least, Miriam cocked the weapon and strode to the front door. Pushing the hairpin behind an ear she clasped the door handle, turned the black steel and pulled open the entrance. A familiar face greeted her. A slave from nearby, the same slave who'd challenged her when she'd been desperate for help as life fled from Vyder's body. *Seems like a lifetime ago.* His master was the fat one who'd suggested she'd killed Vyder and had called for The Watch to be notified. She would have been placed under arrest and probably hung without a trial.

She pulled the weapon into her shoulder, cheek touching the cold, polished wood of the butt stock and stared down the barrel at the servant. Her index finger felt the cool metal of the trigger and took up a little pressure. "What?"

The man took a backward step, eyebrows shooting towards his hairline. His mouth dropped open and he held out open palms towards her. He swallowed. "Don't shoot!"

Miriam walked over the threshold and stopped on the doorstep, weapon still pointing at the man.

"Please, don't shoot."

"What do you want?"

"My master sent me." He kept his hands in view.

Her arms were beginning to ache, but Miriam kept the weapon's maw facing the servant. "What does that fat bastard want?"

The servant's eyes bulged and his hands dropped by his sides. "How dare you speak of the master in that way?"

"You didn't answer my question. What does that fat bastard want?" She lunged forward a step. "Don't make me shoot you."

The man lurched backward one pace, hands flying back up into the air, empty palms facing her. "He sent me to find out the meaning of the noise he heard."

"Noise?"

"A gunshot."

She lowered the weapon to her hips, but kept it pointed in his general direction. Miriam jerked her head towards the East. "Have you heard the fighting on the eastern wall these last few days?"

His hands dropped once more. "Of course!"

"Did that disturb your master?"

He frowned. "No!"

"Well, it bloody should have. You hear any fighting there now?

The bump in his throat rose and fell. "No."

"Can you take a wild guess at what that means?"

"We've won?" he asked with hesitance.

She shrugged. "Maybe." She brought the blunderbuss up and rested the barrel against her shoulder.

The slave's shoulders slumped and a breath of air rushed out of his mouth. "Thank the gods," he muttered.

"But maybe not," Miriam added. "If the Huronians have taken the wall, it won't be long before they are sweeping through the city, ransacking, raping and killing."

"We don't know the wall has fallen, though."

"We don't know it hasn't," she countered. "So, to answer your flabby master's question. I was testing this weapon to ensure it worked. That way if an enemy kicks in this front door, he won't get far. He should have been much more concerned with the incessant roar of battle coming from the east than my single gun blast."

The slave nodded. "I see. My master has asked you not make further noise."

Miriam shrugged. "I shall make as much noise as I require until I'm happy with the weapon."

"I give you fair warning. If it happens again, don't be surprised if the master himself is at your doorstep. And he won't be asking as nicely as I."

There was a time when a threat like that would have sent a shudder of fear through her. But after recent events she felt no fear, only the slow burning ember of anger in her gut.

Miriam's eyelids narrowed to a slit and her brows drew together. "You tell that leech that if his fat arse appears on this doorstep, I'll splatter his bloody head clean off his shoulders."

"The Watch shall hear of this!" he said, his voice

breaking. "Mark my words, you'll be reported!" He stepped back and turned from her.

"I think they may be indisposed at the moment, somehow."

At least I can offer some kind of resistance if the front door is breached by Huronian soldiers.

She slammed shut the door and turned the lock. Leaning against the heavy, polished wood, she chuckled without humour. *If?* She turned and walked towards the kitchen, a cold spark of fear flickering at the base of her spine. *When, Miriam. Not if.*

Gun Commander Humber strode along the gun line, pride swelling in his chest. The guns were silent now, although strands of smoke drifted from one or two barrels where an active ember still smouldered somewhere within the massive weapon's barrel. The gunners stood in groups, each behind their respective weapon. They were bare-chested, having doffed their shirts halfway through the fire missions in a bid to try and keep cool. Sweat glistened on their skin and plastered hair to powder-darkened faces. The muzzles of the cannons were black from the relentless barrages they'd visited upon the unseen Huronian Army somewhere on the other side of Lisfort's walls. The gunners had worked hard, firing the cannons six times per minute. Two rounds faster than the intense rate.

Where the hell is the forward observer?

Some of the soldiers stretched sore arms and tired backs. But the glint of defiance was present in every set of eyes. He knew his gunners would jump to action if another fire mission came in, their aches long forgotten. The guns had been positioned on the Palace Green, forty acres of flat grassland in front of the palace. In peaceful times, gatherings, royal events, parades, festivals and important celebrations had been held here. Now only cannons stood, the once bright green grass fading to dark grey where spent gun powder had settled. Pyramids of cannon balls and crates of varying munitions stood next to each gun. Barrels of powder littered the royal paddock.

If the enemy breached the walls, eventually, it would be here they'd fight the last battle along with whatever remained of the Wendurlund Army. *If we're fast, we could get two maybe three barrages off before being overrun.* Humber stopped by the last gun in line. He touched his sword hilt. *And then it'll be hand-to-hand.* Turning back the way he'd walked, Humber noticed the few guns in question had ceased their smoking.

"Reload!" he roared.

No further fire mission had been requested, but many years as an artillery commander suggested that readiness was better than hesitation, which sometimes led to panic. As he'd predicted, the gunners leapt to action at the order of each gun's sub commander. Black powder was poured down the muzzle, the ball was dropped down the muzzle and then rammed. Fuses were pushed into the small hole at the base of the barrel and a soldier stood beside each brazier, ready to pull the red-hot poker free in order to ignite the fuse.

Shouts of, "gun ready!" rippled up and down the gun line.

Sergeant Deetag, the forward observer galloped into view mounted on his freshest horse. This was the third horse he'd rotated through, allowing the others to rest. The forward observer carried target directions and fire commands from the front line, so a horse worthy of speed and endurance was a necessity.

Ah, here we go. Fresh commands. The guns will be smoking again before long.

Deetag brought the powerful animal to a stop beside him. Dried blood caked one of the sergeant's cheeks and he nursed a cut on his upper arm.

"Are you well, sergeant?"

"I am, sir. Bad news. The wall's fallen. The enemy have overrun the ramparts and are advancing into the city."

Fear blossomed in Humber's stomach. "Where is

Corporal Trask?"

Trask was on foot, listening to the commands from the wall and relaying them back to Deetag.

Deetag's jaw bulged for a moment. "He fell in battle, sir. He took down two enemy before being overwhelmed. I tried to fight to him but was surrounded myself. I cut a retreat through the enemy and narrowly missed being pulled from the saddle."

Humber acknowledged the cold dread in his gut but refused to allow it to take control of him.

A pity. Corporal Trask was a good soldier.

"May he rest with the gods," he spoke with a soft voice.

With no Trask or Wendurlund soldiers on the wall to feed direction and elevation commands, the artillery was blind.

"Deetag, inform the palace guards the wall has fallen."

The guards will be the last line of defence soon enough.

"Yes, sir!" Deetag kicked his mount into a gallop and thundered away.

Humber turned on his heel to face the gun line. "Drop one fifty!" he roared.

The teams jumped to work lowering the angle of each barrel's direction of aim. Without fire mission commands to follow, he'd drop the guns as low as possible in the event enemy soldiers were still charging towards the wall after their comrades. Dropping one hundred and fifty metres meant the cannon shot would be just skimming over Lisfort's eastern wall. If they dropped the elevation any further than that they'd be striking the wall itself.

"One fifty! On!" the words flickered down the line.

Humber returned his focus to the cannons. "Fire for effect!" he shouted.

"Number one, fire!"

Even before the command had been issued another voice was already yelling, "number two, fire!"

"...three fire!"

"...fire."

Ear splitting thunder rocked the green, spewing across the city and echoing from buildings. The ground beneath him shuddered.

Three seconds passed and every gun on the palace green was empty, hidden by a mist of gun smoke. Humber strode down the line, resisting the urge to cough gun smoke from the back of his throat. "Clock face!"

Without a need to fire over the wall at some unseen enemy force, it was time to prepare for defence in case the enemy attempted to storm Palace Green with a view to capturing the palace.

In case? Humber growled. *Only a matter of time.*

Metal spikes were worked free of the ground in front and behind each cannon wheel. Each team gathered behind their respective weapons and pushed them into position. They faced outward of the palace in a half circle from the nine o'clock to the three o'clock positions.

Next, each cannon's pyramid of cannon balls were carried into place next to the new location of the weapons. Powder kegs were rolled next to each pile of balls and smoking braziers were deftly dragged into place by thickly-gloved gunners. With fresh sweat washing their skin, the gun teams stood by their weapons, chests heaving.

He strode across the grass his glare sweeping across his gun teams. "Elevation zero!"

The order was repeated by each sub commander, the wide barrels dropping inch by inch as their elevation was wound down by each team. Only when the open maws of each gun were horizontal to the ground did all movement cease.

Humber clasped his hands behind his back and turned to face the right-hand flank of his gun line. "From the right, number!"

The sub commander standing by the cannon at the three o'clock position came to attention. "One!"

"Two!" the next sub commander roared.

"Three!"

"Four!"

"Five!"

The count was complete when the last sub commander yelled, "sixty!"

Humber waited until the last man's voice had faded to silence and then cupped hands around his mouth. "Even numbers load chain shot! Odd numbers load grape shot! LOAD!"

The teams leapt to action, breaking open wooden crates where the specialty ammunition was kept. They loaded their respective shot and laid out further ammunition nearby ready for a fast reload.

"Now we wait. It's only a matter of time," he muttered.

When the Huronian infantry had swept through the city their final target would be the palace, and their first few ranks would be welcomed by Humber's cannons. If his teams were fast enough, they might be able to fire a second and even a third volley before the hand-to-hand fighting started. Humber closed his eyes and let out a long breath, touched the hilt of his sword – the cold metal feeling foreign against his palm. How would he, a gun commander, fair in a sword fight against professional infantry soldiers? His lip curled. *An easy question to answer. I won't stand a bloody chance.*

The staccato of hooves reverberated through the ground and Deetag reined in beside him. "Sir, the palace guards are preparing for battle."

Relief swept him, although it did not assuage the anxiety pulsing through his guts. "Thank you, Sergeant."

The palace guards were not a shadow of the King's Own, but they were better trained in close quarter battle than he and his artillerymen.

Sergeant Deetag swung down from the saddle and patted the flank of his horse. "It's better than nothing, sir."

Is my face that easy to read? "I agree, Deetag. The guard

might be enough to turn the battle."

The words of doubt both men held remained unspoken.

"Sergeant, pass on fire control orders to the gun teams. Guns one through fifteen to fire on the command, 'fire battery one'. Sixteen through thirty on, 'fire battery two'. Thirty-one through forty-five on, 'fire battery three' and forty-six through sixty on, 'fire battery four'. All guns to fire on, 'fire regiment'."

Deetag leapt back into the saddle and kicked the animal towards the guns. "Yes, sir," he yelled over his shoulder.

Five minutes later and his sergeant returned, this time he remained in the saddle should further instructions required to be carried to the gun line.

"What now, sir?"

Humber released his sword's hilt and focused above the roofs of the closest buildings. Somewhere out there lay the ruins of the eastern wall and between it and his half circle of artillery guns thousands of enemy soldiers ransacked the city. "Now?" he muttered, eyes narrowing. "Now we do nothing."

The words sounded, much less felt, wrong, even immoral. But he couldn't very well have his soldiers push their cannons, each more than one tonne, around the streets chasing the enemy. Much as he hated it, the more practical option was to wait for the Huronians to come to him.

It took but an hour before blackened smoke drifted into the sky towards the east. Enemy soldiers, it seemed, were already burning buildings. Occasionally the distant clash of steel, shouts or screams drifted on the soft breeze. Probably where The Watch offered some kind of defence against the Huronian onslaught. Sometimes he wasn't sure the faint noises weren't a figment of his imagination.

A shout, much closer than the others, rent the air, drowning out the distant battle. Another few yells replied. *Huronian words.* He clasped a hold of the sword's cold, metal hilt and scanned the small alleys separating the closest buildings. The voices bounced down narrow streets and ricocheted from stone fences making it difficult to decipher from which direction the threat approached. The creak of leather came from nearby where Deetag shifted in his saddle.

"Steady, Sergeant."

"Where do you want us, sir?"

The deep voice sent a spark of terror down his spine and he whirled to stare into the face of an officer of the guard. He was dressed in a boiled leather cuirass painted in vertical blue and black stripes. Beneath that he wore a black, long-sleeved shirt, and thickly padded trousers. Although the armour was minimal, it was also light. The guard always favoured agility and speed. He held a long, odd-looking musket. On closer inspection, Humber realised it was one of those new rifles. The small scope on top of the barrel meant it could be shot with accuracy at targets long distances away. A troop of some fifty warriors standing in a tight group behind him were dressed and armed in a similar fashion.

They'd have been useless on the wall where close quarters fighting was the order of the day. The sledgehammer of the infantry was more effective than the much slower scalpel of the palace guard.

And what would fifty of them have done anyway? Probably got in the bloody way!

"Sir?"

Humber blinked and snapped out of his thoughts. "Right!" he said, offering a tight smile. "What's the range of those things?" he slashed an index finger in the direction of the rifles.

"About five hundred metres at maximum range."

"Well, the bastards won't be anywhere near that far away." He clasped hands behind his back. "More's the pity," he added. "I'd prefer you and your soldiers opened fire first. Once my cannons engage, the view of the battlefield will be hidden behind gun smoke for some time. I think if you arrayed your troop up on the upper level of the palace that should suffice. What say you?"

"Suits us, sir."

"Good. Get yourselves up there and prepare to fire a volley. I doubt you'll have much time before the enemy show their ugly faces. Quickly now!"

The guardsmen withdrew at a sprint. The side streets and narrow drives of the buildings closest Palace Green acted like funnels, channelling and enhancing the foreign voices.

How many had breached the wall? A hundred? A thousand?

Humber strode towards the closest gun team, his hands still clenched together at the small of his back.

More?

He stopped beside the sub commander. "How goes it?" he asked, looking at the soldier.

The man's face and upper body was black with spent powder. A flash of bright teeth shone from within the darkness. "All good here, sir. I've never fired chain shot at infantry before." He jerked his head towards his silent gun team waiting beside the pitch-stained cannon. "We want to see what it does."

Humber chuckled and returned his attention to the distant buildings, scanning the dark roads waiting to see movement as enemy soldiers advanced into view. But aside from the nearing shouts and laughs, they remained unseen.

"Pafik over there reckons it'll cut 'em clean in half. Hup and I are in agreeance. Grek disagrees. He thinks it'll fly over their heads and embed itself into a building."

"Let me guess. You've got money riding on it?"

The pearly whites flashed again. "Course not, sir. Don't know why you'd ever think that. Gambling on duty's an offence punishable by hanging."

Humber smiled. "Yes, I'm aware."

Let them have their fun. As long as they carry out their duty as required.

A stream of Huronian soldiers ran into view from the darkness of one of the alleyways. There were perhaps one hundred of them. The smile widening Humber's lips vanished and his brow furrowed. "Prepare yourselves!" he shouted. He pivoted where he stood and strode back into the centre of the Palace Green to better appraise the battlefield as a whole. He flashed a glance up at the palace roof where the small silhouettes of the guardsmen stood in an extended line, rifles pulled into their shoulders.

They disappeared behind a cloud of gun smoke, the sound of the shot echoed over the gun line. The whistle of rounds cut through the air above the gunners' heads. Humber whirled to watch the fall of shot. Even at what he estimated must have been close to three hundred metres, it was obvious the soldiers were marksmen. The hail of bullets ripped the life from half the charging Huronians. A scant few dropped and clutched legs or held hands upon their belly, screeching their death song to the sky.

The remainder filtered out into extended line and broke into a sprint towards the eleven o'clock position of the semi-circle of cannons. He squinted at the group of enemies and judged their distance at two hundred metres. Gunners stood by the glowing braziers, thick gloves clutching pokers buried deep in the coals. Gone were the jokes and laughter.

One hundred metres. He exhaled through pursed lips. *You can stop there, you Huronian bastards.*

"Fire battery two!"

The command was taken up by his gunners. Each man shouted the order to ensure there could be no confusion. Fifteen guns belched their wrath and a quarter of the semi-circle disappeared behind a fog of gun smoke. The dull scream rang deep within his ears, but Humber ignored it, striding forward, hands still clutched behind him. He scowled when the smoke consumed him and ignored the aching need to cough the itch at the back of his throat created.

"Reload!" he roared. That helped alleviate the annoying sensation.

He passed the gun line and continued until the cloud of acrid smoke was behind him. The sword's cool hilt felt good in his hand. Gone was the nervous tension, replaced with a burning drive to defend the heart of his city. Blinking the sting from his eyes, he saw there were no enemy left alive. His battery had torn the life from them. The Huronians who hadn't been cut down by the withering sniper fire had been sliced to ribbons by the cannons.

Several of the dead were without a head. At least twenty had holes the size of a man's fist punched through leather and steel armour alike. One soldier had been cut clean in two. More than a dozen were missing limbs, bright red blood soaking into the ground around them. He looked upon the devastation with grim satisfaction. He always knew grape shot was effective against foot soldiers, but he'd been unsure about the chain shot. Usually, the latter ammunition was used by the navy to sheer through an enemy's sail mast.

Humber had been of the opinion that if it could slice through a piece of wood thicker than a draught horse's midriff, why not take out a troop of soldiers?

A fair assumption, I'd say. He cleared his throat, still refusing to allow the cough to pass his lips.

"Gun ready!" the distant words were shouted along the line as each weapon were made ready to fire again.

He swivelled where he stood and marched back to the safety of the guns. The team he'd spoken with earlier stood in a loose huddle muttering amongst themselves.

"Oi, you lot!"

They jumped to attention. "Sir?" the closest said.

Humber grinned. "Chain shot cuts the bastards clean in half!"

V
Afternoon – fifth day of the siege

Vyder sat astride Storm, the animal ambling behind the five squares formed by the Highland Army. His heart thundered against his chest, although he kept the hope from his face. *Today might be my skane. I hope it is.* Verone's face appeared in his mind. She was smiling, her arms held open. He shook away the image as a high-pitched whine came from below. He leaned in the saddle already knowing the source. Saigh sat, tongue lolling from her mouth staring up at him. Each thump of her tail sent a tiny puff of dust into the air behind her. For a fleeting moment, guilt sank into him. But he knew whenever it was that he made the crossing of the Frost River, his loyal hound would be well cared for.

"You're a good lass." Her tail wagging increased in speed and power at the sound of his voice.

Most Highlanders weren't afraid of death. They believed the gods wove their skane long before they were born, so their death was inevitable. Until that time, they lived their life in whichever manner they chose within the rules of their clans. In battle, that belief made them bold, fierce and unstoppable. But few actually hoped to die.

There'd still been no word from Gorgoroth. The nature spirit had disappeared as if he'd never existed. He'd be back, though. *Of course he'll be back! Otherwise, I'd be a corpse on the ground. He's around somewhere.* Question was, where?

Vyder touched the blackened disc beneath his shirt. A spark was all he needed to summon Agoth. He might have need of the nature spirit's aid in battle, yet. His warriors were tested against infantry. But how would the squares fair against professional cavalry? He frowned and clenched his sword hilt until his knuckles turned white. *Only time will tell.*

Henry was on his right, Ahitika beside him. The pair were silent, although the Kalote woman wore a fierce expression. He'd forgotten just how much she hated the nation of Huron. Hyglak was mounted on his left, war horn clamped in one hand, his other resting on the pommel of his sword. Behind Vyder walked the remainder of the mounted Highlanders in a loose square. Perhaps five hundred in total. A rudimentary cavalry force.

The squares moved well, their shields held low to stave off muscle fatigue. But they'd be able to lift them up at a moment's notice.

Continuing to advance at a walk, the Huronian Cavalry appeared relaxed, unconcerned. It was easy to discern they believed the battle already won. They grossly outnumbered the King's Own, and mopping up Tork's force would probably be a small action in their minds. Vyder stood in his stirrups and squinted, focusing on the tight square in the centre of the enemy force. King Fillip was definitely present.

Tork's force also advanced towards the cavalry at a walk. They appeared just as unconcerned. The elite troops would make a good account of themselves but would it be enough? The remainder of the King's Own had already been overrun on the wall, or so Henry thought. If Tork's force came to a similar end, the full force of the enemy would be focused upon Vyder's Great Highland Army.

"We came to assist, lord, but it seems we might yet win the entire damn battle!"

The voice speared his thoughts and he noticed the wide grin adorning Hyglak's face. Fear found no place in the big chieftain's demeanour.

He smiled, although the bite of concern still emanated within him. "It appears that way. It's no big thing though, my friend." He gestured towards the huge, slow approaching enemy unit with a sluggish movement of his hand. "We'll defeat these bastards and then lay siege to the entire city. It should all be over by, oh, say..." He twisted in his saddle and found the sun high and behind them. "About five o'clock this evening by my reckoning."

Hyglak leaned back in his saddle and roared with

laughter. "Aye, lord! Aye."

The smile faded from Vyder's face. The Huronians had broken into a canter, their progress accompanied by a soft rumble. He called a halt to the infantry squares. *No point blundering into a cavalry charge. Better to wait for them to come to us.*

Tork's unit still advanced at a walk, still appearing to be unconcerned. A distant staccato of *booms* emanated from within Lisfort. He twisted in his saddle and searched the walls of the city, but aside from the dark smudge of Huronian soldiers eager to watch the clash about to occur, there was no battle that he could see. *Keep that blunderbuss close, Miriam.*

A snicker of movement drew his attention and a hail of cannonballs scudded over the walls. They must have missed the Huronian soldiers standing on the ramparts by mere inches. The fast-moving rounds were crackling straight towards Tork. Shouting erupted from within the King's Own closely followed by a series of short, sharp bugle blasts. The elite force split smoothly in two, their slow progress and relaxed demeanour gone, to be replaced with a fierce, determination and freakish, sudden speed. One group broke into a gallop and speared to the right, the other to the left. Saigh's deep, powerful barks were barely audible over the thunder of hooves, shouts and the increasing screech of incoming artillery fire.

The Huronian Cavalry, now closing the distance at a full charge were moving too rapidly to change direction in order to affect a chase. They were advancing upon vacant ground. The cannonballs screamed through the air, hammered into the ground just shy of the Huronian Cavalry and sent up clouds of dirt and clumps of grass. The dull thuds reverberated through the ground, startling some of the horses in the Highland Army. But they were comforted with soft words and a gentle hand.

The cannon shot ricocheted from the earth, reappeared in front of the brown cloud they'd created and smashed through the front rank of the Huronian force. And then the second rank. Horses and men both, were cast to the ground bloody and broken, some injured, many dead. The third, fourth and fifth ranks fared no better. Their momentum and fury lost, the rounds sent from the Wendurlund cannons rolled to a stop, nothing more than motionless pieces of round lead. But the damage they'd wreaked was incredible to behold. The charge ground to a halt. Some men leapt clear of saddles to attend injured comrades.

"Gods, those poor horses," muttered Hyglak. It was difficult to tell whether the high-pitched squeals and screams emanating from the enemy force issued from the throat of man or beast. But it was easy to see perhaps a quarter of their number were dead or no longer a threat. A second series of distant bugle blasts rent the air. The deep, dull blunderbusses spoke in unison. Another bugle blast and muskets crackled to life. The instrument spoke for a third time. The single-worded war cry of the King's Own rolled across the battleground.

Then Tork's unit appeared from within the ranks of the Huronians, battering their way through the rank-and-file wielding razor sharp spears with devastating effect. They erupted clear, galloping straight towards Vyder's Army. A bugle blast sent them in a wide left wheel and their pace dropped to a canter. Even in the saddle, the soldiers were reloading their flintlock weapons.

"They are in disarray," Henry said, watching the Huronian Cavalry with a keen glint in his eye. "Better to keep striking them while they are vulnerable."

Vyder could understand some of the language echoing from the rank-and-file of the enemy formation, but most of it was indecipherable.

"They are in panic," said Ahitika, a hint of amusement in her voice. "They know not what to do."

Those on the flank closest the cantering King's Own kept throwing furtive glances at the elite unit, half expecting them to charge back at them. Then a deep-throated voice bellowed from the centre. The shouting dropped to a murmur, until only that one powerful soldier was the only one making any noise. Even the foreign words he roared were on a par with the dull drum of King's Own hooves thumping against dry ground.

Henry nudged his horse forward a pace. "King Fillip. Gods, Tork, hit them again before they reorganise."

Vyder returned his attention to the allied force in the near distance. They'd reloaded their weapons. Almost as if Tork had heard Henry's plea, the bugle blast that cut through the sky sent them into a hard turn straight towards the Huronians. Within a few paces the elite force was at full gallop and in extended line, the soldiers shouldered blunderbusses. Even before the next blast of the piercing instrument faded to silence, they disappeared in a cloud of gun powder, the shuddering *boom* of the potent weapons washing over Vyder and his Highland Army.

The bugle continued to blare in strange rhythms varying in complexity. Steel spear tips glinted in the sun as they were withdrawn, then the extended line morphed in a much tighter formation. The King's Own war cry peeled across the field and they struck the Huronian Cavalry at full force, smashing through their ranks and disappearing from view. Tork's formation seemed to have been absorbed by the much larger enemy.

Frightened and uncertain shouts and screams rippled across the foreign unit, despite the powerful boom of King Fillip's words as he struggled to regain order amongst his troops. Musket fire crackled from the distant flank and more screaming commenced. That single word roared in the Wendurlund language rolled over Vyder's troops. Tork reappeared leading his troops in a spearhead formation piercing through the heart of the enemy galloping straight towards Vyder.

The bugle continued to cry in varying degrees of length and repetition. The spearhead dispersed into a single file and slowed to a canter. As before, the soldiers reloaded their weapons in the saddle. A group of Huronian Cavalry broke clear and fled the field. Like their resolve, their retreat was conducted as fast as their mounts would carry them. Tork ignored them, but Vyder did not. He stood in the stirrups and held a hand over his forehead to shield his eyes from the sun. They showed no sign of turning back towards either the Great Highland Army or Tork. He settled back into the saddle.

King Fillip's shouting persisted and the Huronian Cavalry looked to regain some semblance of order. The dying were left to die and soldiers leapt back onto their horses. The formation, still massive despite the attentions of the Wendurlund Artillery battery and Tork's elite unit, broke into a trot. Then accelerated into the canter and turned away from Tork's tiny formation. They were back in the fight. Panic, which had swept their ranks like a wildfire was stamped out by their king. Fear had been controlled, allowing training to take back the reins.

"Shit," muttered Hyglak.

Vyder grunted, the muscles of his jaw bulging beneath his beard. "Be ready to call shield wall, they may charge straight at us."

"Aye, lord."

The King's Own shimmered into a new formation at the trot. This time they held spears at the ready, following the Huronian formation and ready to anticipate a move. As if obliging them, King Fillip's formation wheeled back around towards both Vyder and Tork, the tiny elite unit the only thing between the Huronians and Vyder's army.

Vyder nudged Storm into movement. She chewed the ground up between he and the infantry squares. Swinging her around, he galloped along their front line. "Be ready to fight!" he roared. "We'll face them next. Muskets and blunderbusses in the second rank, I want you to fire off a shot before those bastards hit the shield walls. When they hit us, drag them from their saddles, stab them, hack them apart, cut the life from them!"

He steered Storm down the narrow patch of ground

separating two squares. "Pipers!"

"Lord?" a single voice called.

"Play for battle!"

"Aye, lord!"

The deep drone of a single bag pipe rolled across the Great Highland Army, the piercing tunes drifting through the ranks, the sound haunting and powerful. A second bagpipe joined the first and a third, a fourth, then a fifth. Soon a small army of pipers played, the sound empowering, sending chills down his spine.

Vyder guided Storm back towards the enemy. The King's Own had accelerated into a charge aimed straight at the heart of the Huronian enemy. They struck hard and disappeared into the enemy ranks. The hole they'd punched was reformed and the Huronian charge kept coming straight for the Highlanders.

"Ironstone, let me hear you!" Vyder shouted.

The war cry was taken up by Clan Ironstone, their voices adding to the bagpipes. Saigh started barking again, strings of saliva glistening from her lower jaw.

"Waterborne, what have you to say?"

The war cry of Clan Waterborne added to the cacophony.

"Windeagle! Earthforge! Coppersmith! Wintercreek!"

The bagpipes had been drowned out, their tune retreating before the more ferocious song of the Great Highland Army. On the Huronians came, although the rumble of their hooves was rendered to silence by the mingling war cries.

Vyder galloped along the front of the infantry squares, his spear clasped in his hand. He pointed the weapon's tip at the approaching enemy charge. "They'll wish they'd stayed away." He grinned then, his eyes wide.

He guided Storm around the squares and galloped behind them. Throwing a look at his small cavalry force, he held up a hand towards them. "Stay there for now!" he roared. He galloped to them and reined in beside Rafe. The black-haired berserker was smiling, his eye gleaming with madness.

He is but a hair's breadth from going berserk. The madman might not have been the best choice to lead the Highland Cavalry, but depending on how the battle unfolded, it might also have been the best choice Vyder ever made. *Time will tell.*

"Rafe!"

The chieftain's piercing, unblinking stare shifted to bore into Vyder. "Hmm?"

"When the infantry squares are fully engaged in battle, fight your way forward. Create some distance between the front rank and the Huronians. It'll give our second rank time to reload. Then we'll fire on them again once you're clear."

Rafe grinned.

Vyder slapped a hand onto the berserker's shoulder. "Do you understand?"

Rafe grunted.

Did he nod? I think he did.

He looked beyond Rafe at the closest Highlander, a woman who'd adorned her face with stripes of black and yellow. Her eyes gleamed from within the war paint.

"Got it?"

She nodded. "Aye, lord."

He nudged Storm into movement and thundered back towards the infantry squares. When he reached the middle square, he brought the horse to a stop. Hyglak halted beside him, Saigh stood nearby, her hackles up, teeth bared. She'd be growling, but it was impossible to hear the fearsome sound over the noise of the Highlanders. He estimated the enemy were three hundred metres away and closing the distance fast.

He glanced at Hyglak. Wintercreek's chieftain clasped his war horn like a vice, his face grim. He held the instrument halfway to his lips, anticipating the first command.

"Ready?"

Hyglak shot him a glance and smiled. "Oh, I'm ready, lord."

Two hundred metres.

"Call shield wall!"

The blast pierced the war cries and cut through the bagpipes. But only barely. Although the clans were already in their squares, their shields interlocked, the command served to bring their focus back to the war horn. It was a gentle reminder that the first official command wasn't far away.

One hundred metres.

A distant bugle blast followed by a *boom* radiated from behind the enemy charge. *Tork's still in the fight.*

Fifty metres.

Another bugle note pierced the wall of noise. Muskets, almost inaudible over the din, crackled from the enemy rear. Tork's unit continued to deal injury and death to the Huronians. The shouts and shrieks of the Highland Army was savage, fearless. They promised blood and death.

"The Frost River will be well trodden today."

Thirty metres.

"Black powder!"

The war horn spoke, slicing through the cacophony. Front ranks turned side on, lowered their shields and those in the second rank levelled muskets and blunderbusses and fired creating their own thunder. Gun smoke consumed the first few rows of Highlanders. The leading line of cavalry went down and the screaming started.

"Shield wall!"

Hyglak gave the command, although the front ranks had already recovered their position, interlocking their shields and leaning forward in preparation to take the brunt of the cavalry charge. Better to give a command not needed than neglect to provide one and lose entire clans. The following Huronians trampled their downed comrades, some horses tripping in the process, sending their riders slamming into the dirt. One man knelt up, his face creased in pain, but disappeared beneath the hooves of a war horse. Then the remnants of the enemy battered into the Highland squares. The enemy managed to smash their way through to the third, fourth or even fifth rank of some squares. The clatter of steel on steel or muffled *thump* of swords on shields took over, drowning out the spine-chilling screams of the dying.

"Gods!" Vyder swivelled in his saddle. He glared at the Highland Cavalry. "Get in there!" he roared. Rafe was already leading them in a gallop. They hacked and sliced their way into the Huronian flank. One clansman leapt from his saddle, roaring a war cry, his face, painted entirely red, a picture of fury and rage. He was another berserker by the name of Byfros if he recalled. Byfros was airborne for a couple of seconds and then collided with a Huronian. The Highlander wrapped a hand around the midriff of his adversary arresting his travel and stabbed a knife into his opponent's neck. Byfros pushed the dying soldier clear of the horse and took up the reins catching up with his comrades with a couple of kicks to the animal's flank. Rafe was a force in his own right. He was utterly fearless, his blood-stained sword rising and falling with inexhaustible speed.

Relief washed over Vyder. Making Rafe the commander of the Highland Cavalry was the right decision. The mounted clansmen and women pierced the Huronian formation, forcing those advancing back from the squares and cutting off those embedded within the Highland lines. Rafe, already bleeding from slices to his face, arms, belly and back didn't slow. Nor did his reddened sword. He wielded the weapon in a blur, dispatching soldiers to make their journey across the Frost River.

"Lord! Our flanks!" Hyglak shouted.

Vyder stood in the stirrups so as to see better. His stomach lurched into his throat. Huronian Cavalry not already engaged in combat flowed down the flanks of the outer most squares and were hacking their way into the Highlanders.

Vyder cupped a hand around his mouth. "You stay here!"

Hyglak nodded.

He peered down at Saigh. "Stay, lass!" The hound

barked at him and whined. "When Rafe and the others have ridden clear, call black powder again. Understood?"

"Aye lord!" the veins in Hyglak's throat bulged against the skin of his throat.

This isn't going as well as I'd hoped.

A bugle blast cut the sky followed immediately by the thunder of blunderbusses. *Thank the gods. Tork's still harassing them.* He turned Storm towards the Highland square fighting at the extreme left and nudged her into a gallop. He cast a glance over his shoulder. "Stay!" he shouted at Saigh. She obeyed the command, but stared after him, barking. He spotted the airborne spear almost too late. It was scudding straight towards his chest. He leaned back and twisted in the saddle, the weapon slicing through thin air where his body had been moments before.

Had they time, he might have trained the Highlanders in more complex commands given via the war horn. The King's Own could almost hold entire conversations with their bugles. That kind of training took years. The Great Highland Army was privy to a few weeks. Still, what they could do was better than nothing. An enemy soldier charged down the narrow strip of land separating two squares and came straight towards Vyder. He wore a furious frown, lips peeled back revealing clenched teeth.

Vyder swung Storm mid gallop towards the threat. His thighs clasped tight about the animal's flanks to assist his balance. He gripped the spear firm with both hands, stood in the saddle and thrust the weapon towards his adversary. The spear's tip cut through chain mail and slid deep into his guts. Vyder released his clutch on the wooden haft and instead grabbed the sword arm of the Huronian warrior. Mortally wounded and weakening, it wasn't difficult to stop the sword swing from connecting with his neck. Vyder clenched one of the cross-guards and wrenched the blade free of his enemy's grip. Then the horses galloped by one another. He encouraged Storm back the way she'd travelled. The wounded cavalrymen slid from the saddle and smashed onto the ground, the spear haft breaking off. He rolled a few times and stopped, face down.

Wounded? He's dead. Storm passed the confused, riderless animal and he turned her towards the outer square once more. Like the man Vyder had just sent to tread the Frost River, several Huronians had advanced down the narrow, vacant land separating the Highland squares and were harrying the rear of some of the squares. One Huronian was dragged from his saddle and the life cut from him by several swords and an axe.

The enemy cavalry might be professional, elite soldiers but they'd never faced a truly fearless enemy. One soldier remained in the saddle. Vyder stood in the stirrups and swung his blade in a horizontal strike. The sharp edge separated the man's head from his shoulders. Storm galloped past.

"Keep fighting!" Vyder shouted over his shoulder.

Storm chewed the ground, sending thigh length grass blurring by on the left. On the right, the rear most ranks of his Highland squares slid by. Although their war cries and roars of battle-fuelled fury didn't. The noise drowned out all but the flintlock weapons and the occasional bugle blast suggesting Tork was continuing to battle.

Hyglak's war horn tore through the air commanding black powder. The Highlanders in the second row opened fire, sending a hail of lead down onto their opponents. The first few lines disappeared in a cloud of spent gun powder. When the noise of the gunshots washed over them, Storm's powerful muscles tensed for a fraction of a second mid stride.

A dull rumble came from behind and Vyder threw a glance over his shoulder. Rafe, a knife hilt blossoming from his shoulder blade led the cavalry force down the strip of land separating the third and fourth squares. Turning the small force, he led them towards the Huronian's harrying the rear of the Highlander formation. He tore his eyes from the scene and returned his attention to the fast-approaching first square.

Half of the Highlanders were either dead or dying. The enemy cavalry had dealt them a terrible blow. He swivelled in his saddle again and made eye contact with Ahitika.

"To me!" he shouted gesturing for her to approach. "Bring as many with you as you can!"

Rafe had led most of the cavalry into the enemy formation, driving them away from the rear of the infantry squares. But those at the back of the mounted Highland force, Ahitika included, had no task. She gathered a group around her, Henry among them, and thundered towards Vyder. She held a sword above her head, the wet blood upon the blade glistening in the sun. Ahitika whooped in the way of the Kalote people, although he couldn't hear the blood chilling sound over the battle. Alongside her rode the pair of Kalote warriors they had rescued from slavery in Shadolia. Their faces, too, were lined with savagery.

Vyder turned away and pushed Storm on, the animal stretching out into a gallop once more. He passed the second square, the empty, narrow piece of land separating the second and first infantry formations whipped by and then he reached his target: the decimated first square of the Great Highland Army. He guided Storm straight for a Huronian warrior facing away from him. The man was slashing down at a Highland woman. She blocked the cut with her shield, slammed a spear into the man's stomach and then dragged him from the saddle, her brow creased with anger and hatred.

She doesn't need any help. He pushed Storm on past the doomed enemy and aimed instead at a small group of adversaries. Storm barged her way in between them. Vyder stabbed, slashed and cut his way through them. Then he was clear charging on to the next cluster of mounted Huronians.

"Tighten up the shield wall!" he shouted at the beleaguered infantry square. "Pull back and regroup!"

The command was passed from one to the next and the square shrunk to half its original size. Shields were interlocked once again and the few Huronian cavalrymen who'd fought their way deep into the Highland ranks were killed. The shield wall peeled apart a narrow distance to allow the frightened, riderless horses to dart clear, then it closed, shields clacking together and war cries intensifying. They'd taken a battering but were far from beaten.

Rafe, now sporting an arrow in his thigh, galloped at the head of his small force. He reached down, snapped the arrow off close to his leg and cast the remains away with disdain. The mounted Highlanders cleaved into the enemy harrying the front ranks of the squares, pushing them away from so as to create space for the next volley. The rudimentary cavalry force had also taken a few hits. Half of them were down.

Vyder tore his glare from the progress of his riders and returned his attention to the battle at hand. He gasped and lay flat in the saddle, clutching Storm's neck, his cheek resting on her mane. The enemy sword sliced through the air above his head, even though the din of fighting the blade's faint whistle was audible.

He straightened again. Turned Storm away from a group of enemy charging right for him and guided her back the way they'd travelled. If he advanced any farther, he'd be in the thick of the Huronian ranks alone and outnumbered. Ahitika and the other Kalote warriors had entered the fray. Ahitika leapt from her cantering horse and hit the ground sprinting. She aimed for an oncoming Huronian cavalryman and as he galloped by, she reached out and grabbed a fistful of his shirt. Ahitika vaulted up behind him, cut his throat and shoved the dying man out of his saddle. Blood spattered her face. Then she grasped a fistful of hair, pulled back his head and cut free his scalp. She screamed her high-pitched shriek and held the piece of bloody hair above her head. The dying Huronian tumbled from the saddle and slammed onto the ground where he disappeared beneath the mass of jostling hooves.

Vyder plunged his sword deep into the back of an enemy, ripped the blade clear and galloped past. The first

Highland square had regrouped well and continued to fight with ferocity. Rafe, now also carrying a short sword lodged in his guts, led his force down the strip of land separating two squares having successfully pushed the enemy cavalry back from the squares. To his relief the war horn blared and those Highlanders in the second rank opened fire, the wall of lead stealing the life from both man and horse.

"With me!" he yelled at Ahitika.

Her dark, savage eyes stared out from a face of drying blood. She tucked the scalp into her belt and whooped, turning her newly acquired Huronian horse to follow Vyder. Her companions, including Henry followed suit. They streaked back the way they'd come, cutting through the few enemy cavalrymen who'd fought their way down the corridors between each square. Saigh's deep, powerful bark greeted Vyder when he halted beside Hyglak. He stretched down, stroked her face and patted her neck. Straightening, he appraised the chieftain.

"How goes it?" he shouted.

Hyglak tore his gaze from the battle and looked at him. "This is a hard fight, lord," he yelled back and smiled. "But we'll make them pay in blood for every metre they gain."

"Aye. Today has been the skane of many. Keep calling black powder once they've reloaded." He gestured at the fifth square. "I have to reorganise the farthest formation. They've been flanked by the bastards as well."

"Aye, lord."

Vyder was about to nudge Storm into a gallop when something battered into his right leg. Rafe came to a halt beside him. The berserker chieftain was badly wounded, his skin pale. Sweat glistened upon his brow. Various weapons blossomed from his body and through a tear in his armour, Vyder saw a section of intestines bulging through a cut in his guts. The man grinned at Vyder, his teeth stained with blood.

"Well, this is fun, lord!" he roared.

"Keep pushing them away from the front ranks."

He sat bolt upright in his saddle and snapped off a crisp salute, a wide grin still adorning his maddened face.

"On second thought," Vyder shouted and pointed at the wounds he carried. "Perhaps you should sit this out, Rafe? You are badly wounded."

"What? This?" the berserker grabbed hold of the arrow stub and ripped the remains of the head free from his leg and held it up for inspection. A clump of flesh clung to the arrowhead, the metal tip painted bright red. "It is but a scratch." He threw the thing aside as if it were a burr that had lodged in the fabric of his shirt and offered a mild annoyance. "I shall be fine, my lord." He bent double in the saddle and coughed, spitting out a glob of blood. "Although I'll not lie." He clapped a hand onto Vyder's shoulder. "I think today might be my skane, lord." His blood-stained grin widened, if that was even possible. "Now, if you'll excuse us?" He roared an incomprehensible noise and kicked his horse into a gallop, the remains of the Highland Cavalry thundering behind him, yelling war cries.

Vyder returned his attention to Hyglak. "Call black powder once Rafe has finished with them."

Hyglak nodded.

He peered down at Saigh sat at Storm's front left hoof, gazing up at him. "You must stay here, lass." She yapped, a high-pitched noise. "I shall return for you, my girl. I promise."

Vyder pushed Storm into a gallop, Ahitika, Henry and the two Kalote warriors following behind him. Rafe veered down the lane between the fourth and fifth squares, the small force mirroring his lead.

The fifth square was in worse shape than the first. Two thirds had been defeated, the final third almost completely overrun. If they fell, the entire Highland Army would be in trouble.

"Come on, Gorgoroth," uttered Vyder. "Where the bloody hell are you?"

VI

Rone speared the fleeing Huronian soldier between his shoulder blades and ripped the weapon free. His horse galloped past the man who sank to his knees and toppled to the ground where the earth soaked his life blood. The King's Own warrior shook his head and blinked against the sting of acrid gun powder. The dark pall into which he and his tiny force rode continued to hug the land in the immediate vicinity, imbuing its stink into everything. Even through the cloth covering his nose and mouth the bitter taste almost overwhelmed him. A spate of coughs erupted from deep within his chest, muffled by the cloak enshrouding his face.

Jeers from behind followed by a clash of steel suggested his small force of unlikely allies had found more of the enemy. He didn't bother to turn to see how the others fared, they could take care of themselves. From within the depths of the grey mist appeared an overturned, still burning wagon. The horse that once towed it lay dead nearby, still attached to the neck yoke. Several men, their skin stained dark by spent gunpowder batted cloaks onto the flames in a bid to extinguish them. Rone's mount swept past the scene of destruction, and Rone decided to leave the soldiers to fight the fire.

A distant high-pitched scream rent the air, not to mention Rone's soul. He hated that sound. It was second only to the scream of a horse in agony. He turned towards the shriek, coughing again into the cloak. He blinked away the minuscule grains of spent black powder settling upon his eyes and ignored the sting. Shouts and roars of pain exploded from behind where, no doubt, the former Huronian cavalrymen had happened upon those attempting to stifle the flames. He'd chosen to show them mercy but those who'd once considered the flame-beaters comrades, hadn't.

The scream to his front quietened to a dull groan that echoed through the dark cloud. Silence followed, but he pushed the horse onward. The animal picked its way around shrubs, jumped over clumps of corpses that stank of roasted flesh. It weaved around trees and narrowly missed a riderless animal galloping in the opposite direction. A soft clanking escorted the panicked beast as empty stirrups swayed back and forth, colliding with metal buckles. The deep, guttural sound emanating from the environment to his front morphed into a scream once again, this time much louder than before.

A massive tree loomed from the man-made mist, it's trunk as thick as a wagon was wide. At the base, sitting on the ground was a large, dark bundle of what looked to be clothes. But at this distance it was difficult to see properly. As Rone advanced through the pervasive smoke, the scream increased in volume until it was ear-piercing. He pulled Dax to a halt and dismounted with one smooth movement, the spear still clasped in his hand. The screeching appeared to be issuing from the blob of what he'd thought was a mess of dumped fabric. Rone turned on the balls of his feet and commanded the animal to stand fast. A snort and a stamp of a hoof followed, but the powerful horse remained in place. Rone crept towards the noisy mass which loomed clearer into focus with each footfall through the gloom. The thing lunged towards him, a blackened hand outstretched.

"Gods," he muttered.

The skin of the man's hand was scorched from his fingers. Beneath blackened flesh, the white of bone was a stark contrast. He followed the arm up to the elbow. Slews of blackened, crisp skin hung from his forearms. The stench was overbearing. Rone concentrated on mouth breathing to avoid the aroma. His focus moved up until locking onto what was once a face. Now nothing more than a round, burnt mess, lips singed back from his mouth revealing a death's head grin. Eyes long gone, replaced by melted flesh. The teeth parted and another howl of agony assaulted Rone.

He clenched the spear, or tried to, but realised he already gripped the haft as tight as his muscles would allow. "Go with the Gods, Huronian," he said and plunged the weapon deep into the man's chest. Rone withdrew the spearhead and slammed it home again. The scream died to a gurgle and then silence.

The King's Own officer knelt in front of the corpse. He reached out and rested a hand onto one shoulder. The scorched flesh felt brittle beneath his gentle touch. "I'm sorry for your suffering. May your crossing of the Frost River be swift and carefree. You are no longer in pain."

Rone forced the memory of the soul rending sound from his mind. "Gods," he whispered again and stood. No sooner had the smoky surrounds re-emerged, the annoying sting of spent gunpowder returned. He turned away from the dead body ignoring the urge to rub his eyes and hesitated. The small force of former Huronian Cavalrymen stood in a tight semi-circle nearby. Harton nodded once at him and another touched his chest with a fist. A few muttered amongst themselves, casting glances in Rone's direction every so often. Their stares carried respect, or at least Rone thought they did. But he hadn't put the man out of his misery to garner trust or respect. He'd done it to stop the suffering. *Even if he'd been a Wendurlund soldier, I'd have done the same thing.* He strode to Dax and stroked the soft nose. "Good lad," he whispered. The animal nuzzled his hand and sniffed. He chuckled. "I have no food at the moment. Later on, you can have a feed." Even within the mess they found themselves, surrounded by panic, confusion and death, the damn animal could only think of food. He stroked Dax's forehead and smiled. *A true soldier.* Dax pushed his nose into Rone's chest, the warm air of his breath soaking through his clothes and touching his skin. The King's Own soldier walked to Dax's side and stepped up into the saddle. The group moved on.

They found the damaged powder wagon in the deepest remnants of the acrid cloud. One of the cavalrymen reported a large area of ground nearby trampled by countless hooves. *Probably where the main cavalry was staged prior to their advance.* The cordite was settling, the mist thinning with each passing minute. How the wagon had not itself exploded, especially this close to where Garx had initiated the detonation was beyond belief. Rone pointed at the wagon and indicated one of the Huronian horses, then gestured back at the wagon. The cavalrymen sat in their saddles staring at Rone, dumbfounded.

It's so bloody frustrating not knowing their language.

He sighed and nudged Dax closer to the vehicle. Commanding his mount to remain in place, he stepped down and knelt by the neck yoke, clutched the well-worn hardwood in his hand and held it up a few inches from the ground. "We hook up one of the horses to the wagon so we can tow it." Distant blunderbusses echoed to life where Rone's comrades battled against the Huronians. He ignored the noise, but there was never a moment he wasn't thinking of their plight.

The forehead of the closest man creased as his eyebrows met. That was the man to convince. He was their new leader. *Harton.* But understanding was devoid. Rone cursed under his breath. He stood and tapped the wagon's wheel. "This is a now a mobile bomb. We can tow it anywhere we want." One of them muttered something, leaned in his saddle, pulled the cloak free of his face and spat on the ground. Then tucked the fabric back into place.

"Bomb!" Rone repeated as if talking to a brain hurt child. He clenched a fist and wrapped his other hand around it. He pulled his hands apart in a rapid movement, fingers splayed. "Boom!"

Realisation glimmered in the eyes of one man who swivelled in his saddle and rattled off a sentence in their foreign language, his voice muffled by the cloak hiding his face. Harton shifted in his saddle and the deep-lined frown disappeared. The Huronian soldier shouted a few words and the group blurred into movement.

A horse was unsaddled and then attached to the neck yoke. The horse's rider leapt up onto the driver's bench. Another soldier lifted his saddle and dropped it onto a vacant space just behind the bench. Rone held up a hand to slow their fervour. "We need to prepare it to explode first, so we can tow it into place where we decide and detonate it at short notice. Understand?" The confused glances returned.

Rone's jaws bulged against the cloak wound tight around his face. He cursed again, although this time the words did not reach his lips. He kept his open palm facing outward. *Surely, they understand that?* The cessation of their energetic movements suggested so. He let his hand drop to slap against a thigh and walked around the back of the wagon. Unslinging both his musket and blunderbuss, he assisted each cocking hammer forward with gentle controlled movements. A spark was the last thing he needed this close to so much black powder. Once done, he held the weapons up to Harton who took them without a word. Rone swung up onto the rear tray.

More blunderbusses sang their lethal tune and the keening pierce of bagpipes started, quietened by the distance which separated the small clandestine group from the main fray. Between one Highland tune finishing and another commencing the deep but faint roar of Highland war cries rolled across the plain. Flintlock weapons pierced even the bagpipes, then faded amongst the cacophony of war.

Unfastening the metal clasp holding the lid of the rearmost barrel closed, Rone worked the round piece of wood free. It took some time and effort, but eventually it pulled clear and he was rewarded with an aroma of fresh dark powder. He cast the lid aside, tipped the barrel onto its side, then shovelled a good amount of the dark grains out onto the floor of the wagon tray. He worked from one barrel to the next, opening each in turn. Some he pushed over, others he gently dug into the wood with a dagger until a small hole appeared and granules trickled out. *One small spark and we'll be incinerated.*

Finally, he stood, rubbed his hands free of the grit and leapt down from the wagon's tray. "Now we're ready."

A muffled chuckle erupted from beside him and he glanced up at Harton. The Huronian's eyes suddenly became wide. "Boom!" he spoke the Wendurlund word in a thick accent and laughed.

Rone smiled. "Exactly so."

Rone placed a foot in the stirrup and swung into the saddle then took the offered weapons from Harton with a nod of thanks. Turning the animal from the powder wagon he nudged him into a walk, then carefully cocked the hammer of each weapon back, before sliding them into the holster forward of his right knee. When he was at a distance he thought safe, he turned back to appraise the group, ordered his mount to remain in place then dismounted. Picking up a stick he walked back to the ground, knelt and ripped out chunks of grass so that only a large square of bare earth remained at his feet. Looking up at the others, he gestured for them to join him. They did so, one man remaining behind to hold the horses. The soldiers knelt, sat or squatted around him. Some muttered, others chuckled, but at the sharp tone of Harton, they fell silent.

Rone drew a circle in the dirt. "This is us, yes?"

Brows creased, looks of uncertainty glimmered in their eyes. He stuck the stick into the centre of the small circle then swept a hand around at them. "Us!"

One man blurted a foreign word and the frowns eased. Heads nodded and soft conversations commenced. Another sharp command from Harton ensured silence again. *The seige'll be over before we get there.* Rone sighed, pulled the stick clear and drew another circle further away. Then he pointed in the direction of the battle raging in the distance. "Battle. Understood?"

"Bat-ul," said Harton slowly.

Rone stared at the Huronian leader. "Battle, yes good." With a few more deft strokes of the stick, he drew more to the mud map, stopping each time to explain, not continuing until he was sure he was understood by every warrior present.

When he'd finished, confused glances and vacant stares of uncertainty were replaced by the eagle glares of purpose. Now they had a mission, they knew what was to be done. This little group may yet turn the tide of the entire battle.

"Let's get to work," said Rone.

The cool air caressed Miriam's face and tickled her hair. The sudden cannon shot coming from the city's centre had drawn her to the open window. A hint of smoke teased her nostrils, no doubt emanating from the dull, orange glow flickering in the east. *So then, we didn't hold the wall, our troops have fallen and the eastern city burns.* She closed her eyes, clenched the blunderbuss tighter in her grip, the cool wood of the stock giving her confidence.

"What in the gods was that?" a pretentious voice called from nearby.

Her eyes snapped open and she leaned out the window. Miriam had been careful to douse all the candlelight from within the house so she was surrounded by darkness. Her night vision was keen. The fat bastard stood in the middle of the cobbled street below, his dutiful, hand-wringing servant close by.

Cannons! What do you think, you stupid bastard? The words were deafening in her mind, but she kept them from entertaining her lips. There'd been a much fainter explosion earlier in the afternoon before the sun slid below the horizon, but she'd paid no attention to it. Miriam could be forgiven for thinking that detonation had originated from beyond Lisfort's walls. *I hope it did.* That meant someone on their side was still taking the fight to the Huronians. Maybe all was not lost. Although it was nothing compared to the incredible blast which had reverberated through the city earlier in the day. It'd been so powerful she'd felt the vibration through the floor. The recent cannon fire had been much louder, so much so that the blasts had shaken the walls of the mansion. Distant shouting and screams cut the star riddled sky in the east. The obese simpleton swivelled in that direction almost losing his balance. "What is happening?" his voice was much quieter this time, a tone of uncertainty lending his words weakness.

"What do you think is happening you fool?" she whispered. "Lisfort's walls have fallen to the enemy and we are being invaded."

Her grip tightened once again upon the weapon by her side. *Only a matter of time before we are fighting for our lives.* The flicker of orange in the east blossomed into a bright red flash, then faded to a dull light once more. What sounded like a drum struck by one of the gods rolled over the city. Miriam flinched at the sudden sound, heart thundering in her chest, her breaths coming in rapid succession.

"Oh, dear gods help me!" the fat man whimpered.

She turned her attention back to the fat urchin, her eyes bulged and she held a hand over her mouth to suppress the laughter. He'd fallen onto his arse on the street, arms and legs flailing like an overturned tortoise. "Help me up, damn you!" he shrieked. The servant tugged on one flabby arm to no avail. "Let me go, you useless bastard!" the fat man squeaked. He rolled over onto all fours and eventually stumbled back to his feet, his heavy breaths rasping to Miriam, even from this distance. Her shoulders shuddered, but she refused to allow the laughter to erupt from her mouth.

"Back inside!" he panted, gesturing wildly at the manservant. "Away with you, dammit!"

The pair vacated the street, but not before the bastard had slapped the back of his servant's head. She allowed her hand to drop away from her mouth and another flash, less bright this time, illuminated the eastern sky for a moment. A dull thud from that direction washed over the buildings of Lisfort.

The stench of smoke thickened, throwing a blanket upon the city. It was difficult to see what damage had been done to Lisfort, but the light of dawn would bring fresh despair no doubt. She didn't feel tired and knew she wouldn't sleep even if she tried. So, she remained in place beside the eastern-facing window, watching. Waiting. A clatter of steel on steel emanated through the night, so faint Miriam wasn't sure she'd heard it at all. Distant shouts peeled out, the numerous streets and alleys making the noise sound surreal. Another clash of swords and yells were joined by screams of wounded or dying men.

Miriam licked her lips and swallowed. She released her grip of the blunderbuss with one hand and passed a clammy, open palm down the fabric of her dress. "Where are you, Vyder?" she whispered. Her wide eyes turned to the pin pricks of light laced across night's blanket, but there was no answer there. Each passing hour beckoned more smoke and brighter flames in the east. Sometime close to midnight, the once orange flicker developed into a constant bright blaze silhouetting rooftops.

Small battles broke out from the north-east and south-east, indicating how briskly the Huronian Army advanced through the city, fighting, pillaging and burning Lisfort. *And who knows what else?* The blunderbuss trembled in her grasp, the memory of her rape replaying in her mind despite her attempts to push it back down into the depths. If there was to be a repeat of that horrible experience – *and gods please spare me if there is* – Vyder wouldn't be there this time to save her.

Occasionally the crack of a musket echoed in her ears, but it was never repeated and didn't resound from the same place indicating the person wielding the flintlock weapon had been overwhelmed by the enemy. Finally, the memory of her abuse dissipated into blackness and she let out a long breath through pursed lips. Wiping perspiration from her brow, she dried the back of her hand on her dress.

A gentle rattle of shod hooves upon cobbled stones drifted amongst the crackle of faraway flames or distant shouts. A woman's piercing shriek cleaved the heavens asunder but was cut short. Miriam clenched her jaw, eyes narrowing and hands clutching even tighter around the weapon by her side. The clatter of hooves grew in volume and it changed everything. Before she'd had images of a few heavy horses drawing a wagon along behind them at a sedate pace, but as they closed the distance, it was apparent they were approaching at a gallop. And there were more than two horses. Far more. No more was the hint of combat audible, the thrum of hooves drowning it out completely. Then she saw them. A group of about thirty or forty mounted soldiers.

"Regroup here!" shouted a gruff voice.

The cadre clattered to a halt, some of the horses snorting, others nickering. The sheen of sweat, illuminated by the bright orange of burning buildings, glinted from their flanks. Relief washed over her. *The Watch.*

"We'll hit them again from the south," the same voice said. "Gather yourselves."

Miriam leaned further out the window so as to better see the horsemen below. The head of one man was heavily bandaged, the white fabric soaked dark at his temple. She was confident if the light were brighter the stain would be bright red. Others wore rudimentary attempts at first aid on their arms or legs. The hand of one warrior was blotted from view by a large dressing tied in place by thin rope. He leaned over double in the saddle groaning.

"Where's Baramof's force?"

"I saw them fall near the wall," a new voice replied.

"Tragon's troop were overwhelmed, Hadun's men were overrun near the second quarter of the eastern wall." The gruff voice became less aggressive. "Did anyone see Kutter's formation?"

"Yes, sir," another voice said. "They hewed their way into the enemy advance. But I lost sight of them when we were almost surrounded and fighting for our lives."

"And Deraput?"

"Surrounded and fighting for survival. I saw them just before we broke through the enemy lines and retreated."

"Then we must return and aid them!"

"No, sir." The one who'd spoken nudged his horse forward a pace. "With all respect, I wouldn't. Last look I got of them there was only about ten men left in the saddle."

"So that leaves us, then." The once gruff voice was soft now. The man closest the front stood in his stirrups and looked back at the formation. "I count about thirty of us." He nestled back into the leather seat. "Thirty of The Watch against the entire Huronian Army." The aggression returned to the man's voice. "We're all that's left to protect the city. Let's circle around and hit them from behind."

"Then we die, sir."

The warrior at the front swivelled his horse around to face the others. "Would you prefer to tuck tail and run, Gunder? Our city needs us! Our king needs us!"

"Our king? I don't see him out here fighting."

"Silence!" the leader roared. "One more word like that out of you, Gunder and I'll bloody hang you myself!"

"Now let's begone. Weapons ready. On my lead!"

The leader swivelled the beast upon which he sat away from his soldiers and cantered from view. The others followed and the frozen prickle of fear once more worked its way under Miriam's skin. Even outnumbered as they were, the presence of The Watch had given her some comfort, empty as it was. The night drew on and the fires burned closer, as did the shouting and clashes of combat. Soon the enemy would enter her quadrant of Lisfort. She'd attempted to make Vyder's home seem less of a target by extinguishing all light. But that wouldn't stop them kicking in doors or smashing windows. The mansion was built in one of the wealthiest sections of Lisfort; the temptation would be too great for the Huronians to ignore.

A powerful shout broke out, although the voice was too far away to decipher the words. The baritone sounded so much like the commander who'd been talking to his men on the street below recently. A clash of swords followed, then more yells. A roar of pain or anger, she could not tell which. A horse's whiny, another shout. The ting of swords became fewer and then drew to silence as each minute passed with sluggish speed.

The utter quiet was terrifying.

The last of The Watch had fallen in defence of Lisfort, or at least it was her assumption. Miriam sighed, the prickle of fear now a cold wedge lodged in her chest. She latched the window closed, and wandered back into the kitchen to lean against one of the counters. Miriam placed the blunderbuss onto the marble surface, easing the weapon down beside the large tray of socks bulging with black powder and bullets.

The Huronians might kick in the door, but she knew one thing for sure. *I'll take a few of the bastards with me for company across the Frost River.* Muffled shouts filtered in from the window she'd just closed. Cocking her head, she listened with intent. The voice came again. *That's not the Wendurlund language.* Slapping a palm onto the cool butt stock of the weapon she lifted it and brought it close to her body. Snatching a few of the socks, she shoved them into her pockets and strode towards the window. She shoulder-barged a door frame and cursed under her breath. *Concentrate!* Miriam considered opening the window again but decided against it. The noise and movement may draw the attention of the Huronians. *Wherever the hell they are!* More foreign words slid down nearby streets and alleys. She stood on her tip toes and pressed her head against the glass. It was only when the cool surface touched her forehead that she realised how heavily she was perspiring.

Something flashed in her peripheral vision and she jerked, a slight pain jolting her neck as she twisted to look in that direction. The orange glow of blazing buildings was brighter, the stink of smoke imbuing its unwanted presence into Lisfort. *There!* Soldiers sprinted along a road, visible at a distant intersection for a brief moment before buildings swallowed them from view. They followed one after the other, a constant stream. Occasionally, a flash of light offered by nearby flames reflected upon the steel of swords, axes or spear tips.

While they were too far away for her to see their uniforms properly, she was confident they were not friendly.

A pack of them slowed to a halt in the middle of the crossroad and seemed to be discussing something. Or arguing. Then they turned towards her and jogged down the road leading directly past Vyder's home. There must have been more than fifty of them. Although other soldiers behind them continued to run on in the direction of the original warriors, some slowed and turned down the road to follow the group closing the distance with the building in which she hid.

"Shit," she whispered. She slid down the wall into a crouch and clutched the blunderbuss to her chest. Miriam attempted to control her breathing, but the rapid rasp in her ears was deafening. A frozen shard of terror lanced her body. Her legs were weak, her hands trembling. She licked her lips and stared at the ceiling, offering a silent prayer to whichever god would listen to her plea for help. A long-ago conversation with Vyder flitted into her mind, when she'd asked him if he'd ever been afraid.

"Fear, aye and anger are formidable forces. They can promote action, or render someone completely useless, like a fawn in danger. You must be aware of your fear or anger and harness them, use them, control them and force them to drive you forward."

She'd chuckled. *"I'd be the frightened fawn, I think, helpless, lying in the grass frozen. I haven't a courageous bone in my body."*

"Miriam, you can't have courage without fear. The courageous people experience that bone-pitting fear and act anyway."

"And are there those without fear?"

Vyder's laughter had boomed around the room. *"Aye, they're called berserkers."*

"I say, you have no right to come into this area of town, you rapscallions!" The piercing, pompous voice of the fat nobleman drifted to Miriam's ears. She gathered her legs beneath her and stood, although her muscles still quivered. She placed her wet forehead against the cool glass and peered out at the street below. The firelight was duller down this end of the city, but there was still enough to see dark figures surrounding the overweight man. His slave was nowhere to be seen.

"You, stupid, stupid man," Miriam breathed. "You should have stayed inside and out of sight."

More soldiers running down the road stopped and joined the growing circle out of curiosity. Laughter rippled around the multiplying enemy. Some shouted, others jeered. One Huronian stepped forward and punched the nobleman in the gut, doubling him over. The volume of laughter increased, overwhelming the shouting.

The man who'd punched the pretentious nobleman held out his hands either side of his body and turned a full circle, gesturing with his hands in a motion towards the ground. The din of voices faded to a quiet mutter.

To his credit, the obese man pushed himself back to his feet, his chest expanded with one slow smooth movement and then contracted fast. "You'll be whipped for this!" he shouted. He pointed at the throng of warriors behind the one who'd struck him. "All of you!"

"Be quiet, " Miriam whispered. "For your own good, be quiet."

The ring leader's voice boomed. Although the words were foreign, it was difficult to miss the sarcastic tone. Laughter resounded out again. But with another gesture the mass fell quiet. Fat man shouted another few words but a punch in the face floored him. He struck the ground with a dull *thud*. He'd needed assistance to stand up last time, and this instance was no different. The soldiers watching the nobleman squirm thought it hilarious. Miriam had thought it was funny herself, but this was different.

The nobleman had rolled over onto his hands and knees and attempted to gather his legs beneath him. Finally, he managed to put one foot flat on the ground and prepared to push up. One man darted forward, pushing the self-righteous nobleman off balance with a boot to the flank where he struck the cobbled street, rolled over with great effort and managed to move onto his hands and knees.

Some warriors departed in dribs and drabs. *They're growing bored.* The bully leading the circle of Huronians straddled the nobleman on all fours and pretended to slap his rump, moving up and down like he was riding a horse. Fresh laughter peeled out from those still watching the antics. Then the Huronian withdrew a knife from his belt, the weapon's blade catching a glint of distant firelight.

Dread settled upon Miriam and her heartbeat quickened. The soldier leaned forward, grasped a handful of the obese man's hair and pulled back his head. He showed the Wendurlund nobleman the weapon and made a cutting motion in the air.

"Gods no, please!" the man yelled, his voice breaking.

The warrior brought the blade to the throat of the man Miriam had once thought of as an enemy. His scream, filled with terror rent the night sky and passed through the sheet of glass as if it weren't there at all. He sounded like a frightened animal. The Huronian's arm jerked with a swift motion and the sickening scream was replaced with a wet gargle.

Miriam's hand clapped to her mouth. "Oh gods!" she hissed, the words muffled. Her shivering legs collapsed beneath her and she slid down the wall until she met the floor. "Oh gods." *The man was an arse, but he didn't deserve that! No one deserves to die like that.*

The gargling had stopped.

"You must be aware of your fear..." Vyder's voice drifted in her memory.

She clenched her teeth together and pushed herself back to her feet. The muscles in her thighs still quivered, but she locked her knees. Her hand left her mouth, the cool glass touched her forehead once more and she stared out at the cobbled street below. The nobleman was sprawled upon the ground, a dark pool of liquid beneath his head.

The circle of enemy warriors had dispersed, but the muffled shouting, thuds and sounds of breaking glass emanating from the building in which the fat Wendurlund man had once lived, suggested they'd not gone far.

VII

They galloped away from the enemy, holding the swine array formation. Tork led them in a wide circle and slowed to a trot, then a walk. The horses were not winded, but they needed a brief reprieve. He stood in his stirrups and stared upon the right flank. His men had fought well, but sheer force of numbers had whittled them down. He'd lost many of his beloved King's Own. Fury burned in the pit of his gut, but he refused to allow it to take command. He swivelled and assessed the left flank. It was in much the same shape.

Tork glanced in the direction of the enemy still fighting the Highlanders in the distance. A small force about the same size as his unit had broken away and galloped towards them. His mouth stretched into a humourless smile. The little force, overconfident and believing they were on the brink of victory were going to be the ones to finish off the King's Own once and for all, no doubt. Or so they thought.

Tork returned to the saddle and patted Might's neck. "Good lad." His bugler stared at him, waiting for the next command. The patches of Roland's face not stained with drying blood were pale. Although he sat ramrod straight in the saddle, belying any fatigue or weakness he might have been feeling.

"Are you well, Roland?"

The bugler's eyebrows met, lending a powerful, piercing glint to his eyes. "I'm well, sir."

"Good." He clenched the reins tight in his hands and stretched his back. "Then let's get on with it, shall we?" He took one last evaluation of the breakaway enemy formation closing the distance with them, then nudged Might with the heels of his boots. "Canter!"

Roland blasted the command and they accelerated across the plain, still turning in a wide circle back towards the main battle. "Arrowhead!"

The bugle spoke and with smooth provision, the King's Own formation changed shape with expert precision. Finally, they'd turned in a full circle so they were facing their oncoming adversary. Tork guided Might so the powerful animal was cantering straight towards the centre of the enemy advance.

He threw a look over the right flank, the left flank and at Roland to ensure all were still with him. When he was confident all was well, he bellowed, "Charge!"

Roland brought the instrument to his lips and the piercing note cut through the cacophony of the battle in the near distance. The last remnants of Wendurlund's elite unit broke into a gallop, the rumble of hooves competing with the clash of war. When he could decipher individual Huronian soldiers, spears or swords raised over their heads, Tork leaned forward and withdrew his blunderbuss. "Blunderbuss!" he roared. "Fire when ready!"

Piercing notes cut the sky, issuing the order. Some warriors fired almost immediately, but Tork waited. He clenched his thighs around Might's flanks, released the reins and pulled the butt stock of the weapon into his shoulder. *Boom!* The annoying din in his ears turned into a screech and refused to dissipate. More muffled thuds followed as soldiers around him opened fire.

"Muskets!" he shouted, or at least he thought he'd shouted. Even his own voice sounded muffled amongst the high-pitched whine settling into his head. He pushed the blunderbuss back into the leather sheath and pulled clear his musket.

The bugle blast ordered the command. Tork pulled the weapon into his shoulder, stared down the metal sights, steadied his aim and released the shot. The thin cloud of gunpowder blinded him for but a second. A crackle of musket fire broke out around him. The musket disappeared into the sheath alongside the blunderbuss and Tork pulled clear his spear, the sharp tip along with half the wooden haft long ago stained with dried blood.

"Spears!"

Roland brought the instrument to his mouth and gave the command. The enemy charge, cut almost in half, slowed. Their will to fight lost. Too late though. Tork picked one Huronian about twenty metres from him who held his sword diagonally in front of him. To his credit, his eyes remained clear and focused. Fear did not seem to reside there. He was prepared to die fighting. Tork lowered his spear so the weapon was horizontal to the ground.

"OBRAGARDA!" The battle cry rolled over the enemy. Then the Wendurlund and Huronian formations struck.

Tork rammed the spear at his adversary, the weapon scraped up his steel breastplate and bounced clear. The clatter of steel on wood, leather or flesh erupted in the immediate vicinity. Shouted words, incomprehensible roars, screams of pain or panic and curses filled the air. He leaned to the left and avoided the Huronian's sword stroke, almost losing his balance. *Better to lose my balance than my bloody arm.* He straightened, grunted with pain when his knee struck the leg of a Huronian soldier travelling in the opposite direction and slammed his spear straight at a man whose eyes were as wide as dinner plates. The steel tip hammered into his throat and Tork grasped the haft with both hands, ripping it clear before momentum could pilfer the weapon from his clutch.

The razor-sharp metal came free, bright fresh blood glistening where the colour of dried ochre had once resided. A single blunderbuss erupted amongst the confusion. One man had been saving his shot and by the renewed foreign yells it'd been effective.

Tork leaned forward in his saddle, teeth clenched, lips peeled back and drove the spear home for a second time. It found solace in the groin of an oncoming enemy soldier. The Huronian fell screaming from his saddle and disappeared beneath the hooves of jostling war horses. Might erupted clear of the confusion and galloped across vacant land towards the main battle in the near distance.

He stole a glance over one shoulder to ensure the right flank was with him. The King's Own forming that side of the arrowhead formation punched into view from the enemy rank. Tork glanced over the opposite shoulder and the left flank broke into view. He held Roland's stare.

"At the walk! Reload!"

The King's Own slowed, animals taking deep gulps of air, their flanks slick with sweat. They were tired. Not exhausted. Not yet. He patted Might's neck. "Good lad." With rapid, deft movements he reloaded both the musket and blunderbuss. The leather powder bag attached to his belt was empty. Tork pushed his hand in deep, but all he felt was an empty leather bag. This would be the last shots he'd fire. Then it'd all be down to hand-to-hand combat. Some warriors loaded their musket only, indicating they too were out of powder. Others didn't reach for their flintlock weapons at all, meaning the last volley had been their final shots of the battle. He stood in his stirrups and glared back at the enemy. The small Huronian detachment had been cut to pieces, but to their credit they turned at the canter and headed back towards Tork's unit. *They're not beaten yet.*

"Halt!"

The bugle sang and the arrowhead stopped moving. Horses snorted, threw their heads or stamped the ground. For the most part they'd regained their breath. Tork turned Might about to face the oncoming threat. *They can come to us. Better for their mounts to tire than ours.*

"Reform arrowhead!"

The King's Own formation moved, horses accelerating from a dead stop to a full gallop inside a few strides. The flanks of the arrowhead reformed to face the way they'd come. Then all movement stopped once they were in position. Not a word was spoken by the elite soldiers. They patiently waited and watched their enemy break into a gallop towards them. Distant thunder rolled over them as hooves drummed against the ground casting up chunks of dirt and dust. Still, the King's Own remained frozen in place and quiet. The Huronian horses chewed up the ground and as they approached the shouts and high-pitched shrieks of war cries could be heard faintly above the rumble.

Tork tightened his grip on the reigns and leaned a little towards Roland. "Muskets," he said.

He withdrew his musket from the leather sheath even as the bugle's screech cut the sky. The muskets had a better range on them than the blunderbusses, which although a savage force multiplier, was only effective at short range. Tork pulled the weapon into his shoulder and stared down the metal sights, picking one man out of the Huronian mass fast closing on them.

"Fire!" he pulled the trigger. The shot of the weapon deafened Tork to the bugle's call. Musket fire crackled to life around him.

"Blunderbuss! Charge! Fire!"

He nudged Might into a gallop, dropped the musket into the leather holster and withdrew the blunderbuss. There was no time to aim properly, so he held the weapon one handed in a vice-like grip lifted it horizontal to the ground blurring by beneath and pulled the trigger. Strong as his grip was, the wood stock almost bucked out of his hand. A chorus of blunderbusses roared their fury, hiding the arrowhead for a moment behind a grey cloud of gun smoke.

"Battle at will!"

He all but threw the blunderbuss into the leather sheath forward of his right knee and pulled clear his spear, ramming it through a man's throat. Try as he might to keep hold of the weapon, the haft was ripped clear of his grip as the mortally wounded man swept by. Without pause, he lifted the blunderbuss, held the warm barrel and battered the heavy wooden stock into the helmet of a Huronian.

"Obragarda!"

He brought the reversed blunderbuss in a savage overhand cut which battered into another helmet. The heavy wood stock, as good as a beastly club, left a deep dent in the steel of the helm and the man dropped limp from the saddle disappearing beneath a storm of hooves. He tilted forward in the saddle holding a hand on Might's neck to maintain balance. The warhorse's double-barrelled kick connected with a dull *crack*. Tork gritted his teeth and ducked low in the saddle, a sword sweeping thin air a hair's breadth above his head. He sat straight, snarled and sent the blunderbuss's wooden stock in a double-handed horizontal strike which hammered into a man's chest.

Then Might broke clear of the enemy, galloping across vacant, trampled grassland towards Lisfort in the near distance. Tork snatched a glance over his left shoulder checking to ensure Roland was with him. The bugler was mere strides from him, although one eye had now swollen so much it had closed over, fresh blood painting half his face a wet shade of claret. Beyond him the left flank smashed clear of the Huronians. Tork turned in the opposite direction, ignoring the twinge of pain in his spine at the sudden movement and the right flank hammered into view.

"Halt!" he roared.

The bugle called the command and the formation slowed and then stopped.

"Muskets! Fix Bayonets!"

He dropped the musket in the sheath, pulled clear his musket, unsheathed the two-foot bayonet at his right hip and notched it onto the end of the musket. Twisting it into place, the lug on the bottom of the barrel clicked. He pulled on the bayonet to ensure it was fully attached. The razor-sharp length of steel was going nowhere.

He turned Might in a one-eighty to face the departing enemy. He noticed this time the Huronians were not turning back towards his unit. They were less than quarter strength and their will to fight seemed to have fled.

"Reform arrowhead!"

The flanks streaked either side of Tork and in less than one minute the formation was facing the opposite direction, ready to re-engage their adversary.

"Charge! No battle cry!"

The bugle's cry pierced the wind and the King's Own accelerated from a stop into a gallop. Movement caught his peripheral vision. Roland withdrew his spear, the bugle dangling from his forearm from a thick leather strap. Tork clenched his thighs around the saddle flaps, holding his musket with both hands. The reins, knotted together, draped over Might's mane.

Proceeding at the trot, the Huronians were not moving fast enough to evade the threat from their rear. A threat they hadn't yet realised was present. The muscles of his legs burned, but he ignored the discomfort. The musket felt good in his grip. Using his legs, he steered Might to the slight right, aiming for the broad back of a retreating Huronian cavalryman.

Apart from the drum of hooves striking dirt and the intermittent soft blasts of air exploding from the noses of the war horses, the arrowhead formation proceeded fast and silent beneath the clamour of battle and the noise created by the animals of the Huronian Cavalry.

They were upon them.

Might lunged forward, his ears flat to his skull mouth open. He bit the rump of the retreating horse before him. Tork stood in his stirrups and stabbed the bayonet into his enemy. The blade punched through armour and sank deep. He pulled the musket clear, the bayonet screeched from the hole in the metal. The Huronian soldier dropped his sword and sat bolt upright in his saddle attempting to reach behind him to find the wound that would claim his life. Might battered his way between retreating horses. He tore a chunk from the face of one animal and kicked out behind him once he was amongst the enemy group. Tork, still standing in his stirrups, lunged again, this time aiming for the unarmoured neck of a warrior. The bayonet would have been blunted by the initial strike through steel.

The weapon sank all the way to the musket's barrel. Tork grunted with effort and managed to lever the blade clear before Might could gallop past. Screams, shouts and cries of pain behind him suggested the right and left flanks of the arrowhead formation had entered the fray. He'd barged clear of the front of the formation before the enemy were aware of the King's Own presence. The Huronian ranks had been smashed asunder by the charge, their number a glimmer of what they had once been.

"Disperse left and right! Battle at will!" Tork yelled.

Roland sheathed his bloodied spear, took hold of his bugle and gave the command. The spearhead formation broke apart and individuals slowed and turned on the spot, charging back towards the oncoming Huronian Cavalry they had just decimated. The few enemy that remained alive slowed and attempted to turn away, but the King's Own, now fighting without command, broke them apart like hammer upon a rock. Some tried to ride clear but were hunted down in short order. Empty-saddled panicking Huronian horses galloped clear of the fight in all directions.

He drew Might to a gentle stop and patted the neck of his war horse. "To me!"

The piercing cry of the bugle sang and the soldiers of the King's Own turned towards him, stopping in a large circle around Tork and Roland. Confident in their ability to defeat what remained of their enemy, the Huronian Cavalry who had broken clear of the main force had been killed. Not a single man remained alive.

But it hadn't been without cost. He raked the men around him. He estimated four hundred of the King's Own remained in the saddle. Sixteen hundred had died in battle since the very beginning, when the giant spiders had commenced their assault upon the walls of Lisfort. *Gods, that feels like an eternity ago.* The white-hot anger in his chest felt fit to explode through his rib cage. To his knowledge, the unit had never taken such a loss in its history.

The distant clash of battle broke his reverie. They needed to assist the Highlanders fighting for their lives. "It's not over, gentlemen," he shouted. "Steel yourselves. Has anyone any remaining black powder?"

A handful of soldiers raised their hands. "Enough for one musket shot, sir."

"Same as me, sir," another said.

"Me too."

He pointed at those few warriors. "Use your muskets as and when you see an opportunity. Do not wait for the command to engage."

They nodded.

Tork stroked Might's damp neck. "How do you fair, my lad?" he muttered. The animal had regained his breath, but when evening fell all of the war horses would require watering and fodder. They had used up vast amounts of energy that needed to be replenished. He straightened in the saddle, wiped his wet palm against his trousers and looked at Roland. "Swine array."

The bugle screamed and the circle of warriors formed into the swine array within a matter of thirty seconds. They faced the rear of the Huronian Cavalry attempting to cleave through the Highland Army.

"At the walk!"

They advanced at a snail's pace. But when they clashed with the rear rank of their enemy they'd be at full gallop.

The Great Highland Army had been all but destroyed. Oh, they'd fought hard, killing three Huronians for the loss of each of their own. But Vyder didn't see that as any kind of victory. He had failed his people. They had trusted him, followed him, believed in him. And he'd led them to their slaughter. Fury burned in his guts, spreading throughout his being. He roared his fury to the skies, his face hot with rage, the berserk spirit imbuing itself into him. He dismounted and, sword in hand, strode towards the two Highland squares who remained in the battle.

"Vyder!" Henry's voice chased him, but he ignored the young prince. "Vyder, stop!"

Saigh barked at him, but other than a glance and a shout of, "stay!" he ignored her as well.

An enemy kicked his horse towards him. The Highlander sidestepped the charge, grabbed a hold of his breastplate and pulled the man out of the saddle. Vyder stomped on the steel helmet and drove his sword through the leather gorget. Blood bubbled up from the wound, pouring down the metal breastplate. The man struggled beneath his boot. He dragged the blade clear and walked on, leaving the Huronian to his dying.

Another warrior charged him, but he ducked below the sword strike and strode on without a backward glance, rage denying him logic. He negotiated the narrow strip of grassland separating the two remaining Highland squares, advancing towards the main fight. Movement in the side of his eye gave him pause. Rafe slowed his horse beside him. Dried blood painted the corners of his mouth and only his eyes betrayed the berserker's pain. "Are you well, lord?" Rafe asked, a blood-stained grin adorning his face.

Rage burned deep. As he locked eyes with the berserker, Rafe's grin widened. "Yes, you are quite well," he said.

Vyder looked past Rafe. There were only ten Highland Cavalry left alive. He squeezed tight his eyes and clenched his jaw. When he opened his eyes once more, he held Rafe's gaze. "Stay back my friend, take the others with you."

The black-haired man shrugged, the death's head grin still splitting his beard. "I'm heading across the Frost River today anyway, lord. What does it matter?"

"Very well, then."

Rafe brought his horse to a halt. "You lot, back to the rear. Take my horse with you."

There were some shouts of protest. "It is the lord's order!" he shouted.

A *thump* and groan followed. "Take my horse," Rafe sounded pained.

Then the rumble of fading hooves drummed the ground. Vyder didn't bother looking back. White hot fury still laced his veins. A Huronian cavalryman urged his mount into a canter straight for him. The enemy leaned over in the saddle and brought the blade back, focused on taking Vyder's head off no doubt. He maintained his pace and at the last moment ducked low, the sharp steel slashed the air over his head. Vyder swivelled on his haunches, burst to his feet and brought his sword down with all his strength, anger breaching his lips in a guttural roar. His sword cut the man's hand from his arm and the departing enemy's high-pitched scream of agony would have competed against any war horn.

He took the few paces to the limp, lifeless hand clutching the sword and picked it up. Prying the fingers apart, he dropped the lump of cooling flesh and kept the sword so that he held a blade in each hand. Turning back towards the enemy he quickened the pace again, red embers of anger drifting through him no less hot than they were before.

Movement in the corner of his vision suggested Rafe was striding beside him. "Shall we surround them, lord?" he growled.

Vyder looked across into the eyes of madness and couldn't help but return the berserker's smile. Rafe appeared to have not a care in the world. Fresh blood had dribbled from the corners of his mouth and his trousers were soaked through with claret. Pale as his skin appeared, the warrior continued to keep Vyder's pace, seemingly without effort.

"Sounds like a plan, Rafe."

"Aye, lord."

Within a few minutes the pair had left the battling Highland squares behind them. Hyglak's war horn, faint against the noise, called black powder. Musket fire crackled to life and rounds zipped or hissed overhead, cutting through man or horse. Vyder, unperturbed by the rounds of lead whizzing nearby, didn't slow. He bellowed and slashed a vicious sweep, but the blade bounced off a Huronian's chest armour leaving barely a dent. He sheathed one sword, clamped a grip on the wounded man's chest piece and unhorsed him.

Landing face up, the Huronian's fall finished with a metallic clatter. To his credit, he'd maintained a grip on his sword and attempted to stab up into Vyder's groin. He leapt away from the strike, then brought a boot down upon the arm, slamming his enemy's sword hand to the ground. He stamped his second boot upon the chest armour, leaned down and ripped his helmet free. The sweat-soaked leather strap beneath his chin slid free of his face and the steel that had been protecting his head rolled free.

Vyder roared, brought his blade back and sent it scudding through the air to cut through the Huronian's neck. Blood gushed from the vacant neck and the soldier went limp. Foreign shouting blasted the sky nearby and a soft hiss followed by a loud clash of steel brought him back to the present. Rafe had reached over him and blocked an enemy sword stroke that would have cut his head in two. He ducked away and the berserker grabbed the enemy's weapon by the hilt and ripped it clear of his hand.

"Is that all you've got?" Rafe screamed, sending the man's own weapon back at him, the blunted blade bouncing from his armour. The madman laughed. The enemy, now without a weapon kicked his horse into action and galloped clear. "Get back here!" Rafe roared, stumbling after the Huronian.

Vyder drew his second sword and hit a spear thrust aside. Another horse battered him to the ground and he hit the dirt hard. A blast of air erupted from his lips. The hooves of horses stamping, jostling and slamming onto the ground filled his vision. *On your feet, laddie.* The thought bounced around his skull. *You stay here, you'll be trampled to death.* It was only at that point as the berserker rage drifted from his body, that he realised how stupid his advance into the enemy formation had been. Pushing his hands beneath him, each still clenching a sword, he raised his body up, gathered legs beneath him, stood and turned back the way they'd come.

Only horses were visible, their way was cut off. Rafe had vaulted onto a riderless horse and was embroiled in a sword battle with an enemy trooper, the blades bouncing and sliding off one another throwing tiny sparks. *There's an idea!* Hope warmed his guts where his fury had once found residence.

Another almost inaudible horn blast followed by a crackle of muskets. He knelt when the first *whizz* sliced the sky. Men, holes punctured in their thin plates of protective steel, fell from the saddle, their screams of pain muffled by full-faced helmets. In the thick of the enemy formation, Vyder needed a miracle to stay alive. If he died, Gorgoroth, wherever the hell he was, would cross the Frost River with him leaving Miriam to fight for herself. She deserved more than that.

Verone's smiling face pierced his mind. "Soon, love." He gripped the blackened piece of charcoal tied about his neck and pulled. The thin braid holding it in place snapped. "But not yet."

A string of shouted Huronian words erupted around him and a boot slammed into his chest. Wind exploded from his mouth. He left the ground and sailed backward through the air, the cavalryman responsible for the assault galloped by, leaning low in the saddle, swinging sharp steel. The blade sliced the air in front of his nose. His back hit the ground first, then his head. Again, he was surrounded by jostling hooves carving the lush grassland to trampled dirt. One of those powerful hooves would split his skull.

Rafe's pale, sweaty face appeared above him and grabbed his shoulder. "Get on your feet, lord," he snarled. "There is a battle to win." His snarl turned into a chortle, although the good humour didn't make his wide, mad eyes. "We almost had them surrounded!"

Vyder grinned and allowed himself to be pulled back to his feet. The piece of charcoal was still clenched in his hand. The berserker released his hold, looked over Vyder's shoulder, roared with fury and sent his sword end over end like a throwing knife. Vyder swivelled and stepped aside as the warhorse ploughed straight for him. Rafe's sword punched deep into the man's groin and the warrior screamed in agony as he swept passed. Spatters of fresh blood settled upon Vyder's face.

He threw the black sliver high into the air. It reached its zenith and plummeted towards the hoof indented ground. "Agoth!" Vyder roared the name. He brought the swords together with force, sparks sprayed from the colliding steel. "Agoth, I summon your help!" One spark settled upon the falling charcoal. It flared to life, the dark chunk of burned wood hit the ground and the ember winked out.

A Huronian charged him, spear levelled at his head. A faint horn blasted and muskets crackled their voices from far behind, where his embattled Highland Army fought for their lives. Vyder didn't bother ducking. This was his skane. His time to walk the Frost River. The spear cut towards him. Of all the smells that wafted rampant in the air, the one which settled in his nostrils before the sharp point skewered his skull was freshly turned earth. The smell, created by the incessant mash of hooves hammering against dirt was stronger than the iron stink of blood or acrid aroma of stale sweat. Something hissed by his cheek, close enough that the slight wind and heat touched his skin. A hole drilled through the Huronian's helmet just above the eye slit and the man dropped from the saddle and smashed onto the ground at Vyder's feet.

Verone's face faded to darkness again and the raucous of battle drove the scent of fresh earth away. He blinked as the present made itself known to him. He felt fresh, replenishing air flee the vicinity and he couldn't breathe. Horses felt it too. They reared or bucked, eyes wide with fear. Many of the elite enemy remained in the saddle, but some were cast airborne to wage their odds amongst the thousands of hooves slamming the ground beneath. Vyder's chest expanded, but nothing entered his lungs. It felt like he was beneath the water holding his breath.

Immense heat accompanied by a deafening hiss

exploded near Vyder. Flames five times taller than a man erupted from the piece of charcoal on the ground. He backed away from the unbearable heat, sweat beading upon his forehead. He held a hand up to shield his eyes. Bright tendrils of fire flickered across the sky high above the embroiled armies.

Vyder narrowed his eyes, driving his vision into a narrow, horizontal slit. He peered straight up at the blaze's apex. It took shape! Licks of flames widened to form fire-imbued shoulders, arms, and hands. An explosion rocked the landscape sending thousands of sparks cascading in all directions and Agoth's head appeared above the wide shoulders. Horns adorned the temples, tusks protruding from each corner of his fang-lined mouth. His orange, glowing abdomen flickered into view next. Then the blaze closer the ground separated into thick legs, and joining them, Agoth's upper body appeared. His torso was bare but he wore trousers glowing the bright red of molten metal.

In his hand he held a flaming curved sword and draped upon the ground behind him curled a flickering tail, the tip of which was shaped like an arrowhead.

Where is Gorgoroth? The deep powerful voice exploded in Vyder's mind.

"I don't know, but we need your help, Agoth! They have taken Lisfort. I fear for the life of my friend, Miriam."

The fire spirit followed his arm and stared over the heads of the frozen Huronian Cavalry towards the city. "And they'll kill us all very soon."

A molten hand gestured towards the enemy cavalry. **And these puny horsemen are the cause of this all?**

"Aye, Agoth. Will you help me?"

Something brushed his shoulder and he realised Rafe was nudging him. The berserker was staring up at Agoth. "Pardon me, my lord, but you seem to have summoned a demon!" he threw his head back and roared with laughter. The noise peeled off into a racking cough and he spat a glob of blood onto the dirt at his feet.

He glanced at Rafe and noticed that they suddenly had room to move in any direction they chose. The enemy force had withdrawn a safe distance from Agoth leaving the two Highlanders and the giant fire spirit in the centre of a large circle of Huronian Cavalry. Vyder stared up at Agoth and noticed the pair of piercing black orbs in his eye sockets staring back.

I think I will, Vyder.

The fire spirit turned from him and strode towards the enemy force, casually carrying his sword by his side. **And the other cavalry at the very rear. They are dressed differently from the others. They remind me of the horse warriors of whom Gorgoroth once spoke.**

"Aye!" Vyder shouted. He broke into a run in an attempt to keep up with the giant. "They are our friends."

Agoth lunged into a run and brought the sword over his head. The flaming blade hissed and crackled through the air. Vyder advanced at a sprint with a view to support Agoth's attack, but he wasn't fast enough to maintain a pace with the fire spirit.

The massive orange sword swept down and cut through the Huronian ranks, spreading death, and lighting men on fire. Steel chest plates and helmets melted in the heat.

The screaming began.

VIII
Late morning – sixth day of the siege

The wagon's axles squeaked across the uneven terrain, wooden floor creaking. The soldier sitting on the driver's bench clicked softly to the horse pulling the vehicle at a fast walk. Rone had dismounted and walked beside the horse-drawn vehicle, the reins clenched in his fist. Dax needed a break from his lazy weight incessantly sitting in the saddle.

Occasionally, a soft nose touched his chest and gave him a gentle nuzzle. He patted the powerful neck and strode on through the thinning, grey mist. The sound of battle had taken on a distinct new sound. Muskets and blunderbusses had fallen silent, the war cries were muted as were the keening of bagpipes. High pitched screams of agony, terrible to hear, pierced the vicinity instead. Cries of spreading panic and fear swept the area. But a new noise was imbued within the depths of war. A cutting hiss, at times so faint it was difficult to distinguish. At other times, it was a roaring, powerful crackle like a raging bushfire. Rone's brow creased. *Someone's broken rank and flees the field of battle. But who? Highlander or Huronian?* He turned to Dax and stepped up into the saddle. "Sorry lad, your rest is at an end."

He nudged the animal into a canter. A wave of his hand ensured he gained the wagon driver's attention. "Pick up the pace!"

He flicked the long reins against the animal's rump and clicked louder, shouting a few foreign words. The wagon quickened to match Rone's speed of advance.

Rone glanced around him, making sure the other Huronians had the idea. They all cantered along behind, spears held vertical, glistening tips pointing towards the sky. More shouting brought his attention back to the driver, who was on his feet and steering the horse away from him. The wagon rattled on, narrowly missing an overturned carriage painted in the colours of Huron. With deft skill, the soldier steered the horse back onto the original axis. Catching Rone's eye, the warrior made an exaggerated gesture of wiping his cloth enshrouded forehead with a hand, then burst out laughing. Rone grinned and returned his focus to the front.

The cloud of gun powder was petering out and visibility was no longer so difficult to imagine. Rone grabbed a handful of cloak and ripped it free of his head. He shoved the fabric into one of his saddle bags and took in a deep breath of fresh air. A series of coughs exploded from his mouth. *Well, semi-fresh air.* Much better than it had been half an hour ago, anyway.

The driver pulled clear his head shroud as well and dropped it onto the wagon floor behind him. He rubbed the skin of his face with a hand and said something in his foreign tongue, although it was not directed at anyone in particular. As far as Rone could tell, anyway. The more distance they covered, the louder the battle became.

Then the mist faded away revealing the field of battle before them. Shouting a string of words, the driver pulled the horse to a halt. The wagon groaned to a stop. He pointed and another sentence poured from his mouth, his eyes wide. Rone slowed Dax and then pulled the animal to a halt. He leaned forward and patted his neck, "good boy," he muttered, his eyes never leaving the towering inferno positioned in the centre of the Huronian Cavalry. Massive flames licked the orange giant. It swung an enormous sword, flames streaking from the blade as it swept through the air accompanied by a loud crackle. Despite its size, the flame demon wielded the weapon with surprising speed. The sword cut through the Huronians, spreading fire through their ranks.

Ice fear swept Rone's body, wedged in his spine and froze his limbs. Another sweep of that mighty blade and wildfire flickered through the ranks. A soft breeze encourage the stench of roasted flesh over Rone. Dax threw his head and backed away with a snort. The sudden movement and sound broke the piercing grip of fear.

"Steady there, lad," he whispered, stroking the

animal's neck. "Steady."

Dax made to turn away. The powerful muscles of his rump tensed and he was seconds from fleeing. Much like Rone had been moments before, fear had won over the horse's mind.

"Hold!"

Dax relaxed and stamped the ground with a hoof. That one word re-instilled all those months of training, dispersing fear and allowing logical thought to win through. "Hold!" he growled. Dax snorted.

Rone had fought in several minor skirmishes while on missions deep into Huron. Sometimes they'd been badly outnumbered. But he and his sub-unit never lost a fight. There wasn't a human adversary anywhere on the land of whom he was frightened. Training, tactics and discipline had seen him victorious in every encounter. But this. He took in a deep breath. This was different. Whatever this being was, human wasn't the first thing that came to Rone's mind. It might have been cutting the enemy to ribbons, but that was no guarantee it wouldn't turn its attention elsewhere in the blink of an eye.

Only then did the burr of voices around him take hold. The small unit of would-be friends were talking and shouting amongst themselves. Much like the wildfire dispatching the army with which they had once marched, terror, that terrible, insidious beast had taken hold of them.

Where is the Huronian king? Rone scanned the enemy ranks. The tight square wasn't hard to miss. "There you are." The king, to his credit was locked in a bitter battle with... the King's Own. Rone grinned, relief sweeping through him. His comrades still lived. But his smile soon died. *They've been decimated.* The others had to be inside the city walls. There was no other explanation. By his estimate less than five hundred King's Own were still in the saddle and fighting with their usual ferocity.

Rone swung around to face those still bickering behind him. "Silence!" he roared. Yells hushed to mutters.

They didn't understand what he'd said, but the aggression with which it was delivered gave them an idea.

They were tiny. Infinitesimal compared with a fire giant, but equally useless against the powerhouse of the Huronian Cavalry, weakened as they were. However, if they could target the king, Rone and the troops with him could end the fight in one blow. He dismounted, and pointed at a vacant patch of ground nearby that had been chewed to bare earth by the Huronian Cavalry hours before more than likely.

"Briefing!" he led Dax to the freshly turned ground, stooped, picked up a stick and knelt. Dax nudged the back of his head. He drew a circle. "This is us." He paused and looked around at the others. They sat in their saddles staring at him with interest or confusion. "Briefing!" he shouted. "Hurry up!" he pointed at them and then at the ground in front of him. "You lot, here bloody right now!"

Some understood and dismounted with smooth, swift movements. Others followed suit, not because they understood the words Rone spoke, but following the lead of their comrades. Harton was the first to squat beside him. He pointed at the rough circle in the dirt. "Uz?" he asked.

"Us, yes." Others knelt or sat around Rone in a semi-circle. He drew another, much larger circle nearby.

"Bat-tul."

Rone smiled and nodded. He poked a small hole on the outer edge of the large circle. "King." He turned and pointed at the tight formation around the Huronian monarch, then swivelled back to face the mud map at his feet. He pointed at the hole in the dirt. "King Fillip, yes?"

Harton's glare bored into him. "Feleep?"

Rone prodded the stick into the dirt marking King Fillip's position and then dragged a line from him to their location, looked up at the others and said, "boom!"

Silence followed, then Harton blurted a sentence in Huronian. Many of them nodded, their creased brows relaxing as understanding took hold. Others chuckled. Either they didn't understand, or didn't believe it could be done.

Their only problem now was to draw King Fillip to their position. In the past, Garx had mentioned how they'd been driven from the Huronian Army never to return. It was likely that the monarch would recognise Garx, but the officer was long dead. Would he recognise Harton? Or any of the others?

Another crackling hiss echoed across the land and the screaming grew louder again. A rumble gave competition to the piercing, gut-wrenching cries of agony. Rone stood and looked out towards the battle. A large group of Huronian Cavalry were fleeing the field. One man in their midst was well alight, flames engulfing him. The horse which carried him bucked him from the saddle and swerved away. The scorched, limp figure crashed onto the ground, bounced once and came to rest in a heap. A sudden image of the screaming figure Rone had put out of his misery pierced his mind. He squeezed shut his eyes, waited for the image to disperse, then allowed his eyelids to peel apart.

He explained his plan to Harton. With some further drawing in the dirt, the Huronian understood what was required. He took a few other cavalrymen with him and headed for the battle, aiming for the tight square in which King Fillip would be wedged. The idea was rudimentary, but it was better than nothing.

He appraised the remaining soldiers. Some of them sat in the saddle watching the progress of their comrades. Others knelt by the mud map muttering amongst themselves. "We need a fire!" he said, clapping his hands.

Hushed conversations ceased and heads turned towards him. He was greeted with inquisitive stares. Rone made what he hoped was a passing attempt at miming a blazing campfire with his fingers. "Flames." He shoved an invisible poker into the non-existent flames and then pointed the make-believe poker at the powder wagon. "Boom!" he said.

One man's face relaxed and he stood shouting a few foreign words. Another blurted something and dismounted, delving into a saddle bag. His hands appeared from the depths holding a small metal box in one hand and some kindling in the other. Kneeling at a safe distance behind the wagon so as the flames would be hidden from anyone advancing towards them from the area of battle, he opened the tin box.

Rone led Dax closer, his interest piqued. The warrior lifted clear a slice of flint, a small piece of metal and a tiny, loose ball of twine, which he placed upon the hoof-mashed ground. Using the metal, he struck it against the flint. Sparks flew as the metal and flint met. They sparkled down upon the yarn, but no flames burst into life. On what must have been the seventh or eighth strike, the yarn started smoking. The cavalryman knelt lower, cupped his hands around his mouth and blew gently upon the twine.

Rone had been trained to start a fire with nothing more than two pieces of wood, but this new way was far easier and faster. He nodded, watching the small trail of smoke drift up over the shoulder of the kneeling Huronian.

Loud cracks exploded to life nearby and Dax stepped back throwing his head. Broken from his fascination, Rone patted his horse. Soldiers nearby were clambering all over the wagon, levering clear floor slats, they snapped wooden rods used to create the canopy. They kicked clear part of the wall and then broke the pieces of timber over their knee.

Returning his attention to the fire starter, the man had coaxed flames into the midst of the yarn and was placing kindling in a pyramid over the orange flicker. Soon they were aglow and the voracious appetite of the fire grew. More kindling was introduced and then the first of the planks were placed upon the hungry blaze. A sword was plunged into the depths of the growing blaze.

Rone swung around and walked away, Dax dutifully following him, the horse's hot breath upon the back of his neck. Harton and the others had reached the rear of the tight square.

"This might work," he said. "It might just bloody

work."

Harton steered his horse to canter along the rear rank of the tight square formation protecting King Fillip. He slammed his spear into the back of a man and ripped the weapon free. He thrust it again, the tip sliding into the back of a neck. The two soldiers who'd ridden with him joined in.

"Gods above," he muttered, looking beyond the monarch's formation. The demon towered above the circle of Huronian Cavalry. It opened its maw and bright red flame exploded from its mouth. The sword swung down, slicing the sky with a crackle. Back at the powder wagon the noise had been loud. But here, in the midst of battle, it was deafening. Highly trained as he was, Harton's mount attempted to break clear, ears flat to his skull. He clenched his thighs around the barrel of the animal, reached down and gently patted the neck, offering soft words. He turned the animal back and pushed him into a gallop and swung him along the rear rank. Then he went back to work. His spear smashed beneath the lowest point of a piece of armour, skewering the lumbar region. The warrior straightened in his saddle, dropped his sword and attempted to reach behind him to feel what had wounded him.

Harton ripped the weapon clear. "Remember me, *sire?*" he roared. He stood in the stirrups and glared into the centre of the square. Many of the soldiers still faced away from him, those at the front darting forward in an attempt to attack the legs of the flame demon. Despite their courage, they fell inside moments. The heroic warrior king, of course, sat safely in the centre.

If he survives this, he'll no doubt tell tall tales about how he rallied his fleeing men and saved the day. He snarled. *Such a pathetic little man.* However, for all the years he'd served King Fillip, he'd never spotted the grandiose nature of the man. Not until he'd been cast out of the elite unit, anyway.

Some of those at the rear of the formation had

noticed the new threat from the back. One cavalryman rounded on him. "Your king is a coward!" Harton shouted.

"Says a man spearing us from behind without any means of defence!"

The comment gave him pause. The warrior slammed heels into the flanks of his horse and charged Harton, sword swinging over his head in a diagonal downward strike. Harton snarled, and urged his mount into a counter charge. He ignored the sword bearing down upon his neck and brought his spear forward at the last moment in a powerful stab. The sharp, steel head slipped through the leather gorget and pierced the man's throat. His sword tumbled from his hand, the horse swept past and the wooden haft was ripped from Harton's grip.

He turned his mount on the fly and swung back the way he'd come. Asking the animal to halt, he vaulted from the saddle and retrieved the sword. He swung up onto his horse, and pressed the animal into a gallop, casting a glance over his shoulder. The wounded soldier had fallen from his horse and lay limp upon the trampled ground, the spear still lodged in his neck. The animal had fled into the distance and was stood grazing.

Harton returned his attention forward. "Fuck!" he ducked low, the sword sweep grazing the back of his helmet as the enemy galloped past. They were gaining attention. But soon, he and the few who had accompanied him would need to withdraw to the power wagon. It wouldn't take much for them to be surrounded and slaughtered. He steered to the side of another charge so the two war horses did not collide and brought his sword in close. His opponent's face, revealed from within the depths of the open helm glowed hatred. He swung his sword in a horizontal sweep that would leave him without a head if it connected.

The sharp blade, catching glints of sun as it sliced the air continued to approach his neck. It was like time had slowed to a standstill. He could still hear Garx's voice in his mind. When he'd first joined the Huronian Cavalry, Garx had trained him in close quarter combat. *A sword's fastest strike is a straight line.* Swing a sword in an over or under-hand strike or a horizontal blow meant the blade would land with enough force to kill or incapacitate an enemy.

He ducked low in the saddle and his enemy's weapon swept the air above his head with a soft whistle. An incomprehensible roar left his lips and he lunged forward. The sword travelled up at an angle and took his opponent through the throat. A stab always defeated a swing. He pulled on the hilt and the razor-sharp metal glided free of the terrible wound.

He stood in the stirrups and held the sword high above his head. "King Fillip!" he shouted. "You are a coward!" Another opponent charged towards him, but he ignored the warrior. Others in the deeper ranks were aware of the minor threat at their rear and turned to join their comrades. Finally, the monarch turned in the saddle and stared over his shoulder, his eyes locked onto Harton's face. He levelled his sword so the tip pointed straight at Fillip. "Coward!" he screamed. "You remember me, *coward?*"

The king's eyes bulged in recognition, then narrowed to slits. The jaws beneath his thick beard bulged and he snarled. He swung his powerful steed about and kicked the flanks shouting a string of curses. Those around him followed suit, their faces lined with confusion and concern, although none of them attempted to call their commander off or question him. To do so would have been their head.

Harton batted a sword aside and remained stationary, glaring at the oncoming monarch. "That's it," he whispered, grinning, although the good humour did not reach the fury in his eyes. "Finish what you started, *coward!*"

"Time to go, Harton," someone shouted from close by.

He nodded, turned his mount away and pushed the animal into the gallop. The air around him seemed to split asunder and incredible heat exploded against his back. A deafening crackle swept behind him and renewed screaming intensified. He cast a glance over his shoulder and a shard of dread entered his body. The fire demon was close behind them. What had once been the front rank of the Huronian Cavalry were well alight. Some of the soldiers attempted to flee, but engulfed in flames, many of them fell from the saddle.

But King Fillip's hate-filled glare remained locked on Harton. He grinned and faced front. He patted the horse's neck and urged it to gallop with all its effort. The heavy rhythmic breathing exploding from its nostrils suggested it was running as hard as the muscles of its legs allowed. He steered towards the distant wagon. *I hope you're ready, Rone, or it'll all be for nothing.*

Another flick over his shoulder told him the demon was running after them. His eyes widened. *And it's gaining ground. Fast!*

"Oh shit!" a comrade yelled beside him.

A hissing crackle cut the air in every direction and another blast of heat touched the skin of his back. Another chorus of high-pitched shrieks of agony told him the flaming sword had dealt more damage to the elite cavalry. Another few strikes like that and there'd be nothing left of the Huronian force. Harton swivelled in the saddle. Fillip was still giving chase. He seemed oblivious to the flame demon or was unconcerned by its presence. Fury still lined his face, his piercing stare never leaving Harton. He shouted something at him, but over the noise of screams, wind in his ears, the thump of hooves slamming onto the ground he couldn't make out what the words were. He cupped a hand around an ear and grinned. "What, coward?" he roared.

It might have been Harton's imagination, but he was sure the king's face took on a scarlet hue. He shouted a reply, veins in his neck bulging, but Harton turned away and ignored the monarch. Fear gnawed at the pit of his guts. Here was a man he once thought of as a god, a man he'd sworn his life and entire career to protect, and here he was avidly mocking the monarch. He knew if his horse tripped or threw him from the saddle, he'd be dead for sure. If the fall didn't kill him outright, Fillip's attentions would. The bastard'd make his death slow and painful as well.

"That bloody demon better bugger off!" a soldier shouted from beside him.

A single spark would send the powder wagon sky-high and kill everyone around it. "I know!" he offered with a shrug. "But it might yet work in our favour."

He cast another look over his shoulder and the breath caught in his throat. Half of those who'd given chase were down, either actively burning or smouldering black lumps upon the dirt. Curiously, not a single horse was injured.

Rone leapt down from the wagon and pulled clear a barrel half-filled with gun powder. He walked backwards holding it between his legs and shook free a thick trail of black leading away from the wagon. The last of the grit fell clear of the wooden container when he was one hundred metres away from the wagon. He straightened and cast the barrel aside. Stretching his back and ignoring the ache in his lumbar region, he looked beyond the small fire at the oncoming cavalry.

Harton and the two who'd gone with him led the way, steering the chasing group straight towards the wagon. Timing would be everything. If the explosion were initiated too soon, it'd kill Harton and the others while dealing little or no damage to the Huronians behind them. Too late and it'd do no damage at all.

They were riding hard. "What is that bloody thing?" Rone whispered. The orange, shimmering giant was running behind the conglomerate of horses and it was gaining on them. He'd heard of strange giants in mythology, but he'd thought it nothing more than simple stories put to books written by ancient generations. He considered it a possibility he'd imagined the thing, but the reactions of his new comrades suggested they'd seen it as well. He turned his attention to the small group gathered about the powder wagon. Some of them had climbed to the highest point, staring at the oncoming threat. Others stood nearby, whilst one man leaned against a wheel, arms folded in front of him, his demeanour relaxed. Almost complacent. To their credit they remained uncowed, however. Surprised? Yes. Frightened? Probably. Preparing to flee? No.

Rone smiled and jogged back to the group. He untied Dax and mounted. "Prepare yourselves!" he shouted, gesturing at their various horses. Some men held the animals by the reins, while others were content to allow their beasts to graze upon the sparse pick not already trampled to dirt by thousands of hooves.

They didn't understand his words, but the premise wasn't lost on them, especially with the mass of cavalry bearing down upon them at such speed. Soldiers jumped down and ran to their horses. Others led their mounts away before stepping into the stirrups. The relaxed warrior pushed himself away from the wagon's wheel and ambled towards a single horse still grazing. He clicked softly and the animal's head came up, ears pricking and alert eyes staring at the approaching man. He stroked its face and took hold of the reins draped over the powerful neck.

The King's Own warrior raked his gaze over the small formation around him. They were not so dissimilar to him. He held his hand out to a nearby man who wore a thick mitten upon his hand.

"I'll do it, lad," Rone said. "Give me the glove."

The Huronian's face creased into a frown and he spoke a rapid sentence in his foreign language. It seemed he knew what Rone wanted but was refusing. He thought it his duty to set the fuse.

Rone kept his hand outstretched. "It was my idea. Let me be the one to light it."

His face relaxed and he nodded. He ripped the glove clear and tossed it to Rone. He caught it mid-air and pulled it onto his right hand. He gestured to the group. "Move away!"

He motioned into the distance. "Get away from here, you lot. It's about to get very hot and very bloody loud!"

The complacent one, now mounted on his war horse smiled and his eyes suddenly became wide. "Boom!" he said then turned away and pushed his horse into a canter.

Rone grinned and chuckled. "Exactly."

They moved away, leaving Rone alone by the fire. Fresh planks had been placed on the blaze and the sword wedged in the centre showed the first signs of a dull red glow. The metal pommel was smoking and the leather binding around the grip hissed and burst into flame. The leather strips broke away and dropped into the fire leaving the hot, bare steel of the sword's grip. Taking hold of it without a mitt would burn the skin to the bone. Something he'd prefer not to experience.

The dull rumble grew closer drawing his attention away from the retreating horsemen. The Huronian Cavalry were almost upon him. His guts lurched. "Oh shit!" They'd advanced farther than he realised. Stooping low in the saddle, he patted Dax's neck. "You ready, lad?" Gripping the sword in his mitten, he lifted the red-hot weapon free of the flames and turned Dax away. The blistering steel hissed softly in the cool air and the metal smoked. He pushed the horse into a canter and then a gallop, steering him to traverse the thin black line of powder Rone'd poured onto the ground so recently.

The dark trail of grit came to an abrupt halt. Rone leaned back in his saddle and Dax slid to a stop. He turned the animal back and approached the end of the powder trail. Harton and the two who rode with him had passed the wagon and approached at a gallop. Even from this distance, he could hear the sharp blasts of air exploding rhythmically from the horse's nostrils over the drum of hooves and shouts of fury. The animals were exhausted. Harton and the others swept by Rone shouting something in their foreign tongue.

Even through the thick mitten, the sword's heat worked its way into the skin of his hand. His tongue wet his lips and his eyes narrowed, concentration winning the day. The king's square was still advancing straight towards him in chase of Harton. That meant his axis of advance would lead straight past the powder wagon in what he estimated to be about ten seconds. He leaned down in the saddle and touched the sword to the dark stain upon the ground. "Come on, you bastard," he whispered. A flurry of dark blue smoke rose into the air round the blade and then a bright orange flame and loud hiss came to life.

The flame worked along the line of powder heading straight towards the wagon in the near distance. "Time to make ourselves scarce!"

He urged Dax about to follow his comrades cantering away in the distance. He allowed Dax to have his head and laid low in the saddle, the ground blurring by beneath him. "Run hard, my boy!" he shouted.

Dax gained on Harton and his friends. Within fifty metres he was at full stride, chewing the ground up and reeling the other horses in as if they were at a standstill. Rone cast a look over his shoulder, the wind whipping his hair. He snarled. "Fuck!" the king's tight square of cavalry seemed to have spotted the threat and turned away from the wagon, although the blob of the remaining Huronians barrelled straight towards the improvised bomb. They were seconds from galloping past it. The orange glow of the rudimentary fuse sparked up onto the wagon's floor and disappeared into the first barrel.

Rone pulled Dax to a halt and vaulted clear. He clicked and pulled gently down upon the reins. "Down lad!" He tugged on the reins and clicked his tongue again. "Down my boy." The war horse knelt and then dropped onto the ground in a left lateral position. Rone lay prone near him, staring up over the saddle at the wagon in the distance. The Huronian Cavalry galloped either side of the wagon and were suddenly swallowed by a thick, black pall, closely followed by an earth-shattering *BOOM*. Rone jumped, even he wasn't expecting the explosion to be that loud. Pieces of broken wagon scattered in all directions. A shattered wagon wheel flew through the air towards him, skidded once off the ground and scudded straight over his head with a soft hum. A chunk of wood one end aflame, probably part of the axle, flicked end over end high into the sky, like some small twig. What looked to be a human torso span clear of the dark cloud and thudded to the ground. A flurry of hooves battered the sky breaking Rone's concentration. Dax's head came up and his horse attempted to roll to his feet. "It's okay." He stroked the animal's flank. "It's okay, lad." The kicking legs slowed and Dax's head relaxed back onto the ground. He patted the powerful muscles. "You're safe, my friend." The massive chest rose and fell as a snort left the soft snout.

"No one would have survived that," he whispered, his eyes returning to the expanding black pall. He pushed himself to his feet, guided Dax to roll onto his guts and then straddled the animal. He clicked his tongue and tapped the saddle with a boot. Dax gathered his hooves beneath him and stood with one swift movement. As the animal stood, Rone shoved his boots into the stirrups and pushed Dax into a canter.

The explosion had faded to silence and there were no screams from the wounded. Because there weren't any wounded. The detonation would have turned all the riders and their horses to ash. He felt sorry for the horses, but there had been no other way to bring the battle to a swift end. Of course, the king and his small entourage still lived, but the King's Own would take care of them in short order.

He halted Dax beside his new comrades and grinned. "Job well done!"

They ignored him. Some of them had dismounted, but they all stared in the same direction, their faces haunted. Rone followed their gaze to the west and the breath caught in his throat. The horizon in that direction was stained by a dark, moving blanket.

"Gods!" he said. "Giant spiders!"

There are hundreds of them! He swept his focus across the

darkness advancing towards them. *No.* He swallowed. *There are thousands of them.*

At the front of the army of arachnids there scuttled a monster, a spider the size of a house and upon its back... Rone squinted... appeared to be riding an old lady. As the creatures closed the distance, Rone was mesmerised by the multiple eyes of the giant leading the unlikely entourage. They were the brightest blue.

IX
Night – sixth day of the siege

Miriam's stomach gurgled and growled. She sat on a padded chair in the living room, the blunderbuss resting on a table before her. Her pockets bulged with powder-filled socks. Her head hung, eyelids growing heavy and her breathing soft and deep. A powerful, distant *crump* rolled over the city and she jumped in her seat inhaling a deep breath. She clutched the blunderbuss with one hand and rubbed her eyes with the other. Her heart hammered in her chest and fresh sweat broke out upon her forehead.

"What in the gods was that?" she whispered. She allowed the fear to swell and flicker through her, used it to climb to her feet. Burning pain ran up her thighs, but she ignored it, lifted the blunderbuss. Her right hand curled around the weapon's grip, her index finger resting upon the trigger.

I swore I wouldn't fall asleep again! She cursed, the fear morphing into anger. She padded to the front door, carrying the hand cannon horizontally. If what she'd heard was an assault on the front door, she could fire from the hip if need be.

Miriam placed a palm against the thick wood and ran her eyes over the door searching for damage, but there was nothing untoward. The noise had been powerful and sudden, but her sleep addled brain had analysed it as coming from the main entrance. Intermittent cannon fire had blasted from the area of the palace all night. This noise had sounded similar but much more powerful. *Maybe it came from outside the city walls? Is there a battle* still *going on out there?*

"Where are you Vyder?" she whispered.

Thick smoke still pervaded Lisfort and with each new night, more fires seemed to bloom to life. The Huronians would raze the city to the ground by the time they'd finished. An urgent need to sneeze developed deep in her nose. She clutched the skin either side of her nostrils and squeezed, hard. The sneeze died. Good bloody thing, too. Because she wasn't imagining the foreign voices in the near distance, or the dull thud of boot-falls along the cobbled street outside.

It's only a matter of time before they force entry in search of loot. An image of her former master on top of her flickered into her memory and terror mixed with disgust speared her chest. *Stop it, Miriam!* A deep breath entered her chest along with a new aroma of thick smoke. She clutched her nose again to ward off the sneeze. The image faded to darkness. *That's not going to happen.*

Her fingers clutched the blunderbuss's grip once again. Her thumb pulled the cocking handle back with a dull *click* and an index finger brushed the trigger. Warm and comforting in her hands, the weapon gave her confidence. "No, I don't think that'll ever happen again."

Soldiers continued running down the street outside the house, sometimes shouting, calling or laughing amongst themselves. Miriam gritted her teeth. *They're having a great bloody time by the sounds!*

Satisfied the noise had not issued from some bastard trying to batter down the door, she retracted her index finger and placed it outside the trigger guard before returning to the living room. Miriam placed the weapon upon the polished table and sat. She swept her palm along the wood. Her fingers felt every carving. Some of them depicted great warriors from Shadolian, Huronian or Wendurlund cultures. Or they may have been gods or goddesses, Miriam was not sure about all of them.

Her favourite figure masterfully cut into the beautiful table was located at the centre and coloured with different shades of tree sap. It was a tall, lean but powerful woman in the shape of a rainstorm standing upon a cloud, a bolt of lightning clutched in her hand. She held the lightning like a spear, preparing to send it straight down.

Miriam smiled. "Thros." Vyder had told her many times about the Shadolian Goddess of Lightning. Being a seafaring nation, the Highlanders often prayed to her before departing on a journey across the sea.

Along the edge of the tabletop and down each leg there were also intricate carvings. Some of animals, or semi-human figures. Even Vyder had not known them all. One of the pieces cut into the timber depicted a humanoid figure of a tree, a pair of tiny bright, piercing blue stones had been glued into place for the eyes. Her smile faded. "I think I know you," she whispered. "You better be taking care of Vyder."

Another table leg displayed a tall blazing fire in the shape of a demon, some Wendurlund god from what she'd remembered of Vyder's explanation. Other edges were marked with runes of all shapes and sizes. She knew not what the script said, but she found it fascinating. Some people would consider the piece of furniture ugly, of that she was sure. But she'd always loved it.

Other figures she'd never understood and nor had Vyder other than to suggest they were Huronian. One such was the image of a powerfully built man with a thick, flowing beard that reached his chest. His hair hung past his shoulders and in one hand he held a massive sword, a huge round shield clasped in the other. Much like the humanoid tree who she assumed was Gorgoroth, small glittering blue stones had been fastened in place for his eyes. Strange letters were written beneath the god. *He* must *be some kind of Huronian god.*

Miriam's gut growled and her hunger took over. She stood from the table, picked up her blunderbuss and padded to the kitchen in search of food. All of the perishable food was rotten and would make her sick within an hour of consuming it. Those stocks had been placed in a ceramic bin and placed near the front door, the farthest place away from the kitchen. But she still had a few oranges and two apples left over. There was also a thick string of salted meat, but she wanted to keep that for dinner. Or for breakfast, if she had the discipline to ignore it.

She peeled the orange and broke it into segments. She bit into one, fresh juice ran over her lips. The taste was delightful. She savoured each piece, ensuring to chew as slow as she was able. When she'd finished, she ate one apple and left the other. Although she was still hungry after her snack, she ignored the remaining apple and meat. That could wait for later. At least it gave her something to look forward to. A tall, cylindrical marble pot stood in one corner. She pulled clear the heavy lid and peered in. It was still half filled with fresh water. That'd be enough for at least a week if it came to it. She pushed a cup into the cool depths and brought the brim to her lips.

Miriam took small sips of the refreshing liquid to trick her belly into thinking it was filling up with food, or at least that was her theory. When she'd finished the cup, she placed it upside down on a counter, grabbed her blunderbuss and returned to the living room.

She placed the weapon upon the polished wood and relaxed into the chair. Taking a deep breath, she let it out slowly. Although anxiety still eddied around her stomach, boredom was fighting hard to be victorious. More distant shouts from outside, muffled by the mansion echoed to her. *I'm one of the lucky ones.* They still hadn't forced an entrance into Vyder's home, but as the enemy soldiers looted and raped their way across Lisfort, time was only a mistress who stood by her for a short duration.

A ripple of *booms* washed over the city. She flinched and made a half grab for the blunderbuss. It'd been several hours since she'd last heard the cannons fire from the palace. Boredom was defeated and anxiety pushed forward. *At least someone is still fighting these monsters!* She licked her lips and stood, rubbing her hands together. Miriam paced around the table, but that didn't seem to help. Another group of cannon-shot rocked Lisfort and she ducked beneath the table. *You're being stupid.* She took a few, slow deep breaths and forced herself to calm.

She stood and leaned on the table. A soft squeak pervaded the house, almost as loud as the cannon blasts. Her breath caught in her throat. This time her hand snatched up the blunderbuss. "I know *that* sound," whispered Miriam. At least she didn't think she'd imagined the noise. With the erratic thoughts and competing emotions, she was no longer confident of what was reality or imagination.

In a few minutes she stood motionless in front of the massive front door. Silence. She held her breath. Still nothing. Then the doorknob moved and that familiar squeak jarred her soul again. "Oh gods," she whispered. Taking a backward step, smoke soaked into her nostrils and she grabbed her nose, but too late. The sneeze exploded from her mouth, followed almost immediately by shouting from right outside the door.

A dull *thud* battered the locked entrance, the door shuddering in its frame, but it remained solid. It sounded like someone trying to kick in the door. Another boot slammed into the thick hardwood, but to no avail. The doorknob twisted and another *thud* rang out. One voice in particular shouted a string of foreign words which sounded to Miriam like an order. The assault on the front door ceased, although the dull burble of muffled voices outside the threshold indicated a group was still present and not likely to depart any time soon.

She unclamped her nose and cursed in silence, anger swelling inside. *You stupid woman, Miriam!* She sniffed and wiped her nose with the back of her hand, the smoke working its way deep into her nostrils. *Stupid!* She sighed. *Can't be helped. What's done is done.*

Boom! The door shuddered more than last time. *Boom!* The sound carried a metallic after tone, indicating they were using a steel tool in an attempt to force entry. *Boom!* "They're using a bloody battering ram," she muttered. *Boom!* A crack of fracturing wood echoed around Miriam. *Boom!* The door started to separate from the framework and a thick crack striated the length of the door's centre. *Boom!* The shouting, albeit breathless was louder than before and less muffled. *Boom!* The crack opened into a crevice and the partial face of a sweating Huronian came into view on the other side of broken wood. The doorway, however, still held. The piercing blue eye narrowed and an angry glint entered his focus as he held Miriam's glare. He turned away and shouted something. *Boom!* The entrance creaked and almost gave way.

"Wait, Miriam," she whispered. "Not yet." She licked her lips and took a deep breath allowing the abject fear to wash over her.

Vyder's distant voice spoke in the vaults of her memory. *"Miriam, you can't have courage without fear. The courageous people experience that bone-pitting fear and act anyway."*

"I wish you were here, Vyder."

...and act anyway.

Boom! The door split into two pieces. The section still attached to the hinges was flung open and smashed against the wall. The other piece broke free from the main door and bounced once against the floor. Huronian soldiers poured in, the first two casting their small battering ram aside and withdrawing swords. They sprinted for Miriam. One grinned, flashing dull yellow teeth, his eyes wide with madness. The face of the other creased in a snarl. A third soldier tried to barge in between the first couple, eager to claim his 'prize' before the others.

Miriam pulled the butt stock tight into her shoulder and stared down the metal sights. Madman's grin vanished. Her index finger touched the cool metal trigger and squeezed. *BOOM!* The blunderbuss smashed into her shoulder making her take several backward steps and the explosion made the battering ram seem like a toy. She coughed amidst the thick cloud of gun powder. Only one man was groaning and gargling softly. The other two were silent. Probably dead. *Hopefully dead.* Miriam turned away and raced from the main entrance heading for the living room.

More voices exploded from the threshold, overwhelming the quiet gurgles of the dying soldier. She pulled free a bulging sock from her pocket and noticed it was the blood-stained light blue material of her former master. She pulled free the pin from her hair, pierced the fabric and allowed a small amount of powder to trickle down the weapon's maw, then dropped in the sock. She tapped the butt of the blunderbuss upon the floor a few times to help settle the ammunition and powder. Grabbing a hold of the warm barrel she lifted the weapon into her hands, fingers curling around the stock and index finger touching the trigger guard. Leaning against a door frame, she pulled the butt into her shoulder and stared down the metal sight at the fading cloud of gunpowder pervading the destroyed main entrance. With her thumb she eased the hammer back. *Click.*

Then they appeared, the Huronians running straight through the silver cloud. Four of them. One of them broke into a fit of wracking coughs, but the others pushed on, oblivious to the acrid mist. Miriam leaned further against the framework, placing the sight over the chest of the soldier leading the pack. He noticed Miriam, his face creasing into a savage grin. He shouted a sentence and changed direction towards her, barging one of his comrades aside. The others followed his lead, lending their voices to the cacophony.

Miriam waited. She ignored the pounding of her heart and the numbing fear willing the muscles of her thighs to fail her. Her index finger touched the trigger and took up pressure. On the warriors ran, thirty metres from her and eroding the distance fast. Swords flashed into their hands. She tried to ignore the dried claret staining the metal of the blades. She locked her legs to prevent them from collapsing beneath her and ignored the thunder of her heart in her chest. Twenty metres.

The man leading the group was laughing. They knew there was no way a blunderbuss could be reloaded so fast. *They think I'm trying to bluff them.* She smiled, and knew her face would have looked like one of unhinged madness. Ten metres. A moment before she squeezed the trigger, the lead warrior's face grew haunted, his snarl disappeared and his mouth dropped open as realisation filled him. He shouted a few foreign words. Miriam took up all the pressure on the trigger and the hammer slammed forward.

"Never again," she whispered.

A faint aroma of sparking flint drifted to her nose and the blunderbuss bucked against her shoulder combined with a deafening *BOOM*. The group of soldiers disappeared behind a new cloud of choking gunpowder and Miriam turned from them, ducking deeper into the house. A high-pitched scream of agony chased her, but of the other two soldiers there was nothing but the silence of the dead or near dead.

She paused to reload the weapon, pulled the hammer back then continued towards the rear door. That entrance remained silent. If soldiers were trying to breach that as well, she'd be in real trouble. But for now, it seemed she was in luck. Fresh voices echoed down the hallways of the home she'd once held sacred. A tinge of anger touched her. These newcomers could just wander in as they pleased. She halted by the rear door and placed her hand on the doorknob. She made ready to exit the home she'd known for so many years but reconsidered. *I'll give them one last gift.* Miriam turned in the direction of the foreign language drifting to her down the hallways. She lifted the blunderbuss back into her shoulder, leaned forward in preparation for the recoil and waited.

A door crashed open at the far end of Vyder's home and the voices took on a muffled sound as they entered the room. More soldiers made entrance to the house. Miriam thought they might have been bickering, but the context of foreign languages, especially with her limited experienced, were sometimes difficult to understand. A series of dull thuds echoed from above. She kept the weapon pulled into her shoulder and glanced at the ceiling.

They're like rats. They're everywhere! Miriam returned her attention to her immediate front and stared down the sight of the blunderbuss. The sound of breaking glass made her flinch, but she remained in control and urged herself to relax. A group of Huronians appeared around a corner, saw her and froze in place. They laughed and ran toward her. She squeezed the trigger, the hammer rammed forward and there was a slight pause, then the weapon roared to life and bucked against her shoulder. One man collided with her and dragged her to the ground. Of the others there was no sign.

The back of her head collided with the ground and she saw a brief sparkle of stars. Her vision was filled with the Huronian's savage face, he was holding her to the ground. She attempted to roll away but he held her firm. One hand snaked up her dress and pulled her knickers down. She squirmed, but it was no use. He ripped free her underpants, cast them aside and unzipped his trousers. She noticed he was bleeding from one shoulder where one of the blunderbuss rounds had embedded. She snarled and pushed a thumb into to the small hole.

The soldier screamed in pain.

Pushing her thumb into his wound up to the second knuckle, she rolled clear of him, scrambled to her feet and clutched the blunderbuss lying on the ground nearby. The barrel was near scorching but she maintained a grip on it and swung it through the air until the butt stock smashed against the Huronian's head. Ignoring the heat, she brought the blunderbuss over her shoulder and swung it down again with all the force she could muster. The hardwood stock slammed into the man's face knocking him unconscious.

"Never again!" she screamed. She brought the weapon back for one more swing, this time the stock thudded against the man's skull and the integrity of his face collapsed. One eye popped out of its socket. Blood oozed from his ears and his rattled breathing ceased.

"Not ever!" she roared at the corpse.

Reloading the blunderbuss, Miriam brought the weapon into her shoulder and opened the rear door with her non-master hand. She pulled open the entrance with care and took a step back staring down the barrel of the firearm which had become her friend and saviour. The street outside appeared clear. She stepped out of the house casting a fleeting glance over her shoulder at what had once been a place of safety. Then slammed the door closed behind her.

Distant shouts and screams echoed from all areas of

Lisfort. She caught some faint words in the Wendurlund language, but the vast majority of voices were foreign. A clash of steel on steel broke out from nearby but ended as soon as it started. A man's voice yelled in pain followed by the laughter of a group of men. A chill ran down her spine.

BOOM! The sudden explosion was louder out here upon the cobbled street than inside Vyder's home. The cannon fire had come from the direction of the palace. Miriam took a breath and allowed her focus to overwhelm the bone-chilling terror imbuing her body. Staying to one side of the street, she hugged the brick walls of houses and walked in the direction of safety. Or at least, she hoped it was safe.

The coach lamps at the next intersection hadn't yet extinguished despite having not been topped up with kerosene for what must have been more than a day. Their light illuminated a large group of Huronian soldiers who'd darted into view from the right. The breath caught in her throat and Miriam hugged the wall and squatted behind a wooden barrel, keeping a tight grip of the blunderbuss.

She squeezed her eyes shut and whispered, "never again." The fear caused her voice to quiver. Miriam swallowed and peaked over the brim of the barrel at the group. They halted in the middle of the crossroads and one in particular pointed with his sword down the street in her direction. The terror already laying siege to her mind doubled its effort and all strength fled her limbs. Miriam hunkered back down behind the barrel.

Breathe, Miriam! She drew in a lungful of air and let it out slowly. *Breathe. You're safe.* Another breath, released with the same lethargy. The wooden butt stock of the blunderbuss felt cool against the skin of her hands. *You're safe for now.*

A staccato of dull *thuds* echoed down the street, bouncing from walls and reverberating down alleyways. The noise of boot falls and shouting grew in volume. A faint, giant shadow of a man cast by the distant coach lamp ran along the side of a brick home opposite her and then the man himself appeared, sprinting by her, oblivious to her presence.

More shadows hove into view, flickering along the brickwork, then the men responsible for the black, stretched ghouls exploded into flesh and blood running after their leader.

Miriam remained still and quiet, allowing the Huronians to pass. When the sound of their boots had faded to near silence, she peaked over the barrel again. The intersection was clear. *Time to move!*

She gathered quivering legs beneath her and pushed to her feet. Holding the blunderbuss pressed against her right hip, she kept the barrel horizontal to the ground and her finger brushed the trigger. Sticking to the shadows she advanced with care, one foot in front of the other, her movements slow and deliberate. Only when she had no choice but to walk into the dim light cast by the coach lamp did she quicken her pace. With her increased footsteps, her breathing also quickened. That stubborn bastard of fear lacing its icy fingers into her soul and causing weakness to enter her legs once again.

All around her, echoing across the city faint shouts, screams and cries of anger or pain were a constant reminder that Lisfort wasn't safe anywhere. *Boom!* She ducked to the cobbled street, heart in her throat. When the roar of cannon shot faded to silence, she realised even the palace wasn't completely safe. But given her options, it was probably the best one to take.

Miriam suppressed a grunt and stood. She moved to the last building before the intersection and edged along the brickwork until she reached the corner. From here she was able to see down one side of the intersection far enough to observe there were no enemy present. But unable to see in the opposite direction she'd have to peer around the edge of the building. A freezing chill filled her body and worked its way into her fingertips. She almost lost her grip on the blunderbuss.

"Miriam, you can't have courage without fear." Vyder's voice whispered with gentle insistence.

She licked lips with a dry tongue and stepped closer

to the corner of the building. The hard, rough surface of the bricks scraped against the skin of her cheek. She moved closer to the edge and glanced around the corner catching all but the briefest glimpses of the road. She thought it looked empty of Huronian soldiers. But she couldn't be totally sure.

"That's not good enough," she whispered to herself. "Come on, you can do this." She swallowed and wiped the palm of her left hand against her dress, took up the blunderbuss with dry fingers and then did the same with her right hand. That small action seemed to help not just alleviate her clammy palms, but her state of mind. Miriam took a pace forward and keeping her back flat against the wall of the building she stared around the corner and down the street. It was empty. She raked every inch of the cobbled road, paying particular attention to the areas hidden within shadow. Nothing. No movement.

Staving away another sneeze, she pushed off from the wall and walked along the street towards the palace. Looking over her left shoulder down the road from which she'd approached, that too was void of movement. The blunderbuss felt good in her grip, lending her strength and helping to keep the chill from enveloping her spine. The index finger of her right finger was never far from the trigger.

The farther she travelled from the coach lamp illuminating the intersection the thicker the shadows developed. For most of her life she'd never liked the darkness, always afraid of what might be lurking in the unseen. But now it was her friend. The night's shroud kept her safe and hidden from view. She paused and pushed against the closest wall of a house. Within the darkness, Miriam thought she'd heard something. There it was again! Faint boot falls clopping against the cobble stones drifted to her. She sunk to her haunches behind a thigh-high wall protruding slightly from the house and brought the blunderbuss to bear. She squinted, but that did little to help her vision.

Her chest expanded with cool, fresh air. She exhaled

through her nose, allowing the air out slow and silent. Then took in the next breath. The only part of her that moved were her eyes. *Thud, thud, thud.* Closer the boots came. Soft voices mingled amongst the staccato. She closed her eyes, held her breath and listened. Miriam could not decipher any of the words. Her eyes snapped open and she clenched her jaw. *Huronians then.*

From the depths of the black street, shadows much darker than their surrounds advanced, each taking shape as they grew closer. A group of five men. They strode along the cobbled road with a relaxed lack of speed. Something about their demeanour seemed vastly different to those of the enemy soldiers with whom she'd thus far had dealings. They advanced along the opposite side of the street. Miriam remained frozen in place, not even turning her head to watch their progress as they passed opposite of her position. The loose formation disappeared from the side of her eye and continued towards the coach light far behind her. Still, she didn't move.

The men continued muttering between each other, both their voices and boots growing fainter. Yet still Miriam remained rooted to the spot. Her chest ached and a faint feeling spread behind her eyes, filling her head. A blast of air exploded from her mouth and she gulped in a fresh breath, let that out and took in another. The discomfort in her chest disappeared and her vision regained limited focus. She placed the butt stock of the weapon upon the ground and relaxed, staring at the cobbles beneath her.

Her breathing slowed and deepened. When she'd regained control, Miriam rose carefully to her feet and stepped around the fence to continue along the road towards the palace. *Not far to go.* She took comfort in the thought. She'd grown accustomed to the burble of noise issuing from all corners of the city. A shout here, a yell there, the clatter of sword on sword or steel upon wood. But a new piercing scream cut the sky asunder, causing her to slow mid stride. It was the voice of a woman. *May the gods help her.* More shouting erupted from behind her, but like the other noise to which she'd become oblivious, she ignored the voices and walked on.

More yelling broke the immediate vicinity. The deep staccato of boots on stone accompanied the voices and grew closer by the moment. Miriam cast a glance over her shoulder. A group of Huronian soldiers had spotted her and were chasing her down. "Oh shit!" she hissed. "Shit, shit!"

There must have been at least twenty. *Where the bloody hell did they come from?* She looked beyond the group and noticed the five who'd strode past her stood beneath the coach lamp looking back the way they'd come with interest. They wore long, red cloaks. Miriam refocused upon the immediate threat. Fear morphed into terror, the blizzard-like chill assaulting every part of her body. The soldiers were sprinting and shouting amongst themselves. Even though their language was foreign, the cruelty in their voices was plain enough.

Can't have courage without fear. She walked into the centre of the street, turned to face her enemies and brought the blunderbuss to bear, pulling the wooden stock tight into her shoulder. She leaned forward in preparation to absorb the weapon's buck. Using the backdrop of the distant coach lamp to illuminate the silhouettes of the group, she lined the barrel up with the enemy centre. *Can't have courage without fear.* Her finger curled around the trigger and squeezed. The hammer thundered down. *Thud.* A hint of sparking flint flashed in her vision and a moment later the world exploded. *Boom!* Her ears entertained a high-pitched scream and the chasing soldiers vanished behind a thick cloud of burnt gun powder.

Miriam turned away and negotiated the cobbled street at a steady jog. There was no time or opportunity to reload. So on into the darkness she moved. Her breathing came in rapid, steady rasps. What felt like red-hot coals embedded themselves into her thighs, radiating down to her calves. Her chest tightened and sweat broke out upon her forehead. *Ignore the pain, Miriam.* The din in her ears faded to be replaced by the cries of dying men behind her. But others, much closer than those soon to cross the Frost River, persisted in their shouting. Their boot falls struck the cobbled stone with loud thuds which seemed to grow in volume.

Concentrating on the location of the palace, she darted to the right along a much narrower road. The far end of the street was illuminated orange by nearby flames. A silhouette of another barrel, probably a water barrel placed in preparation for the siege sat on the side of the street. She ducked behind it gasping for breath and took out another powder-filled sock from a pocket. Slamming the butt stock upon the ground, the maw of the barrel pointing skyward, she pierced the sock with her hair pin and allowed the powder to trickle down into the depths of the weapon's maw. Dropping the bulging sock in, she tapped the butt stock on the street, lifted it into her shoulder and with a thumb pulled back the hammer. Then she stepped out onto the street, turned towards the direction from which she'd advanced and pulled the trigger.

The blunderbuss roared its fury to anything in the immediate vicinity that would listen and almost caused Miriam to fall backwards. New pained voices competed with the renewed high-pitched scream invading her brain. But other shouts, angry and cruel continued towards her and they sounded to have grown in number. *The noise of the blunderbuss has drawn them.*

She had two choices, stay and rest her exhausted body, which risked death... or worse. Or ignore the pain and flee to the safety of the artillery at the palace. She turned and ran, willing her legs to work.

"Can't have courage without fear," Miriam muttered in between breaths.

At the end of the street, she turned left and squinted against the sudden light of the massive semi-circle of flickering torches marking the outer extremity of the palace. The enemy were closing upon her. She dared not take the time to glance behind. Terror imbued ice into her limbs to compete with the molten steel already residing there.

She dashed past the closest torch. It was a huge thing, six feet in height, driven into the earth at an angle facing the palace still hidden in darkness. As her eyes became accustomed to the new environment, the large maws of multiple cannons stared at her.

"Get down!" a voice roared in the Wendurlund language.

A hand clenched her top from behind and a Huronian voice shouted something close to her ear. She shrugged the hand away and screamed.

"Ma'am, get down! Get down NOW!"

He's talking to me!

"Fire battery one!" the man roared.

Miriam dived to the ground, dirt slammed against her cheek. *BOOM!* The noise made her blunderbuss sound like a toy. The ground beneath her vibrated and all sound disappeared behind a dull hum in her ears. Through the muffled lack of noise, Miriam was still aware of the powerful *whizzes* slicing the air inches above her head. Something heavy fell on top of her, hot liquid pouring onto the back of her neck. It streamed down her face and wet her mouth before dripping onto the earth beneath her.

The acrid smell of blood filled her nose.

X

Rone still held the smoking sword in his hand, although the heat which had cut through the mitten was gone. The steel was black and probably still hot to touch. As the massive spider leading the army of arachnids advanced upon him, he only hoped the edge was still sharp.

"Be ready!" he called without taking his eyes from the giant beast.

He saw in the side of his eye that his new allies weren't going anywhere. They'd spread out in extended line either side of him with weapons drawn. The incessant click and soft hiss of walking and chittering spiders washed over the small group of mounted soldiers. However, they didn't budge. Their horses were beyond exhausted, as were they. But mental resilience meant defeat hadn't entered their heads. They'd die fighting where they stood if necessary.

"Ho there!" a woman's voice called.

Rone clenched his sword tighter and looked at the monstrosity which had halted in front of him. It was so close that he could no longer see the bright blue eyes. He stared up at the underbelly and huge pair of fangs not so far from his face. The spider could eat both he and Dax whole if it so chose.

"I said, ho!"

Rone tore his focus from the glistening razor fangs and stared up at the sky, taking in the giant arachnid's sheer size. His eyes came to rest upon the tiny head of the old woman far above glaring down at him.

"Yes, you!" she yelled.

He raised an arm in greeting.

"I see you blew up those Huronian cavalrymen. I'm not sure why you did so, but it was well done. We mean you no harm!" She gestured at the Goliath-sized spider upon which she sat. "This is Gorgoroth."

"It has a bloody name?"

She frowned. "You speak the Wendurlund language!"

Rone opened his mouth and then closed it. *Of course! I'm still wearing the uniform of a Huronian bombardier.*

"I'm King's Own."

Movement beside him gave Rone distraction. Harton tapped him on the arm. He looked into the Huronian's face and the soldier pointed at the spider and shrugged, a confused look creasing his brow.

Rone shrugged back. "No idea."

A grin split Harton's beard and he cast his arm in a wide, circular gesture at the army of spiders halted before them. He punched his fist into an open palm. "Kill!"

"Surround them?" Rone chuckled. "I like your thinking, my friend."

A soft *thud* nearby caused him to turn back to the arachnid. The old woman had climbed down from her perch and limped towards him. She was old, but not frail. In fact, he had the feeling she could deal real damage if she so wished.

She stopped at Dax's right shoulder and glared up at him. "I'm Endessa."

He leaned down and offered his hand. "Rone."

She ignored it.

"You ride with Huronians." She looked at Harton and the others.

"Very observant. They are my friends and are fighting against the enemy invasion."

"Very well." She swept an arm around at the army of spiders behind her. "Your horses appear exhausted. You are welcome to climb on a spider and let your mounts rest."

A prickle swept up his spine. "Er. Thank you." He smiled and patted Dax's flank. "My lad is fine for the time being."

"And can *your lad* climb Lisfort's walls?" she turned away and walked back to the monstrosity. "I didn't think so!" She shouted over her shoulder.

He patted Dax's mane. "What say you?"

The war horse snorted, lowered his head and started eating the grass at his hooves. Rone closed his eyes and breathed a heavy sigh. "I knew you'd say that," he whispered. He looked up at the quiet army of spiders before him. *I've always hated spiders.* He turned in his saddle and fixed Harton with a glare. "Harton!" the soldier jumped and tore his gaze away from the spiders. A haunted, hollow glaze glistened from his eyes. "We must let our horses rest." He pointed at the nearest spider. "These are our horses now."

The Huronian followed his finger and then his head snapped back around, his focus boring into him. He pointed at the dark blanket of arachnids before them. "Ride?"

Rone nodded.

A string of foreign words broke free of his lips and the snarl that curled his mouth suggested the words did not favour his idea. Huronian cavalrymen nearby chuckled and shook their heads.

Rone leaned across and tapped Harton's shoulder, then placed a hand upon Dax's flank. "Rest." He brought the same hand to his mouth and chewed on thin air. "Eat."

The warrior scowled and stared at the ground muttering under his breath. Then he straightened in the saddle and roared a few sentences. The soldiers dismounted and removed the saddles, placing them in neat rows behind their formation. The bridles were kept in place and a soldier was designated to stay behind and lead the animals to safety where he'd no doubt maintain an eye on them while they grazed.

Rone swung out of the saddle and met the ground with both boots. He unclasped the girth strap and pulled clear the saddle, placing it with the others. Then he rubbed Dax's back down with a bare hand. The hair directly beneath where the saddle had been strapped into place was sodden with sweat. He swept the area as best he could, then offered the reins to the soldier leading the other war horses away.

"It's goodbye for now," he called after Dax.

The horse ignored him.

"Fine."

An elbow nudged his arm. "Horse," Harton said

pointing at the spiders. He pushed Rone forward a few steps. "First."

Rone regained his balance, glanced back at Harton and laughed. "You want me to go first?" He shrugged and strode towards the closest arachnid. "Fine by me."

He closed upon the giant creature. Although it was nowhere near as large as the behemoth upon which Endessa rode, it was still massive. The spider's head was at least three feet higher than Rone. He acknowledged the cold dread imbuing his body but refused to allow it to cow him. Instead, he stared into the multiple, black, glistening eyes which seemed to watch his every move.

"Try anything and I'll fucking kill you," he growled at the thing.

A clicking issued from where he thought its maw might be located and although instinct begged him to flinch, he continued striding forward. The mitten no longer felt hot. He clutched the sword between his arm and body. Although it felt warm, the red-hot blistering heat was gone. He pulled the thick mitten free of his hand and threw it to the ground, clasping the blade's hilt. The weapon felt much better in his grip free of the thick fabric. With better dexterity, he cut the air before him, the sharp steel offering a faint whistle.

He smiled. "Did you hear me?"

The clicking resounded again. The spider seemed to bow, offering its nearest leg for Rone to climb onto. He clenched his jaw and ignored the hair standing on end at his nape. He looked back at Harton who was watching him with wide eyes. He grinned at the Huronian and winked, then turned toward the spider. He didn't feel the confidence his face had communicated, but deception was often the better part of valour. He pushed the sword into his belt so he had the use of both hands.

Rone licked his lips and placed a boot upon the leg as thick as his thigh and stepped up. When he had both feet on the arachnid's leg he leaned forward and clasped a hold of the hairy appendage. The black hair carpeting the thing's leg were each as thick as a finger. His guts rose into his throat. His grip tightened to maintain his balance. The spider was raising its leg off the ground! He pushed his boots together either side of the thick appendage to keep grip. The thick hair caused him to slip. Rone cursed and tightened the clench of both his hands and feet. The creature raised its leg above and behind its head, allowing Rone to jump clear. *The bloody thing's helping me!* He dropped onto the spider directly behind its head but forward of the bulge of its abdomen. He sat and straddled the arachnid, his boots swinging down either side of its body. He shifted his weight and felt stable and comfortable in his seat. The spider's leg returned to the ground and it straightened from the bow-like posture it had adopted prior to Rone mounting it.

"See?" he shouted, holding his arms out either side of his body. The spider turned and Rone almost lost his balance. He clenched his thighs against the thick fur and held on, although he kept his arms out thrust. "Easy!" he shouted over his shoulder at the Huronians standing behind him. He came close to falling for a second time. "Easy!" he yelled, although his voice sounded more confident than he felt. Laughter followed him.

He swivelled and placed a hand upon the creature's rump. *Or is it the abdomen?* The silk hair felt alien to his skin. Whatever that part of a spider's anatomy was called, it was as soft as down. The creature was making way so that others without a rider could move into its original place. With some hesitation, Harton was the first to advance on the closest spider. The Huronian's face had lost all colour and the sheen of sweat on his forehead was easy for Rone to see even from his position. He chuckled and cupped a hand around the corner of his mouth. "Hurry up!"

Harton was clinging onto one of the legs for dear life as the arachnid assisted him onto its back. Face still pale as death, he cast him a haunted glance. Rone burst out laughing. The others weren't long in mounting their new steeds. They all showed the same level of fear as Harton but to their credit, they climbed onto the giant spiders without complaint. Once done they moved out into extended line either side of Endessa.

The old woman glared down at Rone. "Shall we?" she called.

He smiled and nodded. "Why not?"

The monstrosity upon which Endessa sat strode towards Lisfort, and Rone's mount moved parallel to it. He clamped his thighs tight and maintained his balance. To his surprise the mode of travel was faster than he expected. The cloud of gun smoke thinned and Lisfort was visible along with the dark blotch of Highlanders and King's Own formed up about halfway between the spiders and Lisfort.

A distant series of bugle blasts cut the sky and the King's Own turned towards them and accelerated from the halt to a trot. They moved into an arrowhead.

"They mean to attack us!" he yelled at Endessa. Even vastly outnumbered, the thought of retreat or failure hadn't entered the minds of the elite cavalrymen.

She shouted a reply but the words were too faint for him to hear. She turned toward him and held hands either side of her mouth. "Ride out to meet them! Use your boots to steer the creature."

"How?"

He sensed more than saw Endessa roll her eyes. Her cupped hands raised to the sides of her mouth again. "Nudge your left boot to turn him to the left! Do I need to explain about your right boot?"

Him, the things a him? He shook the thought clear. "No!"

"Tap both boots at the same time to increase speed."

He nudged both boots and the spider lunged forward leaving the host receding behind him. "Wait. Oh shit." He turned and looked back at Endessa. "How do I slow down?" he roared.

But the old woman was looking away from him. "How do I stop?" his voice was growing hoarse. Rone lost his balance and almost fell. He slammed his boots into the arachnid's sides to arrest his long tumble to the ground. The thing sped up into what must have been a spider's version of a gallop.

"Fuck!" the word was ripped from his mouth by the wind streaking by him.

Concentrate on the task at hand!

Rone inhaled a deep breath and returned his attention to the incoming King's Own. The formation had pushed into a gallop and spear-headed straight for him, a faint brown cloud of dust following behind them. They were approaching from the left. He nudged his left foot against the soft hair of the arachnid and it obliged, turning straight toward the oncoming charge. Rone held his hands above his head, his right still clamped upon the sword. He waved his arms in long, sweeping movements. The King's Own did not slow. They were close enough now that he could see many of them brandished spears, while some held swords. So, their weapons of choice, the Musket and potent blunderbuss, were out of powder, or ammunition, or both. That was some reprieve at least. He was in musket range. He continued with the mad movements above his head. On they came, the thunder of the hooves audible over the wind streaking into his ears. Now he was inside blunderbuss range.

"Stop! We're friendlies! Stop! We're on your side!" he roared.

The warrior at the apex of the spear-head formation was clearly visible. It was Tork.

"Tork!" Rone yelled. "Tork, it is I!"

The formation boar down upon him. Tork was moments from disappearing beneath the spider where he would no doubt stab up into the underside of the thing's head or cut into the soft belly. What was about to happen played in his mind. He'd be thrown from his seat to the ground and if the fall didn't kill him, he'd be trampled to death by a maelstrom of hooves. The spider hissed, the noise drowning out the thrum of hooves.

"Tork!"

The commander's grim face turned upward and the hawk-like eyes glared at him, his face softened in realisation and he roared a single command. The bugle blasted even as he was shouting the order and the spear-head formation split in two, one file of soldiers galloping by Rone's right side and the other his left.

He lowered his hands and ignored the burning which had started in his shoulders. "Thank the gods."

Now how in hell do I get this thing to stop?

He kicked both boots into its flank again and a flurry of clicking noises issued from far below him where he assumed its mouth might be. *Looks like that's as fast as we're going.* He tapped the sides of the beast continuously and it slowed and stopped. He slammed a hand down to stop tumbling forward. *Right, so that's how it's done.* Nudging his right boot, the spider turned. He replicated the request and the spider turned again to face the way they'd been travelling.

Tork's group had regrouped and were trotting towards him in a loose blob. The spider clicked and took a few paces backward. *In fear? Or is it uncertainty?* During his ranging into Huron, the rest of his comrades had been battling massive spiders inside the walls of Lisfort. *I wonder if this one was part of the attack?* He placed a hand upon the soft hair and patted the arachnid. "It's okay, you are safe my friend, there is nothing to fear from them."

It clicked again, this time a little louder, but stopped moving. Tork raised his hand. "By the gods, Rone, you almost got yourself killed, brother."

The commander gestured at the creature. "Tired of riding horses?" His face creased into a grin. Others shouted greetings to him from within the ranks.

He waved at his comrades. "It's been too long between ales!" Rone fixed his gaze back on Tork and patted the creature. "Thought I'd try something different, sir."

The officer chuckled and shrugged. "Fair enough. Why in the hells are you wearing the uniform of a Huronian soldier?"

"This past while I have battled alongside a group of Huronian cavalrymen. They are deserters and have aided me. Don't have a damn clue what they're saying, but they're a good lot."

The commander's grin lost a little power. "And do you trust them?"

"With my life, sir."

Tork nodded. "Very well."

He gestured at the King's Own formation below. "Where are the others?"

The commander's stern expression returned. He swept a hand around him to include his soldiers. "These are all of us who remain alive."

Gods. Rone remained silent, shock sparking in his guts. *This can't be true. He has to be mistaken.* He shifted upon the arachnid. "Are you sure, sir?"

A hint of sadness glimmered in Tork's eyes. "I'm afraid so, Rone."

"What number have you?"

"Last count we have three hundred and twenty capable of fighting."

Rone closed his eyes, and the world disappeared. *From two thousand to three hundred. We've been decimated.* The ringing in his ears, a gift from the recent explosion, was receding allowing in the normal noises of snorting horses, jingle of metal straps and creak of leather. A dull rumble spread across the plain, issuing from deep within Lisfort. *Another cannon barrage. No time to mourn our soldiers, we can do that later. Now it is time to fight.*

Rone's eyes broke open and the plain, once swept with rich grass now trampled to dirt by tens of thousands of hooves, reappeared. Rone nodded. "May their crossing of the Frost River have been swift."

A cackle peeled out behind him. "I see you worked out how to stop!"

Rone turned and stared back at the oncoming host of

spiders. He appraised Endessa and his eyes narrowed. "No thanks to you, old woman."

The cackle turned into a belly laugh. The army of spiders stopped behind him, aside from Endessa and his new comrades, who halted either side of him. The conglomeration of King's Own warriors stared up at those men who'd once been their mortal enemies. Rone knew his words urging his brothers to trust the small number of Huronians carried weight. But he was also aware the former enemy cavalrymen would have to prove themselves in battle before Tork truly felt at ease with them.

It won't be long and that will be put to the test. Rone stretched his back and looked beyond the King's Own. The Highlanders were advancing at a walk, their small cavalry force leading the way. A large hound walked beside the horseman in the centre. He'd often heard of the fighting skill of the Highland clans.

Tork cleared his throat. "I assume you want the Highlanders mounted up on spiders as well?"

"I do," said Endessa.

Tork urged his horse into movement, leading his soldiers out of the way so the Highlanders could close the distance. The tiny cavalry of no more than twenty and in extended line, halted within a spear's throw. Rone's brow creased. He nudged both boots and the spider upon which he rode scuttled forward. When he was within spitting distance, he stopped the creature. He looked down the length of the cavalry again, but the face for which he searched was not present.

"Where is Prince Henry?"

The assassin patted the neck of his horse, the movement catching Rone's attention. He remembered *that* face. The man who'd rescued Prince Henry by walking into the entire camped Huronian Army. The Highlander glared at him, his dark eyes fierce. The odd blue eye he remembered was gone. "He's ridden with some of the others to kill King Fillip. The coward king fled with a few of his household troops when he saw your spiders advancing."

Rone clenched his teeth, jaw bulging. The knuckles holding his sword turned white. "Madness! He's outnumbered and as frail as a fawn. The prince will be hacked down inside the opening seconds of the first engagement!"

"He's not as frail as you remember, King's Own," said Vyder. "The lad can fight, and he's not alone. He has some of the finest warriors riding with him."

"Which direction did Fillip flee?"

The assassin pointed towards the horizon behind the dark smear of giant spiders. "West."

"The Waning Wood!" Endessa cried. "He'll burn it to the ground!"

The house-sized spider upon which she sat made a hissing sound which drowned out all other noise. "Shut up, Gorgoroth!" the old woman screeched.

The spider's raucous faded to silence.

"Who exactly rode out with Henry?" Endessa called.

Ahitika leaned forward in the saddle, her horse negotiating the terrain at a gallop. Wind ripped her long hair from her face and screamed in her ears. She grinned and whooped a high-pitched shriek. Her fellow Kalote warriors, Anonkas and Hexuka, joined in. Henry, just ahead of her, glanced over his shoulder and smiled. The black-haired Highland berserker whose face was painted red with war paint was mounted behind her. She remembered Rafe had called him Byfros. He was bloody and wounded in so many places that any other person would be long dead. But the man was inhuman. She was wary of him, too, because he was clearly insane, often talking in his Highland language and always with wide eyes and through a blood-stained grin. At the start of the battle the red paint had made him seem demonic, but now it was difficult to tell blood from paint. Not to mention the guts she could see through slashes and stabs in his armour. While she understood him, Henry didn't speak the language of the Highlanders. Sometimes she attempted to translate for him, but often it was simply drivel not worth passing onto the prince. Although pale, the madman showed no signs of weakness. Behind him followed some fifty Highland Cavalry. Bringing up the rear was the giant fire demon, maintaining their speed without effort. They were badly outnumbered, but she'd faced worse odds.

Henry had tried to dissuade her from coming with him. She'd laughed and reminded him that she and Vyder had once walked through the entire Huronian Army at camp to reach him. That had shut any further words from passing his teeth. He had conceded knowing he had no choice in the matter.

They'd chased the fleeing Huronian Cavalry for miles and from a great distance, unable to close the gap. Unlike the Huronians, however, Henry often slowed the pace to allow the horses to rest and gather their stamina. The enemy had taken no such precaution. It was only a matter of time before they caught them. *If the thirteen scalps in my saddle bag don't already class me as a Kalote warrior, the scalp of a Huronian king will ensure it!*

Henry held up his hand and slowed his horse. Ahitika leaned back in the saddle and tugged a little on the reins. Her mount reduced its pace, came alongside Henry and walked, recouping its breath. She stared at him, waiting to catch his eye, a hint of a smile on her lips. But he was glaring ahead, eyes narrowed watching their adversary.

"We are gaining on them!" he whipped a look at her and paused.

She smiled wide and lowered her head a little but maintained eye contact with him. He grinned and blushed. Ahitika broke into laughter. He licked his lips, peeled his eyes from her and returned his focus to the cloud of dust in the distance. Then he adjusted himself in the saddle. "At least I think we are."

Ahitika chuckled and appraised the area of ground at which Henry stared. "Agree."

She patted her saddle bag. "I take king scalp." The bag offered a faint hint of rot. She'd not yet had time to clean and salt the scalps to deter the stench.

Henry glanced at her. "That a question?"

She shrugged. "No. Not question. I take his scalp."

The Wendurlund prince nodded and chortled. She raked a hand through her dark hair and noticed the brown cloud in the distance had split. A second one had formed beside the first and appeared to be heading back towards them.

She pointed. "Henry? Look."

He followed her finger and his eyebrows drew together, his jaw bulging. "They're sending a rear guard back to us to protect Fillip."

Her hand dropped to her thigh. "I thought he warrior king? I thought he fight."

"He might be part of that force, who knows? They're too far away to see," muttered Henry. He held up his hand and halted the formation.

Blistering heat warmed her back and then morphed to her left flank. The giant fire demon appeared in the side of her left eye. Much as she tried not to look at the thing, she couldn't help herself. The massive being stood staring at the oncoming enemy, a gentle crackling issuing from all over its body.

The huge head turned and its eyes bored into her. A chill lanced down her back and she tore her eyes away. She grasped a hold of her breastplate, her connection to her ancestors who were long gone. She offered a silent prayer of protection and the power of her people swelled through her, driving the discomfort from her back. She turned back and held the demon's eyes.

"Fight with us and protect Henry," she spoke in the Kalote language.

Did it nod? Or am I imagining it?

"Or I'll cut your scalp from your head."

It looked straight up into the sky, its shoulders

shuddering, crackles coming in waves, loud and then soft.

It is laughing!

The hot spear of anger warmed her guts. "Do you doubt me, demon?" she spoke through clenched teeth. The being turned to her and dropped to one knee, bowed its head and placed a fiery hand upon its molten chest.

You have my word, little one. The deep, powerful voice exploded in her mind. Ahitika jolted in the saddle and clenched a tight grip of her breastplate. The demon rose to its feet and returned its attention to the oncoming enemy.

Henry stared at her with wide eyes. "What in the hells was that about?"

She smiled and released the clutch of her breastplate. "I talk to demons now."

"Do you?"

"Yes, my prince. Don't cross me." She winked.

He grinned and ripped his eyes from her.

Ahitika nudged her horse forward and squinted at the oncoming threat. The soft rumble of hoof thunder rolled across the plains enveloping them. It wasn't hard to see Henry's force was outnumbered by what she estimated might be as much as four to one.

"Good odds!" shouted Byfros from nearby. He grinned his mad grin, a strand of bloody saliva hanging from his beard.

"What did he say, Ahitika?"

"He thinks we stand a good chance of victory."

Henry chuckled. "I like the way his mind works."

He stopped beside her and placed a hand upon her shoulder. "Can you tell the Highlanders to harry the cavalry force from the external flanks? And seeing as you talk to demons now, can you ask if old fire man over there would mind cutting into the Huronian centre?"

Ahitika passed on his commands to the Highlanders with ease. It was less difficult for her to speak Shadolian than Wendurlund. She pushed her horse towards the flame giant, which turned to glare at her. **I heard what Henry had to**

say, Ahitika. She attempted not to jump in her saddle, but failed. The voice in her mind had been so clear and loud! She nodded and turned her mount away.

Henry raised a hand and his horse accelerated into a trot. Ahitika followed and the thud of hooves behind them confirmed that so did the Highlanders. She unslung her bow from her back, keeping the weapon in her hands. Henry urged his mount into a canter and without looking up, she tapped her boots against the flanks of her mount. Opening the cylindrical container at her left hip, she pulled clear several arrows. Stringing the first, she held the others between the inner left thigh and saddle.

The prince pushed into the gallop and held his sword over his head. She followed and came alongside him, whooping. The wind streaking through her hair and roaring into her ears made her feel free and wild. He glanced at her, his face grim. "Good luck, beautiful lady," he called.

She smiled at him and shrieked. Anonkas and Hexuka joined in. The Huronians were approaching fast and in a tight rectangular formation. Ahitika slowed a little, guided her horse on the inside of Henry and accelerated again.

Clenching to the saddle with her thighs to maintain her balance she brought the bow up and pulled the string back until she was staring directly down the length of the arrow. The razor-sharp metal tip hovered over the distant face of an enemy horsemen galloping towards her. Movement off to the side of her point of aim caught her attention. One soldier stood in his stirrups and threw a dagger. The steel glinted through the air, the weapon somersaulting towards her. She ignored it and returned her attention to the warrior almost upon her.

Ahitika release the bow string and sent the arrow on its way. It struck the soldier in the throat and he tumbled from the saddle. A soft hiss of steel cutting air whispered in her left ear accompanied by the flash of metal on sunlight. The dagger had been closer than she anticipated. She strung another arrow and pulled the string taught. The Huronians were so close there was no point aiming. Another arrow flew true. And a third. She steered her horse away from the enemy charge. The clash of steel rang out behind her where Henry and the Highlanders harried the flank of the cavalry charge.

Stringing another arrow, she sent it streaking towards its target. It embedded deep in a man's upper arm. He howled his pain, but she couldn't hear his cries over the battle. Then she was beyond him, her mount stretching across the ground. The string rested in the nock of another arrow. She looked up, lifted her bow and prepared to aim and release. The breath caught in her throat and fear clawed its way down her throat and into her bowels.

A Huronian had left the rank and file and was upon her. He screamed some war cry, his eyes mere slits, lips peeled back in an animal snarl. His horse slammed into her mount and her saddle was replaced by thin air. The ground rose to meet her. Pain lanced her back and air exploded from her lips. She'd clenched a grip of her bow, but the arrow was gone. Everything was dark. She groaned and tried to move, but agony was her only comfort.

Aggressive Huronian words were bellowed at her and she was aware of a horse jostling near her head. Her eyelids peeled apart and light flooded in stabbing her brain. She blinked and focused. The cavalryman who'd knocked her from her saddle leapt clear of his horse and strode towards her. A sword was clenched in his hand.

"I'm goin' to take pleasure in killing you, bitch!"

She sat up, but he placed a boot on her chest and pushed her back to the ground. She swung the bow with all the strength she could muster. The wood smacked him in the face, but he laughed. He pulled it out of her grip and cast the bow staff aside. Pushing down on his boot, the pain in her back reminded her of its presence. She dropped a hand to her knife, but all she touched was an empty deer hide sheath. Ahitika looked about her, desperation filling her. There! By her left hand was the arrow. It'd been snapped in half, probably by her fall. Snaking out her arm, her fingers touched the cold, thin wood but couldn't grasp it.

The Huronian grinned, reversed his sword so the tip hovered over her throat and placed both hands on the hilt, preparing for the killing thrust. One hand curled around her breastplate, the fingers touching the thin, horizontal bird bone pieces. The power of her ancestors flooded her.

"Be with me, Kalote!" she screamed.

Stretching out her arm, pain filled her shoulder. Her fingers clasped the arrow and she whooped, brought it up and stabbed the sharp tip into the thigh of her adversary. He yelled and released her of his boot. She rolled to her feet, ignoring the scorching agony in her back and dropped into a fighting stance.

He ripped the arrow clear of his leg, blood oozing from the wound. A small chunk of flesh blossomed from the arrowhead. Roaring in fury, he ran with a heavy limp at her and brought his sword over his head. The brown blur of a horse darted behind him and his head left his shoulders. His corpse dropped to the dirt.

Henry brought his horse about, his sword painted with blood, as was half his face. He dismounted beside her and drew her to him. She buried her face into his neck and the smell of sweat, blood, leather and horse overwhelmed her.

"I thought I'd lost you," he whispered into her ear.

"You need to wash."

He held her at arm's length and laughed. He jerked a thumb over his shoulder at the ensuing battle behind. "You mind if we finish this first?"

XI
Early hours of the morning – seventh day of the siege

Piercing, persistent screams assaulted her ears.

They weren't human.

The screams were as if something inside her head sang some continuous, terrible tune. In the background, muffled shouts barely competed with the din. Miriam groaned and attempted to stand, but the weight upon her back held her prone. She blinked and wiped the liquid from her face. Her hand came away covered in fresh blood. Only then did she recall what had occurred. Male Wendurlund voices were closing upon her. The unknown, potent vocalist in residence within her skull hadn't eased, so it was difficult to understand what they were shouting.

She turned her head so her cheek was resting upon the cold, cobbled street leading to the palace. A boot appeared beside her head, then a knee. Relief filled her as she identified the uniform of a Wendurlund artilleryman. The weight holding her prisoner against the hard road jostled a few times and then suddenly vanished. A powerful, but gentle hand grasped her shoulder and rolled her over. She stared up into the powder-blackened face of a young man kneeling over her. His lips moved, however his voice was nothing more than a deep, muffled burr. "I can't hear you," she said. Even her own voice seemed muffled to her.

He spoke again and this time she watched his lips. She tried to smile and allowed him to assist her into a sitting position. "Yes, I am unhurt." Miriam took hold of her blunderbuss lying nearby and drew it to her. She checked her pockets. *Still plenty of ammunition.*

She stood with his help. He glared over her shoulder, the soldier's eyes darted left and right, watching for any new threats. Miriam almost tripped on the inanimate body at her feet. The enemy soldier had a hole in his chest she could place both fists inside. His dead eyes stared beyond her at the sky, his mouth open and half-dried blood painting his cheeks and chin in deep hues of claret. The others who'd given chase to her weren't far away either. One had lost both legs and another corpse was without a head. Nausea assaulted her.

The soldier guided her away from the slaughter. "Come with me, ma'am." His voice seemed much louder than it had before.

"Thank you," she offered. The unwanted vocalist in her head had faded a little.

Distant Huronian shouts exploded down nearby alleyways and lanes. The foreign language echoed against stone walls, bounced off cobbled streets and promised nothing but death. Miriam swallowed. *Or worse than death*. His hand pushed her towards the cloud of gun smoke hiding the cannons. A lone soldier stood out in front of the dark grey mist. He scanned the distant buildings.

"What's he doing?"

"Forward observer ma'am. Guns are blind behind the smoke. He'll give direction and target indications to the gun commander so he can give fire orders."

Some of what he'd said made sense, but she was still a little confused.

"Hurry ma'am. We don't have much time!"

She increased her pace, but his hand continued to place pressure upon her. "We need to go faster, ma'am!"

"You lot!" a deep voice roared from within the embrace of the grey mist. "'urry up!"

Gun powder assaulted the back of her throat and attacked her eyes, but she ignored the discomfort. A large, dark object loomed from within the acrid pall.

Her escort pulled her gently to one side. She realised the black behemoth was a cannon. He guided her away from the obstacle. She covered her mouth and coughed. Miriam rubbed her eyes which seemed to force more grit under her eyelids. She blinked away the discomfort and noticed movement from within the gun smoke. Shirtless soldiers were moving near the cannon.

"Gun ready!" a gruff voice roared nearby.

The cloud was dissipating, but at the pace of a snail. The distorted silhouette of another soldier came into focus from within the depths of the murk. Dull, flickering torch light illuminated him from behind. He stood ramrod straight, hands clamped behind his back.

"Bring her this way, lad," the silhouette said. He pointed behind him.

Then as suddenly as she'd advanced into the acrid mist, it was gone. She took in a deep, clean breath of fresh air. The warrior came into view. Unlike the shirtless boys attending to the guns behind her, this man must have been nearing fifty and dressed in the uniform of an officer.

"Gun Commander Humber," the young man said by way of introduction.

The officer offered her a nod and tight smile. "Hurry now, lad."

"Yes, sir."

Torches lit the open ground leading to the nearby palace. People were everywhere, hunkering for safety behind the guns. Some stood or sat in small groups whispering amongst themselves. Others lay in various positions attempting to find slumber, but as far as Miriam could see, none had been successful. This was the last bastion of hope for these people. The Wendurlund gunners their buffer between life or their death at the hands of cold, Huronian steel.

"Join the group, ma'am. Stay back from the guns for your own safety." He grinned. "I'm sorry we can't offer light refreshments, but the situation kind of precludes it."

She chuckled. "I understand. Thank you for your help, young man."

He turned away and jogged back towards the gun line. "Welcome, ma'am."

The screaming in her ears had retreated, allowing the distant foreign shouts in. Many of them. *There must be hundreds of the bastards!* She reloaded the blunderbuss and clicked back the hammer. If they managed to advance beyond the gun line, she'd at least be able to take a few down before she succumbed.

A new Wendurlund voice shouted from the far side of the thinning grey pall. "Enemies all quarters! Two hundred and charging!"

Gun Commander Humber clenched his hands behind him so tight, his fingers hurt. "Shit!" he breathed. "Fire regiment!" he roared. "Sustained fire!"

He strode behind the gun line. "I expect the intense rate, gentlemen!"

Shouts rippled up and down the gun line. And then the cannons spoke.

With every weapon engaging the enemy, the smoke cloud soon tripled in density. Humber strode along, refusing to cough, hand still clamped firmly in the small of his back. The soldiers and the cannons which they fed with powder and shot were no longer visible. All that suggested they were still in the fight were the bright muzzle flashes from within the acrid pall.

The last cannon roared its fury. Curses and shouts echoed along the line of cannons as the reloading commenced. Distant screams and groans of pain cut through the acrid, thick cloud of gun smoke. Humber counted the seconds in his head. When he reached fifty the first cannon opened fire again followed almost immediately by a second, then a third. Pride swelled within him. *Well above the intense rate. Good.*

Then the rest of the gun line followed suit. When the deafening sound of the cannon shot had ceased once more, Humber noticed the wounded and dying enemy were silent.

"Enemy neutralised, sir!" the forward observer's voice carried from the far side of the guns.

"Cease fire!"

Humber walked further into the smoke and couldn't help but cough. He approached the nearest gun team. "Good work, soldiers," he offered walking past.

"Sir," one of them replied.

When he cleared the grey smog, he spotted the forward observer and approached him.

The soldier noticed him and grinned. "We cut the bastards down like a scythe through grass, sir!"

He cast his gaze across the killing ground. Mangled and mutilated bodies lay in all manner of disarray. The sickly-sweet aroma of death mixed with the bitter, iron scent of spilled blood pervaded the area.

Musket shots crackled out from the direction of the palace followed by shouting and the clash of steel. The noise persisted for a short time before silence regained the initiative. Humber turned, a frown creasing his brow. The voice sounded frightened. The screams of women and children drowned out all else.

The artilleryman beside him tapped his shoulder. "Sir! Look!"

Humber, brow still furrowed in concern, followed the young man's finger. On the far side of the killing ground silhouettes appeared. Looming out of the flickering shadows created by the torches, moved a veritable army. They walked slow, the dull glint of flames catching the edges of swords or spear tips. The Huronian soldiers seemed to ooze out of every street, alley and lane which led towards the palace. *Must be more than five hundred of them this time, and there're still more appearing. I'll need every gun firing again.*

The screaming behind them intensified. "Enemy must have clambered from the opposite direction to assault our rear. This might be it for us young man, I fear. Let's give them sheer bloody hell!"

It had only been a matter of time before it happened. The cannons could only face outward of the palace and over the open green. He knew it'd eventually come down to hand-to-hand combat. But at least they'd held out as long as possible.

The young man's face was stern, the cheerful grin having long ago departed. "Yes, sir."

"With me, lad!" Humber turned and ran towards the gun line. He entered the shroud of gun smoke. A cough behind suggested the lad was on his heels. Cannons appeared from within the mist. He veered to one side so that he was in between two of them and that they could open fire without cutting him apart.

"Fire regiment!" Humber roared. "Sustained fire!"

The closest cannon exploded to life and a wave of intense heat washed over Humber. The weapon's explosion left him reeling. He almost lost his balance but continued onward. Shot rippled out from the maws of the artillery pieces. Intermingled with the shouts of gun commanders controlling their gunners who were busy reloading their weapons, were the screams of wounded Huronians forward of the gun smoke and those of women and children behind Humber.

He withdrew his sword and clasped the hilt tight. The first gun to be reloaded belched another blast of death. "Good work!" he yelled in the direction of the gun crew responsible. "Keep up that rate!"

The rest of the gun line followed suit in short order. He turned on his heel and walked towards the palace to see for himself exactly what was happening. The mist left by the continuous artillery barrage was thinner towards the rear of the gun line. He cleared the smoke and stopped in his tracks, his heart rate quickening.

Huronians had clambered over the palace to assault the citizens from behind. The palace itself had been barred from the inside, so whilst the king was safe, his subjects certainly weren't. The fifty palace guards had put up a fight but had been overwhelmed. Anger burned in him. *Long gone are the warrior kings of old!* His lips parted to reveal bared teeth. Many civilians lay dead, their corpses being looted by a group of enemy soldiers. One screaming woman was being dragged away by her hair. She kicked and scratched, but it was useless. Her adversary was pulling her towards a large patch of darkness, where no doubt, she would be raped and killed. *Not necessarily in that order, either.*

Humber cursed under his breath and swept his gaze across the killing ground. There were at least three, perhaps four hundred soldiers between he and the doomed woman. Movement caught the side of his vision. He snapped his head in that direction. The older frumpy woman with the blunderbuss who he'd steered to safety so recently was running in the direction of the female being yanked along the ground. The woman clasped both her hands on the weapon. She leapt over a body, launched a savage butt strike which landed on a soldier's cheek and ducked under a sweeping sword.

Her bravery lent him strength. He launched forward, legs pumping beneath him, the sword's cold steel felt good in his grip. Mistress Blunderbuss slowed to a walk, levelled the weapon at hip level and fired an un-aimed shot. Even over the noise of screams, shouts and the constant rhythmic battering of artillery in the near distance, the blunderbuss's fury drifted to him. She disappeared in a cloud of gun smoke. A moment later she reappeared clasping the hand of the woman who'd so recently been doomed to a truly terrible death.

"To me!" Humber roared, waving the sword over his head. He cupped one hand around the corner of his mouth. "Come to me!"

Miss Blunderbuss saw him, pointed the weapon in his direction and shouted something over her shoulder. The pair changed direction toward him. An enemy yelled a foreign sentence and charged straight at him. He carried a spear two-handed, his intention to bury the bloodied end deep into his flesh. Humber backed away and brought his sword to bear. Without a shield, sword against spear was no fair fight. A small pothole in the ground almost lost him his balance, but he regained it fast and continued retreating from the threat with slow methodical paces.

He watched the soldier, trying to learn something of the man in the fleeting seconds he had left with a view to find a weakness. Any weakness. He was right-handed, had a slight limp on his left side. A patch of dried blood over his left hip suggested that had something to do with his affliction. Humber was no swordsman, but he'd had formal training many years before. Studying an opponent to find a chink in their armour had been one of the teachings. Although the trainer was a master. Humber, in comparison, felt clumsy and outclassed.

The Huronian soldier screamed something incomprehensible, his face creased with an animal snarl, a cruel glint in his eyes. He was almost upon him. Humber ceased his withdrawal, ran to the right and brought his sword down in a horizontal cut. His adversary was forced to deviate to follow, forcing him to cause increased stress on his injured leg. The savagery adorning his face morphed into one of pain and the enemy slowed.

He seized his chance. Humber darted forward, narrowly avoided a deft stab that brushed his arm, shoved the spear aside and slammed his sword into the Huronian's belly. The high-pitched scream that came from him startled Humber causing him to release the hilt of his sword. His adversary fell backwards onto his arse, continuing to groan and cry out. A dull, sickening thud brought silence. The woman had swung the blunderbuss by the barrel, smashing the heavy wooden butt stock against the Huronian's skull. She was short of breath, her eyes wide with fear, but there was a glint of determination there as well. As for the other one, she was utterly broken. Fear had consumed her and there was no fight left in her face. Her vacant eyes stared past Humber, her body flinching with each cannon blast.

Humber stooped, ripped clear his blade and wiped it clean on the cloak of the downed man. He sheathed the blade and turned to Miss Blunderbuss. "And whom might you be?"

"Miriam."

He greeted the second lady but she ignored him, her wide, puppy-like eyes staring over his shoulder. She was trembling with terror. Humber looked past the women at the slaughter in the distance. Most of the civilians were dead and those that weren't were either wounded, or about to be put to the sword.

"Let's get moving!" Humber shouted. "There's nothing we can do for those people now, we are too few."

Miriam nodded and gestured for him to lead the way. The trio ran back to the gun line, Miriam dragged the other woman behind her. When the odd comfort of gun smoke teased his nose and throat, Humber slowed to a walk. He waited for a lull in the cannon fire and then shouted, "cease fire!"

The order was taken up by the gunners.

"Odd numbers, face guns about!"

Further yelling rippled along the line. Grunts and groans ensued as half the cannons were swung about to face the palace. The gun smoke was thick and it was difficult to see exactly where the weapons were.

Humber gained Miriam's attention. "Follow me." He walked further into the murk until he spotted the dark behemoth of an artillery piece through the acrid mist. Now that the gun formation was facing in both directions, the only safe place to stand was directly in line with the weapons. To be located in front or behind them when they opened fire was to court death.

"Stand here, Miriam. Don't move from this spot. Do you understand?"

She nodded and through a series of coughs, reloaded her blunderbuss.

"Fire when ready!" he shouted.

The deafening artillery song recommenced spewing more spent powder in all directions. What little visibility there had been disappeared from view. The black grit soaked into everything. Humber tasted it in his mouth, it irritated his throat, his eyes stung and the skin of his back itched where it had worked its way through the fabric of his clothing. A scream rent the air by his feet and he jumped back, his sword flashing into his hand. The terrified woman had collapsed in a heap her head buried into her hands. With the weapon re-primed, Miriam knelt beside her, placed a hand upon her shoulder and offered a few words that never reached Humber's ears.

He sheathed his sword and rubbed his eyes, but that seemed to make the discomfort worse. A voice yelled his name. *Or is it my imagination?* He shoved a finger into an ear cavity and twisted it around, but that didn't seem to alleviate the high-pitched tone which bounced around his skull. The gun fire had slowed he noticed.

"Keep up the fire!" he roared. "I expect the intense rate!"

The voice came again. "Commander Humber?" The man sounded distant.

He cupped hands around his mouth "Over here!"

He repeated himself to give the soldier a bearing to follow. In addition, the shouting helped alleviate the itch in his throat. The gunner loomed from the grey cloud. His face and arms blackened.

"Sir!" he took a deep breath and spluttered into a series of coughs.

"What is it, lad?"

The cannon shot had slowed even further, only a few maintaining their fire. "What the bloody hell's going on?" He swung away from the man. "Get your arses in gear!" he roared. "Keep up the fire!"

"Sir?"

He turned back to the young soldier and glared at him. "What is it?"

"The cannons, sir."

One more cannon blasted its fury into the night and then fell silent.

"We're out of powder."

Prickles of ice needled the skin of his back. Dread

laced its long, black fingers around his guts and squeezed. His legs were weak and he felt short of breath. Humber inhaled several deep gulps of smoke-filled air, but it didn't help. He swallowed, even though his mouth was dry. Then he heard them. Huronian voices in the near distance coming from all quarters. They were advancing upon the last bastion of hope in Lisfort: Humber's gun line.

"Sir? Your orders?"

The fear, morphing into terror, threatened to overwhelm him. An irritating, muffled voice continued to nag him, although he ignored it. His legs were moments from collapsing.

"Sir!"

He blinked and looked at the soldier. "Right," he said. He stamped his feet upon the ground and snarled. *Get a hold of yourself, man!* "Tell the lads to arm themselves! Tell them to stick together and fight as a team."

"Yes, sir. And sir?"

Humber glared at the young man.

"Good luck, sir."

He slapped the gunner's shoulder. "You too, lad."

Miriam continued to kneel beside the woman, attempting to console her. But it was clear terror had her in its grip. She was as good as useless.

He tapped Miriam on the shoulder. "Best we be going, Miriam."

"I'll not leave her."

He squatted beside her. "I understand how you feel." He gestured at the crying woman. "But she is beyond helping now. Best leave her so that—"

"What? So that we can tuck tail and run?"

Where once the freezing touch of fear had worked into his skin, the heat of anger resided. His eyelids narrowed and he clenched his jaw. "I didn't say that."

Miriam placed the butt of the blunderbuss upon the ground and stared at him. "You may as well have."

Shouts broke out from the left flank of the gun line

closely followed by the clash of steel. The Huronians had advanced onto their position.

"Listen, Miriam," he kept his voice low and gentle. "We don't have much time. Soon the enemy will be upon us." He held his hands up, palms open. "I'm not suggesting we run. I'm suggesting we bloody fight."

Miriam's eyes widened a little, realisation ebbing in.

He waved a finger at the distressed woman sat upon the powder-stained grass. "And kneeling down consoling her puts you in no place to use that thing." He tapped the weapon's maw.

She whispered some soothing words to the helpless woman and stood. Humber rose with her. He gripped the sword's hilt and dragged it clear of the scabbard at his hip. The song of steel was resounding from the entire length of the gun line.

"They'll fight hard, those lads." He attempted to keep the sadness from his voice and failed.

"I sense there is a but," Miriam murmured.

He sighed. "But they're exhausted. Nor are they infantrymen."

Screams of anger mixed seamlessly with those of pain and the clash showed no evidence of dissipating. If anything, more Huronian warriors had joined the fray.

"You stay here, Miriam, and look after your friend," he said, offering the distraught woman a fleeting glance. "But run to safety if you have to. Try and get into the palace if you run out of ammunition or think you might be overrun."

"Where are you going?"

He shrugged and smiled. "I can't leave my soldiers to fight them off alone."

"You'll die, Humber, you know that don't you?"

He nodded. "We all die someday."

He turned from Miriam and strode into the thinning cloud of gun smoke. *Tonight's as good as any.* The weakness in his legs had long departed and dread had released its tight grip of his guts. The silent behemoth of an artillery piece loomed amongst the mist. He headed for the weapon, the din of war growing louder with each pace. He felt somehow disconnected from it all. As if he were viewing the scene from outside his body. He cared little for the fact he was advancing into certain death.

Bodies lay strewn about the gun. Most were still, but a scarce few soldiers – Huronian and Wendurlund both – writhed and cried out as the last vestiges of life fled from them. Humber gritted his teeth and increased his pace. The cold metal of the sword's hilt felt good against his palm. He brought the blade up to rest upon his shoulder and headed towards the battle occurring around the gun. One of his soldiers, his skin blackened from gunpowder fought with a pike, another with the heavy ramrod used to ram the shot down the cannon's barrel. The rod battered a man's head, blood exploding from his forehead. He dropped to the ground without a sound.

One gunner, fighting with a sword hadn't noticed a Huronian who'd approached from behind and was about to stab him in the back. Humber roared and broke into a run. He took the hilt two handed and brought the sharp steel down in a lightning cut that took the enemy's head from his shoulders.

"Friendly behind you!" he shouted, slapping the man on the shoulder.

The gunner batted a stab aside and plunged his own blade into his adversary's guts, stepped back and kicked the dying man away. Sweating and breathless, he turned to Humber, pearl white teeth flashing from within a powder-darkened face.

"Sir! Nice to see you here. It's turned into a real occasion!" he yelled, mirth glinting in his eyes.

Humber couldn't help but chuckle. "It looks that way, lad! Watch your front!"

The soldier whirled in time to block an overhand cut that would have sliced into his chest. Humber advanced until he was standing shoulder to shoulder with the man. Orange torch light glimmered against the stained steel of an axe wielded by another Huronian pushing in from the right flank. Humber ducked, a soft hiss passing over his head. He straightened and drove the sword into the Huronian's throat. He dropped the axe, the fury on his face replaced with wide-eyed terror and pain. He clenched both hands to his neck, but it didn't help to stop the bright red blood leaking from between his fingers in rhythmic spurts.

Miriam knelt by the woman she had come to know as Gab. She clenched her shoulder. "Gab! You must listen to me!"

She peered at Miriam through a thick lock of hair, eyes red-rimmed and tears staining her cheeks. She took a shaking breath.

"If we're to survive, you must be ready to fight. Do you understand?"

No reply.

Miriam sighed. "Sitting on your backside sobbing won't stop the Huronians from killing you." She held out a hand to Gab. "Or worse," she added in a softer tone.

The locks half hiding her eyes bobbed up and down. Gab sniffed and wiped her nose with the back of a hand. She reached up and allowed Miriam to help her to stand. They moved together, withdrawing from the battle ensuing around Humber's gun line.

Miriam's hope at being saved and brought into the protection of the cannons had been short lived. Fear, that bitch's presence was all too familiar, teased the edges of her mind, but she refused to allow it to gain purchase.

"Let's find you a weapon."

"I've never been in a fight in my life, Miriam."

"Neither had I before all of this. But rest assured, very soon, I fear you will be."

"Then so be it," Gab said. She attempted to put on a brave voice, but the words were spoken with shaking tones.

Miriam patted her shoulder. "Best we hurry."

The fight behind them had grown in volume. More Huronian soldiers must have joined the battle and it wouldn't be long before Humber and his troops would be overwhelmed, allowing the enemy force to gain free roam of the entire palace area. They walked clear of the cloud of gun smoke, which had dispersed somewhat from what it had been when the guns were firing.

Gab stopped beside her but Miriam grasped an arm and dragged her along. "Don't stop now," she muttered. Miriam too had been shocked by the destruction with which she was presented. Where so recently there had been Huronian soldiers attacking the men and women with whom she had taken refuge before Humber appeared to help, now only corpses littered the ground. The cannon shot had been effective, cutting enemy warriors down in scores. Some had been cut clean in half. Others sported huge holes in their chests or guts. Nor was the palace itself free of damage. It was peppered with holes the size of a man's fists. Two cannonballs were lodged in the once pristine brickwork, a thick chain attaching the two balls together.

Miriam tightened her grip on Gab's arm. "Come on, keep up with me!"

She stopped by the first enemy. He was lying face first upon the blood-stained grass. Part of his head was missing and a ragged hole had shattered one leg. Miriam released Gab and stooped to pull clear a sword and held it up to her new-found friend. "I take it you've never used one of these?"

She shook her head and sniffed.

Miriam thrust the hilt towards her. "Neither have I. But from what I hear, you stick 'em with that pointy bit."

Gab chuckled. Miriam laughed despite the terrible scene which surrounded them. She took hold of her friend's arm and picked her way across the carpet of dead. Miriam stopped by another corpse and ripped clear a sword for herself. "Come on."

The pair moved fast. Miriam squelched over sodden

ground, the stink of blood and death strong in her nose. *I prefer the smell of gun smoke.* She swallowed bile, kept her grip of Gab and continued. She misplaced her foot on the blood-slicked thigh of a dead soldier and fell to the ground. Miriam released her grip of Gab and landed on her knees, halting her face from hitting the bloody dirt with an open palm. Miriam managed to keep the blunderbuss from being covered with cold, congealed blood.

Gab doubled over and vomited. Miriam concentrated on breathing through her mouth and climbed back to her feet. She wiped her palm upon her skirt, but the skin of her hand remained the colour of claret.

The younger woman approached her and touched her shoulder. "Are you hurt?"

"No, let's keep going."

Humber kicked the knee out from under an enemy soldier and the man fell screaming, clenching the injured joint with a hand. He dispatched him with a deft sword stroke. The gunner beside him fell, a blade lodged deep in his midriff. He didn't even make a sound. Humber took a backward step. Three adversaries advanced on him. The one in the middle, a savage grin lighting his face, lunged. He slapped the weapon aside with the flat of his sword and moved another pace to the rear, his focus flicking from one man to the next. In the side of his eye, Humber was aware that all but two of his soldiers had fallen to the enemy.

As one, the trio charged him. He dodged to the right, parried a strike and slammed his weapon into a soft throat. Ripping the sharp steel clear, he blocked another attack and ended the second warrior with a slice to the groin. He fell to the ground with an inhuman shriek. A searing pain exploded in his side and Humber drew a breath in through clenched teeth. He'd not been fast enough to face the third Huronian. Warm liquid slid down the skin of his flank beneath his arm. It saturated his leggings. He felt light-headed and weak.

Humber grunted and stabbed at his opponent, but he could barely lift his sword. The Huronian laughed, batted the clumsy strike aside and buried a knife up to the hilt into Humber's chest.

His legs collapsed beneath him and his cheek slammed onto the ground, throbbing agony his only companion. He drew one last shuddering breath. Then darkness took him.

Behind them, the roar of battle was subsiding. That indicated one of two things. The enemy had been vanquished. Or Humber's soldiers were dead.

"Do you think they defeated the Huronians?" Gab whispered, attempting to keep up.

Sinking despair descended the back of her throat and settled in the pit of her guts. "No, I don't. We must hurry."

They made the palace and ascended the steps on the exterior leading up to one of the barred entrances high above. Miriam cast a glance towards the silent cannons and she almost lost her footing. Had it not been for Gab grabbing her, she might well have fallen over the side to the ground below. From out of the thinning cloud of gun smoke, silhouettes were stalking towards the pair in extended line.

Hundreds upon hundreds of them.

Huronians all.

XII

Darkness swept the trampled plains leading to the great walls of Lisfort. A half-moon peered from its position just above the battlements, lending sparing light upon the Great Highland Army. An orange, flickering glow emanating from all quarters within the city lit what the moon could not. Many of the Highlanders had been remiss in mounting their spiders – fear, in some cases; abject terror and long-bred superstitions causing their pause. But with coaxing that was sometimes gentle, and where Rafe attempted to help motivate people often far from so, the Shadolian warriors sat upon their spiders.

Vyder urged his new mount forward, finding his seat surprisingly comfortable. Eight legs seemed to maintain a more stable platform upon which to sit, than did four. Perhaps two hundred metres in front of them, the tiny formation of what had been the small force who had linked up with the King's Own approached the wall. The remainder of The King's Own, still mounted upon their horses, trotted towards the huge gate. They'd wait outside for their comrades to make entry and open the entrance from the inside. The Highland Army followed them. Only a small force was required to open the gates. The cannon fire had ceased but minutes ago, causing whispers amongst his people. Has the enemy been vanquished? Is it over? Are we still needed?

"Lord?"

He glanced across at Rafe beside him. The berserker looked worse for wear, his eyes sunken, skin whiter than snow, beads of sweat gathering upon his forehead. His breathing was shallow, but he still grinned like a berserker.

Rafe held his sword out before him aiming the tip at the walls. "It's very quiet in there. Are we too late?"

"I don't know, my friend. We shall find out for ourselves soon enough."

The berserker rested his blade upon the long, spindly

hair of his mount. He cleared his throat. "Because it appears to me, lord." He swivelled where he sat and looked back at the Highland Army, which followed. His voice dropped to a whisper. "If the bastards are still alive in there, we could actually surround them this time."

Vyder smiled. "Think so?"

Rafe's whisper had died to be replaced with a roar. "Of course! If you and me almost had the Huronian Cavalry on the back foot, imagine what all of us could do against mere foot soldiers?"

"I like your positive thinking, Rafe."

The dark-haired berserk patted the giant spider beneath him. "And we have these... things, to aid us."

A loud hiss issued from the arachnid. "I meant no offence, my great, ugly friend," Rafe crooned.

They closed the distance with Lisfort, the walls growing in height with each step the spider army placed. The moon winked from view behind the closest battlements and so too did the orange glow of the endless fires raging across the city. They were now in the black shadow cast by the vertical, man-made cliffs of beautifully crafted bricks and mortar. Vyder leaned back and looked up, spotting the silhouettes of the spiders carrying their human riders towards the top of the wall.

Vyder tightened his grip on the sword. "Luck, lads."

Rone remained in his seat but leaned far enough forward his face was buried amongst the thick, soft hair of the spider on which he rode. Each hand firmly clenched a tuft of hair. With every vertical pace the creature took, Rone was aware they were higher from the ground. The farther up the wall the arachnid negotiated, the less likely it would be of survival if he were to slip from his precarious purchase upon its back.

As if that thought brought the worry to life, Rone slipped, but clenched his thighs and tightening his fists upon the fur to keep his seat. "Are we there, yet?" he growled into the spider's back.

A soft hiss was his only reply. Relenting, he pulled his head out from the soft forest of hair and looked straight up at their direction of travel. A sudden rush of dizziness swamped him and he brought a hand to his face, wiping away beads of sweat. Then he slipped again. This time his fall accelerated and he cried out. He reached down and clenched another clump of hair and renewed the vigour with which his legs clamped upon the arachnid. Releasing his grip to clean his face had been an instinctive movement. *You fool, Rone. Concentrate!*

From the little he saw prior to the vertigo assaulting him, they were within spitting distance of the top of the wall. "Almost there," he whispered. "Almost bloody there, just hold on a little longer."

Then they were over the battlements. Sitting horizontal once again, relief was his companion. The spider stopped and Rone clambered down. He leapt clear, his boots slamming onto stone. His legs, weak with fear, nearly collapsed beneath him. He smacked a hand upon a nearby battlement to retain his balance and stamped his feet. "Work, damn you!"

When his thighs ceased quivering, he released his grip of the stone and glanced around. The others had either dismounted or were in the process of doing so. When the boots of all soldiers were firmly upon stone, the spiders scuttled down the inside of the walls towards the streets of Lisfort far below. Rone was grateful not to be taking the journey with them. He strode along the rampart and gestured for the Huronians to follow him. The fires blazing across the city lit the stone well, which was some comfort considering the terrible damage the cannons had done. He didn't fancy walking along the damaged rampart in pitch darkness. One wayward step or loss of balance and it was a sheer fall into thin air, which would result in a sudden stop on the cobbled streets far below.

He slowed his journey and picked his way across the dozens of corpses littered before them. In some areas the bodies were two or three high. Amongst the uniforms, he spotted a few King's Own cloaks and tore his gaze away before he could focus upon the dead faces. *I don't need to know who they are. Yet.* When he'd climbed across the stinking human obstacle, Rone pushed onward to the only remaining stone steps still intact. He reached them, threw a glance over his shoulder to ensure the others were following. They were, but spread out, some of them taking their time negotiating areas of the rampart where the dead were scattered in thick piles. He waited until the warriors had pushed up in a tight single file behind him.

"Ready?"

Harton nodded and grunted.

He thumped down the steps. A growing staccato followed. The first half of the stone stairs languished in an orange, flickering glow that made for a sure-footed decent. Then they advanced into a black murk and their speed slowed. Rone placed a boot down and felt something soft under it. He stopped and hissed, "halt!"

Harton careened into him and grumbled something under his breath. He whispered a string of Huronian words that seemed to be passed back along the line of men making their way down. They ceased all movement and waited for further instruction. Rone had clenched a hold of a large crack in the wall where he'd been able to wedge his fingers to maintain his balance.

He knelt. With his other hand he felt around just forward of his boots and found what it was that had almost sent him into the vacant darkness awaiting him on the left side. *Dead body.*

Rone pulled his fingers clear of the wall so as he could use both hands. "Sorry, lad." He grabbed the sword belt of the deceased, clenched his teeth and pushed the dead weight over the edge. A few seconds passed before a dull *thud* indicated the body had reached its destination. He winced and stood.

"Okay, time to move," he whispered.

Nine times Rone was forced to halt the warriors so as corpses could be removed from their axis of advance. Had daylight been present their decent might have taken but half the time. But shadowed in the towering buildings near the wall, light was not an ally upon which they could rely.

They reached the road and squelched across patches of coagulated, stinking blood. The incessant *click* of the host of spiders followed them. Much as he was aware the arachnids were allied with his soldiers and he, Rone couldn't stop the hairs of his nape standing on end. He cast a brief look over his shoulder. The giant spiders scuttled behind them. Some climbed on the walls of buildings, others leapt from roof to roof. The breath caught in his throat and he turned away, the lump in his throat rising and falling.

Not so long ago and his comrades had been battling to protect Lisfort against such creatures while his sub-unit had been ranging deep in Huron. He threw another glance behind him, the nearest spider seeming to watch him, a sliver of orange light escaping down an alley illuminating its numerous eyes. The black orbs arrayed around its head glittered in the light. *Maybe these exact monsters.* He imbibed a deep breath and reminded himself they were allies.

The group of men avoided bodies as best as possible, but a few times men were sent sprawling to the fetid cobbles. A hard lesson to learn for a moment's lapse of concentration. A pale orange glow illuminated the massive gates outside which the rest of their army stood. The light was funnelled down the wide road that led from the barred entrance, deep into Lisfort's heart.

A crane built into the wall was used by The Watch to lift the thick, heavy timber bar off the brackets. The timber must have weighed at least ten tonnes, he surmised. *Maybe more.* With some distance still to travel, he was unable to spot the crane. *If it's been damaged, we're done for.*

Harton nudged his shoulder and pointed at the beam.

"Lift?"

He nodded. "That's the idea, my friend."

Harton burst out laughing and gestured at the men around him. "We strong, yes, but not strong enough."

"There's a crane here somewhere."

The crease of Harton's brow suggested he didn't understand what a crane was. *There it is! Bloody bastard of a thing and it's intact!* He grinned and pointed at the huge implement. "We use that to lift!"

The Huronian's brows disentangled themselves and his mouth widened to display pearl white teeth. "Crane." The warrior laughed.

He approached the circular wheel, which was connected to a series of thick ropes interlinking an intricate pulley system. The wheel would be turned by two men, which provided the capacity for the machine to lift and lower its load. A rope, nigh on as thick as a man's leg draped to the ground. The remaining soldiers would be heaving on it to steer the direction of the crane arm.

Rone explained the workings of it and where they would need to stand to do their jobs, to no avail. The Huronians stood in a semi-circle around him and stared at him with blank faces. Apart from one man who tried to hide a snigger.

Harton spoke through a smile. "I sorry, your word crane, similar to Huron word. Dirty word. Very dirty."

Rone laughed. "Right." His good humour vanished almost as fast as it'd approached. "But do your soldiers understand what it is required of them?"

Harton turned on the balls of his feet and presented Rone with his back. The Huronian roared a few sentences and gestured at the crane. Men ran to their places, two standing by the wheel and the others clenching the thick rope, staring up at the massive wooden machine built into the wall high above them.

He strode to the pair near the wheel. "Are you ready?"

One of them, a fierce looking warrior, nodded but remained silent.

"Turn!"

They bunched their arms, grumbled, groaned and strained.

"No, no, the *other* way!"

They complied and the huge chain at the end of the arm descended with slow rattles. He turned to the crew standing at the rope. "Okay, you lot!" he shouted. "Pull on that bastard and swing the arm out!"

They did.

A loud, long wooden *groan* echoed around the immediate area, bouncing from walls and ricocheting down alleyways. Rone ran to a ladder beside the crane and jogged up it to the small ledge leading out towards the crossbeam. He stepped onto the colossal piece of timber locking closed the gate and darted along until he was in the centre. The chain descended toward him with a frustrating lack of speed. Darting a glance at the pair far below, they continued to work the wheel.

"Faster!" he roared. If they were caught out in the open here by the enemy, they'd be slaughtered inside seconds.

Rone glared down at the team heaving on the rope. He waved his hand towards the city. "Pull the arm out a bit further that way." They grumbled and strained but complied with his command. Finally, the cold chain touched the hand of his up stretched arm. He guided the thick metal.

"Keep turning that wheel!" he shouted.

When the chain had descended to what he thought necessary, Rone called a halt. Dropping to his guts on the thick beam, he passed the chain under the timber, pulled the steel link up the opposite side of the wood. Or tried to at least, the metal was much heavier than it looked. Bunching his muscles, he strained. His brain felt as if it were but seconds from exploding clear of his skull. Finally, he latched the chain onto itself. Out of breath, he stood and appraised the pair at the wheel who'd stopped all movement, staring up at him.

"Turn the wheel!" They did. "No, the other way. The *other* bloody way!"

Rone felt the beam creak beneath him and thought it prudent to retreat to the wall before the timber swung clear of its brackets. From the safety of the city's wall, he crouched and watched proceedings. A deep, wooden scream washed the area with piercing noise and the huge piece of timber broke from its brackets, swinging freely in the air.

"Keep that thing tight!" he snapped at the crew working the rope. The crane arm remained straight, maintaining the cross beam from smashing into the wall and damaging it beyond repair. The Watch could carry out this operation in under a minute, but then they were practised and would have more hands to help than Rone could currently supply.

He rose and darted back down the ladder. "Okay, that'll do you." Rone held up a hand to the men at the wheel. Both were running short of breath and sweat streamed down their faces. They stopped, arms quivering.

Rone licked his lips and grabbed hold of a large handle beside the wheel with both hands. From what he'd seen, he was sure this would disengage the gears and send the beam plummeting to the ground. Cracked, smashed and missing cobbles all along the road under which the timber hovered suggested as much.

Checking the team on the rope were far enough back that they wouldn't be crushed, he was satisfied. He exhaled and paused. Then he slammed the lever forward. The beam dropped like a stone. Men shouted, roared and cursed, darting out of the way of the heavy behemoth dropping toward them. The beam smashed onto the road sending a shudder through the ground. It bounced a few feet and came to rest upon the ground.

Rone ignored the angry Huronian words directed at him. "Get that gate open!" he pointed.

A piercing metallic screech washed the area accompanied by a deep, creaking groan of wood on wood. A split appeared between the city's gate in front of which waited Vyder and his army. The gap widened and the doors seemed to shrink in width. They were swinging inwards with desperate lack of speed. When they were only partially open, the King's Own accelerated into a canter and moved into single file as they advanced, each mounted warrior disappearing into the widening darkness beyond which lay uncertainty.

He nudged the spider and clicked his tongue out of habit. "Come on, great one," he muttered. A gentle hiss from beneath him and they were underway, skittering towards the half open gates. The increasing clicking behind him suggested the army was following.

They passed beneath the widening entrance and pitch blackness consumed him. Groans of wood and gentle whistles of protesting steel surrounded him. A pleasant smell of ancient hardwood and oil settled in his nostrils. Soon the scents were joined by the aroma of rope and rust. Then he was on the city side of the gate. *We're in. Miriam, I hope you are safe, lass.*

The King's Own had disappeared, likely having advanced further into the depths of Lisfort to start trouble with the Huronian occupiers. Vyder steered his massive mount along the main road skirting the wall. The pleasant smells were long gone, desecrated by the stink of blood and rot and death. Movement caught the corner of his eye and Rafe came alongside. "The plan, my lord?"

He chuckled. "Kill all the Huronians."

Rafe nodded with solemn sincerity, the good humour Vyder having offered not being shared. "A good plan." He smacked a fist against his chest and snarled, a dark savagery glinting in his berserk eyes. "A damn good plan!" he shouted, globs of phlegm exploding from his mouth.

The berserker stood on his spider and looked back at the Great Highland Army, many of whom were still appearing through the city's entrance, snaking behind the pair. "We shall kill them all!" he roared, holding his sword above his head.

Vyder grinned and turned the spider onto the main road leading into the heart of the city. Rafe's arachnid mount followed suit and the furious, terribly wounded warrior lost his balance and squatted to avoid falling to his death. He roared with laughter and howled at the sky.

The road, being much wider allowed more Highlanders to come alongside Vyder. Seven spiders clattered abreast of one another along the cobbled road allowing the remainder of the Highland Army to bunch up. Instead of a narrow snake, they were a thick wedge, pushing into the depths of Lisfort.

Copying Rafe, Vyder gathered his legs beneath him and stood, both arms hanging by his side, a blood kissed sword in each hand. He appraised the Shadolian people who'd entrusted themselves to him. When he was sure all spiders had turned onto the road, he sat, shifted until he was comfortable and then urged the arachnid into a faster pace.

A group of Huronian warriors strode out between two buildings in the near distance. They turned away from them and continued along the road, speaking between one another. The man on the left flank raised his head to the sky, his shoulders shuddering. But his laughter did not reach Vyder. The giant in the centre rested a battle-axe on one shoulder and the soldier on the right carried a decapitated head by the hair. He coaxed the spider into a more rapid advance. The faster they travelled, the more stable his seat upon the creature.

Only as they were almost on the trio, did the tall, well-built soldier in the centre turn and appraise them. His mouth dropped open and the arrogant glimmer in his eyes faded as fear took control. The spider reared and Vyder clamped a fistful of hair, leaning forward to maintain his balance. The arachnid lunged forward and the Huronian disappeared from view, consumed somewhere beneath the giant animal. Only one high-pitched scream rent the air, but even that was cut short. The host of giant spiders didn't slow. They left the dead bodies strewn upon the cobbles to be stamped and battered by those following.

There! Weak, flickering orange light glinted against the skin of the tiny palace nestled in the centre of the city. They were still some kilometres from their target, but at least it was visible. *For now, anyway.* Then it disappeared behind the walls of a much closer building.

A howl gave him pause and he looked across at Rafe. The berserk was still crouched upon his eight-legged steed staring at Vyder, a flicker of madness sweeping his eyes and a wide grin adorning his face.

"I'm getting used to this, lord!" he roared.

The madman looked even worse for wear, although his demeanour suggested otherwise. The madness flickering on his face seemed foreign against his pasty white skin and dark rings beneath his eyes. His shirt was still damp with blood, and the terrible wounds were still visible between the cuts, stabs and tears in his clothing. But he seemed not to notice, or care. Rafe's berserk rage was carrying him through. *Anyone else'd be dead by now. Long before. Stay strong, Rafe, we have need of your sword yet.*

Another enemy jogged into view, stopped to stare at the spiders clattering towards him, turned the way he'd approached and sprinted from view, shouting.

Rafe's laughter bellowed out. "We scared the shit out of him!"

The palace hove into view, its flanks still bathed in the orange light of nearby fires. The building was much larger. When they arrived, the behemoth would dwarf even the spiders. He hoped Miriam had the forethought to flee to the palace. At least the artillery had been mounting a defence against the invaders. *Not anymore, though.* The thought darted into his mind. Dread drove a cold spear deep into his guts.

Vyder encouraged the beast to increase its pace again, but it hissed and continued at the same speed.

Huronian voices, gathering in number, burbled throughout the streets, growing in intensity. One voice, louder than the others roared what he could only assume were commands. A Huronian soldier sprinted into view further down the road, stopped in the middle of the road, watched the host of spiders for a moment, then ran from view.

"They're going to try and ambush us," Vyder muttered.

Rafe chuckled. "*Try to.*"

"Lord," someone hissed from behind.

Vyder turned and saw one of his Highlanders pointing towards the King's Own officer who had been trying to gain Vyder's attention.

"He wants to speak with you."

Vyder managed to drop back in the formation, allowing other spiders to push past his own until he was riding beside the one called Rone.

He switched to the Wendurlund language. "What is it?"

"My comrades here," he swept his arm to indicate the former Huronian cavalrymen nearby, "are saying that they can hear a high-ranking officer." The Huronian voice in the distance burst back into life, echoing down side streets. Rone pointed towards the noise. "*That* high ranking officer in particular, is attempting to organise three groups of enemies to come at us."

Vyder grunted. "I thought as much."

"But they are waiting for us to pass a certain point and then will try to assault us from behind."

"Which point?"

"That's the difficult part. The enemy are referring to a street they are calling Street Fillip but I don't know where that is."

"Neither do I. Which is the closest main street to our

current position?"

Rone's chest expanded and he exhaled a long breath, his eyes raking the dark sky. "We're in the second east quarter on the road closest the wall, so... well, the secondary east-west arterial is coming up in about another mile or so."

That made sense, as they had entered the city via the main east-west arterial at the city gate.

"So, we can only assume that the secondary east-west is Street Fillip."

Rone shrugged, then nodded.

Vyder thanked the man and accelerated his spider towards the front.

What is your plan, little brother?

He inwardly flinched at Gorgoroth's voice booming in his mind.

"Where the hell have you been?" he breathed through clenched teeth.

Endessa and I have been at the rear of the column, just relaxing.

"Not for long."

So, I hear. My question still stands.

He arrived back beside Rafe.

The berserker shot him a glance and a wide, blood speckled grin. "What news?"

"The Huronians intend to attack our rear," he responded, answering Gorgoroth at the same time.

"Typical bastards, always only interested in hitting the arse end."

"I believe we should divert our advance to the west and come around to hit them either from the flank or rear, giving us the element of surprise."

Rafe stared at him. "With respect lord, it's better then, to stop talking and start doing."

I agree with him, little brother. Would you like me to help with directing the spiders?

"Aye."

Tell your people to grab a hold of their mounts

with all their strength, some of the spiders will be climbing up and over buildings. We will attack them from all sides.

Vyder twisted and bellowed the order over his shoulder in the Highland language. He caught Rone's eye and shouted the same in the Wendurlund language. The officer turned slightly pale, nodded slowly and started his attempt at translating to his Huronian comrades.

Let me know when you are ready.

"Do you know where they are exactly?" he muttered. His soft words were drowned out by those around him, excitement or war spirit garnishing their voices.

Endessa and I went and had a quick look when we entered the city. I have a good idea.

He noticed Rafe staring at him and turned to meet the berserker's eye.

"I talk to myself, too," he spoke, wide unblinking eyes boring into him. He lifted his hand and made a fist, apart from an index finger which pointed at the sky. He placed the finger upon his wide smile, blood-stained teeth visible beyond. "I won't tell anyone." The berserker chuckled, looked away and allowed his hand to drop into his lap.

He swivelled in his seat to appraise the Highlanders around him, they looked ready, weapons were sheathed, hands clenched clumps of spider hair.

"Hold on tight!" he roared as a last-minute reminder. "We are ready, Gorgoroth," he breathed, facing front again, his legs clenched around the spider.

Let us get this done, little brother.

The spider beneath him hissed and lurched forward in a veritable gallop straight for a nearby building. Shouts, screams and screeches echoed out behind him as fellow arachnids took a similar approach. An unintended grunt left his mouth when the creature clattered vertically up the building's wall, scuttled onto the roof top and then leapt straight out into thin air. Vyder couldn't help but cry out as fear enveloped him. Gorgoroth's soft laugh echoed in his mind. A neighbouring building was beneath them a moment later and the spider halted. Vyder pushed his fists into soft hair to stop his forward momentum and the risk of somersaulting forward towards the ground far below them.

A piercing scream rent the air nearby. Vyder shot a look in that direction and saw a Highlander had lost his purchase and had fallen from the spider. However, the creature, fast as lightning, arrested his fall with a couple of spindly legs and assisted him in climbing back onto the spider.

Vyder's attention was drawn away from the Highlander's brush with death as the hairy behemoth beneath him turned, stepped forward and once more launched out into the night. He was ready this time and even allowed himself to grin as the cool night air whipped through his hair and whispered in his ears. They landed on the next building, then the next, negotiating across the city at a rapid pace. Others too had become used to this new mode of transport. Cries, gasps and shouts had been replaced by an ever growing raucous of Highland clan war cries.

The stable structure of the building upon which the arachnid stood disappeared beneath them. The creature leapt onto the next building, thick, fresh thatch coming up to meet its many legs. He looked over his shoulder and the Great Highland Army were progressing behind him. Giant spiders leapt, climbed and scuttled across and onto buildings in every direction. A small, tight cluster of creatures moved as one, in some semblance of formation. *The King's Own officer and his section of soldiers.* The arachnids jumped together onto a nearby building and then descended to the street below, disappearing into the night leaving nothing in their trail but thick ropes of spider silk draping from roof tops. Vyder returned his attention to his own advance. He jostled in his seat to regain some balance, then they were on the move again, cool night air whispering through his hair and in his ears.

Clutching a fistful of soft spider hair, he arrested his forward momentum to again avoid flying over the spider's head and looked down at the street far below. Tiny figures were streaming along a main road in two columns. They were moving fast.

"Get me down there, Gorgoroth," he muttered.

A grunt unintentionally escaped his lips when the creature tilted forward and scampered straight down the wall of the tall building. His arse started sliding forward, hands pushed deep into a forest of soft hair. Then they were on the ground and he breathed a sigh of relief. They were pressed against the deep, dark shadow of the huge structure they had just descended and remained undetected by the soldiers. As he expected, they wore the uniforms of Huronian infantry. Scattered amongst them were the red-cloaked warriors of The Mortals.

"These are the enemy, Gorgoroth, bring the others and let's show them the Frost River."

Within minutes, Vyder found himself surrounded by a host of arachnids bearing screaming, yelling and hollering Highlanders. He pushed his boots a few times into the arachnid's bulging abdomen and the thing instinctively knew what he wanted. It barged its way through the others so that Vyder was at the front of Great Highland Army. He drew both his swords and held one high in the air.

"Kill them all!" he roared. "No prisoners!" the spider galloped on, straight toward the enemy host. "No mercy!"

He burst out of the protective shadow and into torch light, dull yellow light catching against the sharp steel of his raised sword. The closest enemy troops noticed then the threat and most broke and ran. Others, most with red cloaks draping from their shoulders, turned towards the charge and made a tight square formation, spears bristling from within their ranks. But even these small formations were retreating, but to their credit, they never presented their backs.

Vyder caught movement in the corner of his eye and noticed Rafe's spider had barged past him, carrying the howling berserker to war. The madman stood on the back of his steed, sword drawn, face turned towards the dark night.

He went into a half squat and then jumped off. He landed on the back of a fleeing soldier, dragged him to the ground and cut his head from his body, then moved onto the next.

Lifting one leg over the spider, Vyder slipped from his purchase and dropped to the ground, both boots hitting together. Darting forward, he advanced past his multiple-legged mount and ran to join Rafe. One Huronian soldier sprinted at him, face creased in fury. He brought his sword over his head in a powerful slice straight towards the Highlander's head. Vyder stepped to one side and cold metal cut empty air. He stabbed his sword into the man's belly and ripped it clear just before his second sword opened his adversary's throat.

Two soldiers advanced on him. Vyder watched them, the one on the right, red-cloak draped from his shoulders looked more confident. He was the one to take down first. Vyder turned his body a little to face the new threat. Red cloak shouted something at him through a sneer, but his words, foreign as they were, were swept away in the roar of battle. They disappeared behind a blur of movement from the left. Both enemy warriors fell to the ground, Rafe standing over them. Then the berserker hacked the life from them, shot a fury-filled glance in Vyder's direction, grinned maniacally at him and sprinted from view to take the fight to some new opponent.

Striding onward he appraised the situation. A throng of Highlanders, all dismounted, advanced upon one of the small enemy squares and closed with them. The combat was savage, the forces an equal match. Courage, fury, hatred and savagery being held at bay by discipline, good leadership and excellent drills.

Returning his attention to his own advance, another Huronian was charging at him. Vyder ducked under an axe blow, the thick, sharp steel whispering over the top of his head. He swivelled and cut the man's hamstring as he passed by him. Grabbing the back of his mail shirt, he pulled the man off his feet. The axe clattered to the road, the weapon long forgotten by the man who yelled his agony to the sky. Vyder slammed a sword into his throat bringing the piercing shriek to silence. Another cluster of warriors made a beeline for him. He was the only Highlander with two swords and he wore the tartan bearing the colours of all the Highland clans, making him a target.

Raking his gaze across the group, they were all grim-eyed, confident in their ability and meant to end him. An image of his beautiful Verone flickered into his mind. Was this the night he would be reunited with his lost love? It felt like years since he'd seen her on the far side of the Frost River. Like an eternity.

Not yet, little brother.

They shouted amongst one another and sprinted straight at him, weapons held above their heads. One wielded a spear which he held two handed, the bloodied tip pointing at Vyder's chest. They arrived together. Vyder dropped a sword, stepped aside, grabbed the spear's wooden haft and directed the weapon's stab over his shoulder. He met the spearman with his forehead, smashing the man's nose in an explosion of a blood. The flat of a sword smacked him in the temple and his vision disappeared for a moment behind a flutter of white spots.

Vyder lost his balance and fell to his knees. Piercing pain emanated from his side and he cried out through clenched teeth. The Huronian sporting a destroyed nose was lying on the cobbled street nearby clutching his face with both hands. Vyder climbed back to his feet still holding one of his swords and with a clumsy slash, blocked a blade that would have beheaded him. He kicked a man's knee out from under him and the soldier fell to the ground clutching the joint and allowing his weapon to clatter to the ground, long forgotten. More pain exploded from his guts this time and he felt breathless.

Allowing a quick glance down he saw a sword buried into his midriff up to its hilt. His flank was adorned with a knife. He grabbed the handle of the knife and ripped it clear, growling through the pain. Acrid blood was all he could taste and tendrils of blood mixed with saliva dangled from his half open mouth. He bared his teeth at the last two remaining enemy warriors in his immediate vicinity. One of them, his eyes wide with panic, lunged in a poorly judged attack. Vyder danced back, ignored the searing pain in his body and leapt forward, bringing his sword in a fast, powerful attack that sliced the air in a horizontal attack. The Huronian's head departed his body. The final opponent seemed more measured and disciplined. His eyes flicked between Vyder's face, his sword hand and the wounds he displayed. He was calculating where and when to attack. Then his eyes widened and looked beyond Vyder, his mouth agape.

Darkness surrounded the Highlander, nearby flickering torches blotted from view. A familiar scent settled in his nostrils and huge, hairy, spindly legs settled either side of him. The Huronian turned on his heel and ran, but the spider was faster. Leaping over Vyder it struck the soldier fast as a snake, enormous fangs plunging through armour, skin and bone. The arachnid spent a few moments feeding on the dead man, then allowed the body to drop to the ground. The creature turned and approached Vyder, it hunkered down in front of him, seeming to stare at him. He felt it was somehow appraising his wounds. A large leg reached out and gently touched his shoulder.

He smiled. "I shall survive, my friend."

Wiping his mouth with a sleeve, the material was left stained with fresh, bright red blood. Vyder coughed, spat blood and pushed the knife into his belt for later use. He stooped to pick up his second sword. Straightening he clenched his teeth against the agony permeating his being and forced a grin. "Shall we?"

The arachnid pushed itself back up to its full height, tapped his shoulder with a soft staccato and then withdrew its leg from him, turning around faster than its bulk might suggest and walked in front of him.

He had time to look around from his immediate

surroundings to take in the battle proper. The all too familiar din of battle had morphed from shouts, yells, clashes of steel on steel, or steel on shield to the abject screaming of terrified men. Spiders had advanced beyond their human comrades to take the fight to the Huronians.

The once tightly packed, disciplined enemy squares were in disarray and the fleeing started. Battle once joined and equally matched became a route. Each boot-fall caused him pain, but he refused to allow it show on his face. Rafe fell in beside him and watched the slaughter unfold in front of them.

The berserker slapped him on the back. "Turns out those spiders are rather handy, lord!"

"Aye," he grunted.

Rafe gestured at the sword hilt jutting from Vyder's belly. "It appears you have a flesh wound."

The Highlander chuckled. "Looks like a damn fine sword, too!"

Rafe grinned. "It does! Better to leave it in there, though. For now, at least, else I fear it'll kill you."

He nodded and smiled. *It'll kill me regardless, my friend.* One Huronian taken in the full throes of terror and devoid of all logic, darted in between the spiders and attempted to sprint past Vyder.

"Wrong way, lad!" roared the berserker and swept his head clear of his shoulders with a single, powerful stroke. Rafe glanced at Vyder, his eyes wide with fury and teeth on display beyond the grin stretching his mouth. "Someone gave him the wrong directions, Vyder!" he tapped the headless corpse at his feet leaking blood onto the road. "Can you believe that?"

Despite his discomfort, Vyder laughed, each shudder causing new waves of agony. But it didn't matter, he was in good spirits. Soon the streets, cast into flickering shadow, were silent, the shattering roar of battle having fled. Only the soft sputter of nearby torches remained. One torch had been knocked clear of its metallic bracket during the fight and rested on the cobbled street, its once mighty flame dying. A Huronian soldier lay on his guts nearby, dry, dead eyes seeming to watch the tiny orange glow of the torch disappear to leave in its wake a long, thin ascending trail of black smoke.

Vyder kicked the torch to the wall and strode past. Arachnids, having defeated their enemy returned to their Highland riders. He stopped in front of the hairy behemoth in front of him, stepped up onto its proffered leg and climbed up onto its back. "You'll have to forgive me, my large friend. I am wounded, so slow moving." A gentle hiss was his reply.

The army of spiders bearing their human warriors moved further into the depths of the city. Occasionally, enemy Huronians were overwhelmed and sent to the Frost River. Others fled. It was an hour later when they halted before the towering palace at the centre of the city. Vyder pushed his spider onward until it was standing at the very front. The gunners lay where they fell. They'd died in small groups around their cannons, defending the city and their comrades until the last man. Even now the faint smell of spent gunpowder hung in the air. A hint of what had once been. Not a single gunner had fallen with their back to the enemy.

Around the semi-circle formation of cannons was a heavy blanket of Huronian dead. They stained the ground in every direction. Many of them were dismembered in some form and in most places the corpses lay two or three deep.

"Who are these men?" Rafe pointed at the deceased Wendurlund gunners.

"Artillerymen."

"Brave warriors, all," the berserker said in a soft voice.

"They were."

Vyder clambered down from his huge, hairy mount and wandered across the ground towards the cannons. He ensured he placed his boots carefully to avoid slipping. A small clump of bodies on the far side of the cannons caught his eye. They were all civilians. He passed the mighty weapons, the smell of gun powder much stronger. Touching the barrel of one cannon, the black metal still held warmth. He made his way beyond the groups of gunners. "Travel well, warriors," he offered their still, silent bodies.

When he reached the pile of Wendurlund civilians, Vyder looked at the faces, stared at the clothing trying to see something familiar. But nothing caught his eye. He smiled, despite the terrible scene within which he found himself. Somehow, somewhere, Miriam survived.

XIII

Afternoon – eighth day of the siege

The Huronian rear guard were dead. They'd fought long and hard, but ultimately were no match for Henry's force. King Fillip was not amongst the dead, though. Much to Ahitika's chagrin. The Wendurlund prince stared at the fire demon who sat upon the ground nearby resting, a small grass fire surrounding him. *Well, the enemy were no match for* him *more like.* The thing had decimated the Huronian ranks. A soft crackle permeated the air around the flame-covered giant. Its head turned and two jet black eyes stared into Henry's soul. He held its gaze and nodded once in thanks.

You are welcome, little prince. The words boomed in his mind. The hair stood up on his nape and a bolt of ice shot down his spine. **But it isn't over yet.** One blazing arm came up and a single finger pointed off into the distance. Henry followed it and saw the main group of Huronian Cavalry had stopped and turned to face them. They were formed into a spear head and were making ready to charge. Henry returned his attention to the fire demon. *Will you help us fight this last time?*

The thing climbed to its feet. **I will, Henry. For Gorgoroth, I will help rid the land of this...** he gestured at the force of enemy cavalry who'd moved into a canter. **Rot.** The giant held his arms by his sides, hands horizontal to the ground. As if on command, the tiny grass fire spreading out around him died out, to be replaced with a thin fog of smoke.

Henry adjusted himself in the saddle and patted the horse. Its hair was wet with sweat, but the beast had regained his breath.

Ahitika came alongside him. "They charging." She was right. The formation had accelerated into a gallop, a haze of dark dust trailing in their wake. The faint thunder of hooves echoed across the plains to them.

"This time, King Fillip will be amongst them."

Ahitika grinned. "Good!" Her hand dropped to the sheathed knife at her side. "Good."

Anonkas and Hexuka stopped beside Ahitika. She spoke to them in the Kalote language and they held their bows to the sky and whooped. It appeared they were keen to close battle with King Fillip. So was the prince. It was anger that kept him in the fight. Exhausted as his body was, the memory of his capture and suffering at the hands of the Huronian savages was what kept him going. Ultimately, King Fillip was to blame for his experience. An experience which had nearly killed him were it not for Vyder and the Kalote woman at his side.

Henry turned in the saddle to look over his shoulder. "Prepare yourselves!" he shouted. "Here comes the second wave."

"About bloody time!" roared Byfros. "I'm getting hungry. Let's get this over and done with." He brandished his blood-soaked sword above his head. "I need to go and eat!"

Henry couldn't help but grin at the antics of the madman whose face was still painted bright red with a mix of both paint and blood. Crazy as he might be, he had to admit the Highlander was a demon in battle. A soft crackle rattled from the fire giant nearby. A bystander could be forgiven for thinking the growing thunder signalled the coming of a storm. The enemy charge was closing the distance fast.

"In extended line!" Henry shouted.

His force obeyed, arraying themselves as commanded. Some shifted in their saddles as nerves or war spirit ebbed through them. Others leaned forward to stroke the necks of their mounts, offering soft words. He nudged his mount forward and trotted along the line of warriors.

"At my command we will turn to the left and gallop. Then we will slow, turn back towards the enemy and counter charge. Is that clear?"

Some nodded, others sat and stared at him.

The thunder cast by the Huronian hooves grew

louder still, the noise rolling over them and drowning out all else.

"Turn to the left!" Henry yelled, pointing in that direction. He looked along the extended line and was relieved they'd all turned as instructed.

"Let's go!" he nudged his horse into the gallop. Whipping a look over his shoulder, the extended line was following, making a thunder of their own.

Ahitika came alongside him, black hair streaking out behind her. "Why we galloping away from them?" she shouted. Her dark eyes flashing anger.

"I'll fight them on my terms. Not theirs!" he yelled, the words whipped from his mouth. She looked doubtful but accepted his reply. Looking beyond her, the once neat arrowhead of the Huronian charge was in disarray. They'd expected the Wendurlund Cavalry to simply counter-charge straight at them. Their formation slowed in order to turn towards their adversary. Henry steered to the right and stood up in the stirrups. He waved his sword over his head and pointed in the direction he'd turned. The single column turned to follow suit so they were moving along the flank of the Huronian force.

Henry remained standing in the saddle, glaring at his adversary. There in the centre flew the flag of the king. The enemy. His lips drew back in a snarl. Henry levelled his sword at the Huronian king as if in challenge. "I see you!" he roared.

The Huronians had slowed to a walk to change their formation to face the mobile cavalry attempting to circle around behind them.

Henry slowed his mount and faced his opponent. "On me!" Then he kicked back into the gallop. He threw a glance over his shoulder to ensure his warriors had followed him. They had. Still standing, he held his sword and his non-sword arm up above his head in a makeshift 'V' to signal arrowhead formation.

"Arrowhead!" a distant voice roared and the order was repeated down the line. He sat back into the saddle and clenched the hilt of his sword in a tighter grip. From the side of his eye the fire demon loped from their original position towards the Huronians.

Focusing on the enemy was difficult at the speed of a gallop. The oncoming horsemen, horizon and ground seemed to shudder and shake. An arrow streaked past his head in the direction of the enemy and lodged itself in the leg of the man leading the Huronians. Another two arrows followed the first, one slammed into the man's throat and the second pierced his shoulder. He toppled from the saddle and disappeared beneath a battering of hooves.

He steered a little to the left and aimed straight at one particular man, his focus never leaving his target. Holding his sword in close to his body his elbow pushed hard in against the armour directly over his right ribs, he ensured his arm wouldn't be hacked off if he was caught waving his sword above his head like some madman.

Foreign yells and war cries erupted from the Huronian Cavalry, their voices mingling with the near deafening thunder. Henry's target was close. Close enough to see the whites of his eyes. The Wendurlund prince screamed anger and hatred. He tensed every muscle in his arm and tilted his sword tip up a little. Then they collided. His sword slid into his opponent's throat and then he was beyond the man, his sword nearly torn from his grip. Bringing the weapon up onto his shoulder, his horse battered into another mount a loud grunt coming from the animal beneath him. They slowed and then an ear-piercing clash of steel and animals exploded behind him where his arrowhead formation impacted the enemy.

A blade flashed through the air towards his face. He met the attack with the flat of his sword and smacked the sharp steel away, leaned forward and stabbed the attacker in the throat. The man's eyes widened, he dropped his weapon and clutched the terrible wound in his neck. Ripping his weapon free Henry sliced the shoulder of the Huronian on the left of him and, bringing his blade back, used the force of his arm to elbow the man on the right in the face. Then he urged his horse deeper into the maelstrom of enemy horsemen.

A warrior came at him, levelled a spear and lunged at his chest. Henry pushed the power of the thrust away, and the spear tip flashed over his right shoulder rather than pierce his ribcage. He kept a tight grip of the wooden haft and brought his sword down in a savage overhead cut that battered the man's helmet. The weapon dented the steel and knocked the man unconscious. He slid from the saddle and disappeared beneath the jostle of hooves in every direction.

Something smashed into the back of Henry's head and pain exploded in his skull. He saw stars, nausea washed over him and he slumped in the saddle. He groaned. The spear toppled free of his hand, but somehow, he maintained a weak grip on his sword.

"Protect the king!" a nearby shout reverberated around his skull. A horse barged past him, slamming into his left leg. Another animal pushed by on his right side. A clatter of steel on steel, shouts, roars and screams of pain followed. Then a hand slammed on his shoulder.

"Are you well, young warrior?" Byfros's face painted now more with fresh blood than paint filled his vision.

A soft chuckle broke free of his lips. "You called me a king, my friend."

Byfros glared at him. "You think your father tucked safely away in his palace refusing to fight for his kingdom is a fucking *king*?" The berserker burst out laughing. "You are a king, lad, he is one in name only. Remember that!" He slapped Henry on the shoulder and charged further into the enemy screaming some Highland war cry.

Nausea continued to assault Henry, but he separated himself from the feeling and nudged his horse forward. His warriors pushed in either side of him advancing deep into the throng of the enemy. He caught a glimpse of Ahitika on the outskirts of the battle at full gallop, standing in her stirrups, drawing back on her bow, eye looking down the arrow shaft.

Then she disappeared from view behind desperate warriors fighting for their lives.

On the far side of the fight high-pitched screams washed over the clash of steel and a flash of the flame demon appeared between the gaps of horses. Then the smell of burning flesh pervaded the air. Henry swallowed back his nausea once again and nudged his mount onward. With blood-stained sword rested on his shoulder he moved alongside Byfros, then pushed his mount on harder. He lurched forward and reached a canter before he barged into a Huronian cavalryman. The man wore an open-faced helm, his skin marred with dirt and deep rings beneath his eyes suggested lack of sleep. Henry blocked the sword stab with his left forearm, ignoring the sting of cut skin. He leaned forward and punched the man in the face, drew his fist back and punched again. Then brought his own sword down in an overcut which lodged in the man's brow. Blood exploded from the wound and the Huronian released his weapon, howled in pain and held a hand to the wound. Henry ripped free his blade and brought it down again in the same place, hacking free fingers and half a hand before cutting deep into the warrior's chin. The howling morphed into a scream. Flicking the sharp edge free, he stabbed and the point of his sword found solace in his adversary's throat. Hot blood pumped rhythmically from the large hole in his neck and the screaming suddenly stopped.

He grabbed a fistful of chain mail and pulled the dying warrior from his saddle. The soon to be corpse slid clear to the hoof pummelled ground below.

"On!" he urged his mount deeper into the fray.

Byfros pushed beyond him and battered into an opponent. A spear lodged in the berserker's hip, but the man didn't flinch. Instead, he roared a war cry and hacked the life from his enemy. Then he pulled clear the spear, stood in the saddle and threw it high out over the battle deep into the enemy formation where some poor bastard would probably receive the sharp steel in the face.

Henry charged past Byfros and slammed into the fray. He ducked under a sword swipe, blocked a spear thrust and smashed a man in the face with his fist. Huronian shouting erupted around him and enemy heads turned his way.

They came for him en masse.

"They know who you are, Henry!" shouted Byfros. "They mean to overwhelm you!" Byfros stood in the stirrups. "Highlanders to me!" he bellowed. "To me!"

A blade hissed through the air towards Henry's head and for one brief moment a sliver of sunlight flashed on the beautiful steel. His own blade blocked the attack. Another weapon, poorly aimed, glanced from his hip. Pain assaulted him and warm liquid trickled down the skin of his leg beneath his trousers. The attacker died with Henry's steel in his chest. He pulled, but the edge was lodged deep inside his enemy. The hilt ripped clear of his grip as the lifeless warrior fell from his horse.

"Make way!" Byfros shouted and thundered by Henry, pushing back the foe.

A throng of Highlanders closely followed. Their foreign cries and battle screams filled the sky. A clearing opened up around him in a semi-circle where the adversary had been pushed back. A grim Highlander halted beside him. He offered Henry's sword to him. A chunk of flesh was still skewered on the tip.

"You dropped something," the Shadolian spoke in a deep voice, a hint of a smile tugging at the corners of his mouth.

Henry nodded his thanks and took the weapon. He attempted to block out the dull nausea and sharp pain in his hip. Failed. Pushing his mount onward, the animal lunged forward and found a gap between Byfros and another warrior. Movement high above the battle caught his eye and he glanced in that direction. It was the flag of the Huronian king and it was advancing towards him. Word had spread to the enemy king as to Henry's whereabouts.

"Come here you bastard!" he roared, anger warming

him and driving away both the nausea and pain. "I'm waiting!"

Molten rage devoured the anger, and Henry roared his hatred, urged his mount onward and hacked the life from an opponent. His sword found a brief home in the guts of some unfortunate enemy, then it kissed the skull of another. Henry brought down the sword, the blade singing through the air and separated a head from a neck. The Huronian foe backed away from the prince who'd clearly gone berserk. A bow appeared in their lines where Henry and Byfros fought side by side.

Henry blocked a clumsy spear thrust, grasped hold of the haft and ripped it clear from the hands of his assailant. His own sword found the man's throat and then spine. Bright blood spilled from the man's mouth and his eyes rolled back in his head. Ripping clear the blade, Henry left the man to his dying.

His fist found a nose, sharp steel met flesh and bone beyond, Henry's sword edge blocked a spear, then a counter thrust punched into a mouth and out the back of a skull. Huronians fell like wheat before a scythe.

Loud crackles grew closer, vying for pride of place. The noise of war mingled with the screams of the dying. The flame demon fought on towards Henry, ploughing through the ranks, burning those who stood before him, their screams almost unbearable to hear.

The Huronian Cavalry backed away from Henry as Byfros and the Highlanders moved in to protect their flanks. The adversaries turned and attempted to flee but their lines were too thick with warriors trying to push back and away from the flame demon. They had nowhere to go and were decimated by Henry's forces.

Soon all that remained was a tight circle of enemy warriors facing out, King Fillip in their centre. Beside him was mounted the flag bearer. Ahitika came to a halt beside Henry.

She flashed a smile at him. "We are victory." She

returned her attention to the circle of enemy cavalry and the smile fled before the hatred that appeared on her face. "Now time to kill the king."

Henry placed a hand on her arm. "Wait. Translate for me."

He nudged his warhorse closer to the defensive circle. "King Fillip." Ahitika's voice closely followed his own.

"My name is Henry."

A horse snorted nearby, saddle leather creaked as someone readjusted themselves and all the while a soft crackle emanated from the flame demon towering over them. The entity's black eyes bored into King Fillip's back. It didn't need to speak for Henry to know that it wanted to wipe Fillip and all of his men from existence.

"*Prince* Henry," Henry elaborated, sheathed his sword and placed his hands on the mane of his horse. "You took me prisoner. Held me ransom. You had your guards torture me endlessly. I remained alive, malnourished, starving, thirsty and in the end, dying. I was a shadow of a man." He held his arms out. "Yet here I am!" he roared.

The enemy king replied, Ahitika giving sense to the foreign words, "I did not order them to torture or—"

"Silence! You say that now, yet in all the time I spent as a captive in your dungeon, you did not come to see how I faired. Not a single time. You gave me no quarter. Were it not for this woman beside me and a Highland warrior sent by my father, my skeleton would now adorn a cell in your stinking dungeon. You showed me no mercy."

He allowed his hands to drop back onto his horse. Then he reached for his sword hilt and drew the weapon, still slick with blood. "Now I will show you the same."

Henry's lips peeled back and his brow furrowed to deepen the hatred glinting in his eyes. "Kill them all except the king!"

Ahitika whooped, stood in her stirrups nocked an arrow, drew her bowstring and a sent an arrow that thudded through the throat of the flag bearer. The king's colours fell, landing upon the churned earth beside the dying bearer.

Highlanders roared their war cries and charged either side of Henry, slamming into the thin line of Huronians still left alive. It wasn't a battle. It wasn't even a fight. It was a massacre. The Highlanders formed a massive circle around King Fillip, larger than the Huronian Cavalry had recently provided. They walked their horses around the enemy monarch, staring inward at the lone king shouting war cries, yelling profanities or staring at him in silence, battering their swords against shields.

Gone was the cocky, confident king and in his place sat a man on a tired horse, his shoulders slumped. The sharp, clear, calculating flash in his eyes had disappeared and now only fear resided.

Henry pushed through the circle of Highlanders, followed closely by Ahitika. He dismounted and the Kalote woman leapt clear of her horse to land lightly beside him. The Highlanders fell silent, but they continued walking their horses in a slow circle.

"Get off your horse!" he shouted, striding towards his enemy. Ahitika translated.

The defeated man did not move. He simply stared at Henry with a blank expression. Henry pointed his sword at him. "Get off your bloody horse. *Now!*"

Fillip swung down from the saddle and stood upon the hoof trodden earth. He drew his own sword. The blade was pristine, unmarked, unstained and beautifully clean.

Henry gestured at the weapon and chuckled. "Been fighting hard I see."

Fillip swiped the air expertly and smiled. "You mean to fight me one on one?" he spoke through Ahitika. "You think you can best me? I am the greatest swordsman in Huron, maybe the world."

He turned to Ahitika. "Do you still want this kill?"

She somehow smiled through a face of savage fury. She nodded. "Then I will take scalp."

Henry turned back and laughed. He pointed at the

spotless sword. "Your weapon would suggest otherwise. I will not fight you, it would be over in a matter of moments. No, Ahitika will fight you."

Fillip looked beyond the pair and at the mounted Highlanders beyond. "Where is this warrior?" he shouted.

Ahitika stepped forward and dropped her bow and quiver, placing them on the ground. She knelt, took a fistful of dirt and stood. She whispered to her closed fist and allowed the dirt to trickle gently through her fingers. Then she clenched a hold of her chest plate and glanced at the sky, offering a short, muttered sentence.

Henry swallowed. *Be safe lady.*

Fillip's eyes returned to the pair and focused upon Ahitika. Confidence reignited in his eyes. "A woman?"

"Last time I checked, yes," she replied in the Huronian tongue.

He ignored her, staring instead at Henry behind her. "A *woman?* You mean for me to fight a *woman?* You mock me!"

His gaze returned to her and he laughed, shrugging. "Very well then. I've killed plenty of women in my time. What then is one more?"

"You are such a *mighty* warrior king, aren't you?"

"And where is your sword?" he yelled, advancing towards her.

She reached for the small of her back and her hunting knife flashed into her hand. "Sword? I need no sword to defeat you. All I need is this little knife."

He roared his hatred and ran at her, his rage all consuming. He brought cold, sharp steel down in a blistering overhead attack, the blade cutting the air like lightning. Ahitika ducked aside, darted around him and cut open his bicep with a neat swipe. He whirled to face her, blood dripping from his elbow. He feinted a stab then, with expert skill, altered his strike into a low sweep. She leapt aside, ran in with lithe agility and plunged her knife into his guts. She sliced him open and stepped beyond him.

He cried out in pain, holding a hand to his midriff. "You bitch!" he growled through clenched teeth.

Fillip ran at her, then at the last moment sidestepped and swept the sword in a fast, horizontal strike meant to behead her. She ducked, steel whispering through the air where her neck had been moments before. Ahitika stepped into his attack and sliced deep into his groin, then spun away behind him. He screamed and almost fell into the dirt. But somehow remained on his feet.

She waited for him to turn to face her. "I'm going to kill you, great warrior king, then I am going to cut the scalp from your skull." The crease in her brow deepened and her eyelids narrowed to slits. "Or maybe it'll be the other way around."

His eyes flicked around him, tongue appearing for a moment between dry lips.

"There is no escape *mighty* warrior king."

A dull thumping echoed out around them. Highlanders slapped swords, spears or axes against round shields. Although the warriors themselves remained silent. To Ahitika, the staccato seemed to speak to her. Two words in particular. *Finish him!*

He took two faltering steps toward her and lunged with a clumsy movement. She slapped his sword aside with the flat of one hand and rammed her knife under his chin at an angle, the sharp blade lodging in the spine just below his skull. He dropped without a sound. Then she scalped him.

She held the scalp above her head and offered a high-pitched whoop, fresh blood oozing down the skin of her arm. Anonkas and Hexuka joined in, shrieking their victory to the sky, holding their bows high. The Highlanders roared their triumph, their voices drowning out all else in the area.

King Fillip was dead.

XIV

A cold, wet nose touched his hand and Vyder looked down at Saigh, she returned his stare, her tail wagging slowly. He patted her head and knelt. She nuzzled his face. "There is a lot of death here, lass."

A long, warm tongue licked his cheek. The Highlander swept the area with his eyes, still amazed by the sheer amount of courage the artillerymen had shown in their final stand. Perhaps the pile of civilian dead would be twice its size if they had abandoned their positions and fled. A dull *thud* beside him and Rafe stood nearby, hands on hips. Would-be mortal wounds still adorned his body, his chain mail and clothing beneath displayed slits, cuts and holes, from which fresh blood still dribbled.

"Some battle," he muttered.

Vyder nodded, continuing to stroke the powerful animal sat beside him. "Aye."

The berserker stretched and groaned. "I need to sleep."

"Soon, my friend. We're not finished yet." He looked over his shoulder at the pitiful number of Highlanders still mounted on their spiders. Some had departed with Henry, but the loss of Highland life had been immeasurable. Guilt still ebbed around his being. He closed his eyes. *I need to sleep too. So tired.*

His eyelids parted and a piece of cloth caught beneath the corpse of a man close to him caught his eye. He frowned and stood. Grabbing the shirt of the deceased, he rolled the body over, attempting to ignore the sickly-sweet aroma which pervaded the air. The piece of cloth was cool and soft in his hand. It was somehow familiar to him.

"I didn't pick you for a man eager for women's fashion, lord."

He turned to Rafe and grinned. "I know this clothing." He held the material up to show the berserker.

"By the look of it, I'm sure you do."

Vyder's eyes widened and his lips parted, mouth hanging open. *It is Miriam's shawl!* He knelt again and pushed the material towards Saigh. The hound sniffed it, tail still wagging with lack of speed.

"Can you find Miriam, Great One?" The animal locked eyes with Vyder and cocked her head. "Do you know where she is?"

Saigh returned her attention to the item of clothing and recommenced her sniffing, her dark nose moving over all areas of the shawl. Then she stared back up at Vyder.

"Where is Miriam?"

The dog stood, smelled the ground briefly and then trotted towards an alley. Vyder followed her at a jog.

"Lord!"

Vyder ignored the berserker.

"*Lord!*"

He entered the dark alley and even there the hint of gun powder had settled into the cobbled stones and walls of empty, silent buildings. Saigh darted to the right and disappeared. He followed and found himself in a wider street. A toppled wagon lay in the centre, the horse which had once pulled the vehicle lay dead nearby.

"Slow down, lass!"

But the hound appeared to have the trail and showed no sign of listening to her master. Another alley, even narrower than the first, saw his shoulders brushing the walls either side of him. He leapt over a dead Huronian soldier, then another. He slowed and scrambled through a throng of dead Wendurlund warriors and then ran on. The dog was well in front, but still visible. She disappeared around a corner and her thunderous barks ensued, followed by a deep growl.

"Saigh! To me!" he shouted between breaths.

A staccato of barks followed. He increased his pace and ran around the bend in the road. Two Huronian soldiers stood before Saigh. One was knelt before her holding out his hand and speaking in hushed tones, the other was standing nearby, watching.

Vyder didn't slow. He drew his sword and killed the first with a powerful sweep of the weapon and cut through the throat of the second, before kicking him to the ground where his life blood soaked into the road. The hound bounded off and the Highlander followed. His whole body ached and a deep exhaustion dragged at him, its thick tendrils seeming to encircle every fibre of his being. A distant blast echoed over the immediate area. *That sounded like a blunderbuss.*

Saigh trotted down an alley and out of sight followed closely by a scratching and whining noise. He attempted to call the animal's name but he couldn't manage to speak between the ragged breaths. Vyder came around the corner. The hound was stood on her hind legs clawing at a closed door, whining. She looked back at Vyder, pushed herself from the door, darted to him and pushed a nose into his hand then returned to the door and stared at it.

"Is she in here?"

The deafening, single bark was enough of an answer. He turned the handle and pushed but it was locked. A scream echoed from inside. Stepping back, Vyder kicked the door and it flew open on protesting hinges. He stepped over the threshold. Stumbling down the hallway he passed a room on his left. Empty. Another on the right was the same. The kitchen was a mess, rotting food littered the table and a dead Huronian sat on a chair nearby, a hole the size of a fist punched through his face. Near his feet lay a woman, her throat cut and congealed blood in a pool around her.

The smell of faint gunpowder floated in the air around the corpse and for a moment he thought his memory carried the scent from the artillery guns.

"Get your stinking hands off me!"

"Miriam!" he roared. "Where are you?"

"In here!"

He whirled and darted for the closed door. Kicking that door open too, he ran inside. Miriam was on the floor, held down by a Huronian soldier. Vyder bellowed an incomprehensible sound and stabbed the soldier in the back. Ripped the sword clear, grabbed a fistful of his mail armour and pulled the dying man to his feet, then threw him against a wall and slammed his sword into his throat and ripped it clear. The soldier slowly slid down the wall painting a bright red trail down the wall.

He turned back. "Are you hurt?" he knelt and helped Miriam to her feet.

Saigh pushed past him and licked her hand.

Taking her by the arms, Vyder helped Miriam to her feet.

"I'm not hurt, Vyder. He was trying to… he tried to…"

Vyder pulled her into his embrace. "You are unhurt. That is the main thing."

"I had no strength left. I couldn't hold him off. Oh, thank the gods you are here, Vyder."

They held each other for some time. Then Miriam pushed him away and wiped her eyes with the back of a hand. She stooped down and came up with his trusty old blunderbuss in her hand. "This thing has saved my life more times than I care to remember."

He chuckled. "She is a good weapon." His brow creased and he spotted a sock on the ground. He picked it up. It had been cut down and a lump bulged from within.

"Powder and shot together." She held it over the maw of the blunderbuss pierced it with a hair pin so powder started to trickle into the weapon's barrel, then dropped in the sock. Still holding the blunderbuss upright so the barrel pointed towards the ceiling, she tapped the buttstock on the ground a few times. "Saves time on reloading."

He nodded. "Bloody ingenious." He jerked a thumb towards the room behind him where the dead Huronian took solace on the chair. "I take it that is your work?"

A haunted look returned to her face. "Aye," she whispered. "They came into the house together. Poor Gab. I couldn't save her."

The front door squeaked and boot falls thudded upon the wooden floor. Miriam pulled the weapon into her shoulder. Vyder raised his sword and turned towards the advancing noise but noticed Saigh's tail wagging and knew no threat was present.

"Lord?"

"In here, Rafe." Vyder placed a hand on the barrel of the blunderbuss and gently pushed it away. "He is a friend."

"Is that the Highland tongue you are speaking?"

"Aye, lass."

"I've never heard you speak it before." She placed the buttstock back upon the floor.

Rafe appeared in the doorway. "I see I was not needed." He looked even worse for wear, if that was possible. The man was ghost white. All colour had fled every aspect of his skin. Rafe looked more akin to some creature from the myths than he did a human.

Even so, Saigh pushed forward and smelled his hand, then licked it. Rafe patted her head.

"No, my friend. Miriam did most of it all by herself."

The berserker pointed his chin at the dead man in the chair. "I see you punched a hole in that one's face."

Vyder grinned and held up a fist.

"I take it the king has been killed?"

Vyder shrugged. "I know not." He turned to Miriam and switched to the Wendurlund language. "Was the king slaughtered by the Huronians?"

She scoffed. "He has remained holed up in his palace throughout the entire battle. As far as I know he remains quite well."

Vyder relayed the message to Rafe. The berserker glowered. "The king did not even show his face to defend his people?"

"Things work a little differently down here than they do in the Highlands, my friend. The days of the warrior kings of old are dead and gone."

Rafe's eyes widened with disbelief. "He is a king…

but not a warrior?"

"Aye."

His friend stared at the floor. "Makes no sense to me. I think we should go and speak with him. I want to understand his weakness."

Vyder laughed at his friend's genuine honesty. He looked at Miriam. "He wants to go and speak with the king."

She stared at the wounded berserker. "Why? If he sat down, I could dress his wounds and clean him up a little."

"Trust me, lass, he cares not about that. Rafe wants to look the king in the eye." He shrugged. "It's a Highland thing."

Her brows drew together and her mouth narrowed. "Gladly. I wouldn't mind giving the bastard a piece of my mind."

He turned to face his friend. "Miriam agrees."

The berserker stood on tiptoe so as to look over Vyder's shoulder at Miriam. "Does she have Highland blood in her?"

"No."

Rafe lowered himself from his toes and stared at Vyder. "You sure?"

He grinned and pushed past. "Come on, let's go. Saigh, to me!"

The trio moved out into the night and made their way back towards the palace where the army of spiders waited. They passed a side alley and movement caught their eyes. Saigh growled, fangs on display. A Huronian soldier who was hugging a wall and hoping not to be seen flinched from his position and sprinted away. Rafe loped after him and disappeared from sight.

Vyder patted Saigh on the rump. "Leave it. Come on girl." She stood rooted in place staring at the place where the berserker had darted from sight in pursuit of his quarry. She licked her jowls and followed Vyder.

"Will he be safe by himself?"

Vyder's laughter boomed around the surrounding

buildings, which was the only answer he provided her. "It is good to see you are well," he said. "I feared for your safety for a long time, especially once I knew the Huronians had breached the city's walls."

Miriam tapped the blunderbuss she had rested on one shoulder. "As I said, this thing has saved my life more times than I'd like to admit." Her voice wavered. "I thought the Wendurlund Army had been all but destroyed and it'd be only a matter of time before I joined them in death." She sniffed and attempted to withhold a sob but failed. "The best I was hoping for was a swift death."

He stopped and pulled her close. "You are safe now, Miriam. I'm so relieved I found you." He reached down and stroked Saigh's face. "Well, Saigh found you."

"Come on, Vyder." She broke from his embrace. "Let's go and meet this coward king. I'd like to give him a piece of my mind."

He smiled and followed the former slave. Relieved as he was, the exhaustion which had settled upon him grew more intense. The great muscles in his legs seemed like they were filled with rocks and his arms were heavy.

Boot falls on the cobbled street behind them gave warning of Rafe's advance. The Highland berserker slowed to a walk beside them, a fresh splatter of blood adorning his cheek.

He grinned at Vyder. "Didn't put up much of a fight." He sheathed his blood-soaked sword. "These Huronians are bold when they are surrounded by their own. But they are like mice when they are caught by themselves in the dark."

Within minutes the trio were walking into the Palace Green. Well at one time, before the siege, the field had boasted beautiful green, well-cut grass. Now only dead bodies grew there. Where grass could be seen, it was either blackened by gun powder or, closer to the cannons, burned to bare earth by the heat of the gunfire.

Miriam halted and drew a sharp breath. Vyder's arm

snaked around her. "You are safe, Miriam. They are friends."

"Spiders," she breathed. "They are huge."

He squeezed her. "They are friends. They helped us get into the city. See?" he pointed at the closest arachnids where Highland warriors were perched. "We rode them into battle."

She looked up at him. "By the gods, Vyder."

"Come, let us see the king."

The climb up the long flights of stairs had winded Vyder. He was much weaker and growing more by the passing minutes. Or at least that is how he felt. Finally, they arrived at the top. A group of riflemen lay dead facing out where, no doubt, they had been firing upon the advancing Huronian soldiers. Enemy warriors lay in death all around them but it was clear the riflemen were vastly outnumbered and had been overwhelmed.

The palace doors were made from wood some several feet thick. They were at least fifteen feet tall and barred from the inside. Vyder approached and hammered his fist upon the wood.

"Open the doors, your grace. We are friendly." He bashed on the entrance again. "The Huronians have been defeated."

Silence was his answer.

"He is deaf!" Rafe thundered. He gestured at the dormant cannons in the square below. "Perhaps the gunfire destroyed his ears."

"No, my friend," Vyder muttered. "He ignores us."

Rone appeared from the stairs and jogged to them. "No luck?" he asked.

Vyder stepped back to allow the King's Own officer room. "None."

Rone walked to the massive entrance and banged the

side of his fist against the wood. "Sire, it is I, Rone, one of your King's Own officers. Open the door. The siege is at an end!"

Again, silence was their solemn reply. Rone cursed.

Vyder took a step back and then darted forward, delivering a powerful kick onto the wood. "Your grace! Open the doors. We are friendly. We mean you no harm."

"You might not," Miriam said.

They made more attempts over the following hours without success. As dawn broke the eastern horizon projecting hues of orange and pink across the sky, a clatter of hooves drew their attention. Vyder strode to the edge of the stairs and looked out over the square beneath. Many of the Highlanders had dismounted their spiders and sat in groups, chatting.

On the far side of the corpse riddled clearing rode Tork leading the remnants of the King's Own. They were in a tight formation moving slowly. He spotted two horses the riders of which were lying belly down over the saddle, dead. Some of the elite soldiers had rudimentary bandages covering wounds on their hands, arms or legs.

Rone brushed alongside Vyder and raised his hands above his head. "Ho! Tork! Up here!" he roared.

The formation of warriors halted and Tork cantered towards the palace. He took his musket out of its sheath, dismounted and took the stairs two at a time.

"We can't make entrance," Vyder explained by way of greeting.

The King's Own commander nodded but made no reply. He strode to the entrance and smashed the buttstock of his musket against the wood then took a backward step. "By order of the King's Own Commander, I demand the doors opened," he shouted. "The battle is over and I must see King George."

Nothing.

Tork advanced and attacked again with his musket's stock. "If the guards inside can hear me. My name is Tork, commander of the King's Own. I demand entrance. If you refuse me, I'll see you hang. You have my word on that."

Vyder heard a *clunk* and a series of *thuds,* then silence. One final *bang* and a widening crack appeared between the two doors followed by a prolonged screech of hinges in dire need of oil. After a few minutes the doors had been pushed outward to their fully open positions.

Vyder followed Tork inside.

The commander halted in front of a small group of guards. He pointed at them. "Who is in charge here?"

A haggard looking, thin man stepped forward. "I sir."

"Name?"

"Prichard."

"Rank?"

"Captain, sir."

Tork pushed past the man. "Not for long, Prichard."

Rafe tapped Vyder on the shoulder and gestured at Tork walking away down a wide corridor. "I have no clue what he says, but I like him."

Vyder nodded and followed Tork. "He is a good warrior and leader."

"Halt!" Prichard called. "You can't bring a dog into the palace!" he glared at Saigh.

The hair on the hound's back stood on end and a deep rumble reverberated from her throat.

"She goes where I go."

"The hell she does!" Prichard called.

Vyder approached the guard officer and glared down at him. He pointed at the sheathed blade at the man's hip. "Your sword is clean, polished and free from any scratches. You haven't raised a finger to defend this city, never mind this land. I have."

"What did the tiny man say?" Rafe's voice boomed from behind him.

He ignored the berserker and dropped a hand to rest on Saigh's head. Her growling stopped. "And so has she." He jerked a thumb behind him at Rafe. "And so too have my

Great Highland Army. We have done far more than you and your men have, and likely more than you ever will in your lifetime." He leaned into the man who seemed to shrink away from the Highlander. "So, like I said, she goes where I go."

Prichard nodded and stepped aside. "Very well."

Vyder strode on. Rafe sneered at the guards as he walked past them.

Another few minutes and Vyder found himself in the throne room. It stank of rotten fruit and off meats. King George sat in a corner on a beautifully crafted wooden chair, elbow on the armrest and chin in hand. The throne itself was vacant. *That's fitting.* He stared at the newcomers. Anger warmed Vyder, but he quenched it.

The king rose to his feet and stretched. "Gentlemen!" his voiced boomed, echoing around the massive room. He spotted Miriam. "And lady! Well done!"

Vyder came to a stop beside Tork. The King's Own Commander dropped to one knee. "Your grace, we have bested the Huronian Army. They are routed. Some still remain in the city, but we'll flush them out over the coming days."

Vyder remained on his feet, refusing to kneel, as did Rafe and Miriam.

"Excellent work! I had no doubt. Stand, man, stand."

Tork returned to his feet.

"Losses?"

"Our Army fought hard. Their number have been decimated. Perhaps one quarter are fit to fight. As for my King's Own, I have maybe three hundred left alive of the original two thousand."

The king chuckled. "*Your* King's Own."

Silence filled the throne room. Vyder glanced across at Tork and realised the commander of the King's Own was struggling with his anger.

"Yes, your grace," Tork spoke. "*My* King's Own. Forgive me but I did not see you leading them on the field of battle."

The monarch's mouth drew into a thin line and he frowned, anger glittering in his eyes. "What did you just say to me?"

"Watch yourself, Tork, take care how you answer!" Prichard said as the group of guards made entrance to the throne room.

Tork took a step forward and stared straight into King George's eyes. "You were not there on the battlefield." He looked over one shoulder and then the other, gesturing at the room around him. "You remained here, locked safely away while your soldiers fought to protect their city, their families and their homes." His hands dropped to his sides and his piercing glare returned to the king. "Many of your soldiers died carrying out their duty, and thousands of your citizens were put to the sword. I know not whether my own family have survived yet."

King George shrugged. "We won the battle, it is an acceptable loss of life as far as I'm concerned."

Vyder switched to the Highland language. "There's going to be a fight. Be ready."

The berserker's eyes grew wide and a large grin split his beard to reveal blood-stained teeth beyond. The Highlander's hand dropped to the pommel of his sheathed sword. "Oh, aye?"

"Miriam, you can fight if you want," he muttered. "But I suggest you wander over to the far side of the table. That blunderbuss is a good weapon, but here where Rafe and I will be amongst the enemy, it has just as much chance of wounding or killing us as it does anyone else."

The woman nodded and walked away.

Focusing on King George, Vyder strode forward a few steps and glared at the monarch.

"And I suppose you want payment for services rendered?" the king asked. "When I see that my son survived the fighting, then I shall pay you and not—"

He pointed at the monarch. "I couldn't give a shit about my payment. You are a bloody coward!"

Vyder heard a slight inhalation of breath from Tork beside him. He cared not. He was willing to voice what the Wendurlund officer was thinking. "Your son is twice the man you'll ever be!" Vyder gestured at the throne. "And he should be sat on that throne, not you. You gave it up when you ran and hid."

"That is sedition!" roared Prichard. "Guards, seize the Highlander! You'll hang for that!"

Vyder spun around. "I voice only the truth! You guards are as much cowards as your king."

"Take him dead or alive!" King George boomed. "Preferably dead."

"We fight!" Vyder shouted in the Highland tongue.

Rafe's sword appeared in his hand and the berserker darted amongst the advancing guardsmen with an incomprehensible bellow of rage. Vyder ran at the group, unsheathing his blade. He ducked under Prichard's attack and cut the man's head free of his body. The guard was dead before he hit the floor. Blood geysered from the wound, spilling across and soaking into the pristine carpet.

Rafe had already downed two soldiers. Saigh sprinted at another guardsmen and toppled him to the floor where Rafe's sword skewered his throat. Vyder's sharp steel cut deep into the last man's gut. He stepped back and kicked the dying guard off his blade and turned back to King George. He levelled his sword at the monarch. Blood tripping from the steel. "I should kill you as well. But for Prince Henry I shall not cut the life from your worthless body."

The monarch glared at Tork. "Are you going to let this man speak to your king like this?"

Tork turned on his heel, ignored the king and strode away.

"Commander Tork! Return to me at once!"

Vyder sheathed his weapon and advanced on the monarch. The king's tongue darted between his lips, eyes wide like some doe. "I'll have you relieved of your command!"

"Do the right thing, King George," Vyder growled. "Relinquish your crown. You're not fit to fill the position it signifies. It is time for Prince Henry to become monarch."

"Do not speak to me of affairs of the palace, you savage!"

Rafe whose blade had not yet been sheathed sauntered up beside Vyder. "What does the pathetic king say, lord?"

"He won't give up his throne to Henry."

Rafe's laughter boomed, full of life and humour. "As if he had a choice." He stepped within inches of the monarch and glared at him. "As if you have a choice!" he roared in the Highland tongue. King George attempted to step away and ended up falling backwards into the chair behind him.

The berserker thrust his sword into its scabbard and turned his attention back to Vyder. "He makes a good point. I'm tired. I'm going to sit down, too."

Miriam pushed in beside Vyder. "How dare you sit there in this protected palace while your people died and your city burned. You are a pathetic excuse for a man! I can't count the amount of times I was almost killed. Had it not been for Vyder, I would have been raped!" She was red in the face, her eyes wide with fury. She whirled to take in the long table. "And all the while you filled yourself with fancy food and wine to pass the time! You're a *despicable* man. You are no king of mine."

Rafe moved to the nearby long table and sat on the closest chair. He poured himself a cup of wine and picked at some of the less rotten fruit. Distant shouts echoed from outside but Vyder couldn't hear the words that were spoken.

Henry cantered into the square, Ahitika at his side. "Gods," he muttered casting his eye over the cannons and the artillery gunners who lay dead near the massive weapons. It was clear they'd made their last stand and gave an incredible account of themselves. A formation of King's Own stood nearby. He turned and approached them.

"Prince Henry!" one of them called. "It is good to see you alive!"

"Likewise. Hell of a fight!" He scanned their number. "Where are the rest of you?"

The man pushed his warhorse forward a pace and held out a hand. "This is all that remains of us, sire."

"By the gods," he whispered. "I'm sorry to see that."

"Not your fault, sire. Each one of our brothers killed at least ten Huronian soldiers before they died, if not more."

Sadness washed over him; the elite unit had been all but decimated.

"Prince Henry!" a familiar voice shouted from behind him.

He twisted in the saddle and saw Commander Tork striding towards him. "Tork, it is good to see you!"

The warrior stopped beside him and grinned up at the prince. "Likewise." He offered a cursory point behind him at the palace. "Your father awaits your arrival. He is none the happier for seeing me."

"That was to be my next stop. Why is that?"

"It appears he doesn't like home truths, sire." Tork patted Henry's horse and then moved past. "I'll speak with you later, my prince."

Henry grunted. He could only imagine the conversation that had taken place. Commander Tork was not a man to mince his words and would not have been pleased the king had remained in hiding while his city had burned. "I look forward to it."

He turned his mount away and cantered towards the palace. Henry stopped at the base of the long climb and tied the reins of his horse to a rail. Or at least one of the few that had survived the battle. Ahitika did likewise.

He negotiated the stairs and strode into the throne room. The first man he noticed was the Highland berserker sat at the table chewing idly on an apple. Rafe was his name from memory. He looked worse for wear. Blood stained his beard and multiple wounds littered his chest and arms. The table itself obscured his stomach from view, but if he was in any state like Byfros, Henry bet there were wounds there as well. His skin was bleached a sickening white, dark circles adorned the skin below both eyes. The warrior glanced up at his arrival and offered a single nod.

Vyder towered over his father who sat in a chair against the far side of the room. A woman stood nearby glaring at the king. Henry stopped and his hand instinctively snaked around the pommel of his sword. "What the bloody hell is the meaning of this?" he roared, looking over the group of slaughtered guardsmen on the carpeted floor between he and his father.

The Highlander turned and a look of fury melted away to be replaced with genuine welcome. "Prince Henry!"

The hound bounded to him and licked his hand and then went to Ahitika for a pat. She knelt down and rubbed Saigh's face. He looked from the dead guards to Vyder and back again.

"There was a misunderstanding, Henry. It was regretful, but alas, had we not defended ourselves, Rafe and I would have been killed ourselves."

Henry approached his father and held out a sack. He untied it and emptied the contents. King Fillip's head hit the carpet, bounced once and came to rest on one cheek, his dead eyes staring at King George's boots. His father leapt to his feet, a look of disgust etched across his face.

He'd never seen his father display behaviour like that. "Father? It is King Fillip. He's dead. Bested by Ahitika."

"You've cut the hair from his head!"

Henry pointed at Ahitika's pouch. "Ahitika took his scalp. This means she will be known amongst the Kalote people as one of the tribe's mightiest warriors."

"Barbaric!" the king whispered.

"What the bloody hell is wrong with you, Father? I don't remember you ever being like this."

"Perhaps you didn't know your father as well as you might have thought, young prince," Vyder said. "War has a way of revealing once boisterous, mighty men for the mice they actually are."

The monarch took a pace toward Vyder and flinched when the decapitated head nudged one of his boots. "Be gone, Highlander!" although his voice did not command the authority the words required.

Vyder held out his hands and chuckled. "Very well, I shall retire."

"You should be ashamed of yourself," Miriam offered as a parting shot before following Vyder.

He turned and walked to Rafe. The berserker sat at the long table, head resting on the expensive wood, wine goblet still clutched in a hand.

"Wine gone to your head, Rafe?" he smiled. He placed a hand on the warrior's broad back. "It is time to leave, my friend." He nudged the berserker. "Rafe?" He shoved the warrior. "Rafe, wake up." Vyder moved closer so as to better check on the man. It was then he noticed Rafe was not breathing.

Rafe, the berserker, his friend and chief of Clan Waterborne was dead. Vyder placed a hand on his shoulder and knelt beside the dead Highlander.

"Goodbye, my friend," Vyder whispered. "They shall write sagas about you."

XV

Vyder, assisted by Miriam and another Highlander he had called to help, carried Rafe's body from the palace. A sword thumping against a shield drifted from the waiting Highlanders below. Then an axe joined the beat, then a spear added its song. With each footstep the rhythm grew in volume, until the beat drowned out all else. Clan Waterborne shouted their war cry and it was taken up by other clans until the whole Highland Army was chanting the war cry of Clan Waterborne. They reached the square where the gunners had made their last stand and gently laid Rafe upon the ground. Saigh licked Rafe's face.

Vyder touched the hound's back and rubbed the soft fur. "Aye, lass, he has walked the Frost River." She looked at him and whined, then sat on his boot. He rested a hand on her head.

Little brother?

Vyder stared at the huge spider upon which Endessa sat. *I wondered when I'd hear from you, my friend. Thank you for your help, Gorgoroth. We could not have done it without you.*

No, I doubt you could have. It is time, now, for the spiders to return to their homes.

Vyder held up his hands and finally the din died down. "You have all fought hard to help the people of Lisfort. But it is time now to dismount the spiders. I'm sure some of you will be relieved by that!"

"Damn right, lord," a Highlander called from somewhere mid ranks.

Others climbed down from their eight-legged steeds and patted them, offering soft words of thanks in the highland language. Some nodded at the arachnids before walking away. One man bowed before the spider which had carried him into battle.

The spider as large as a house led the other arachnids away and they disappeared, heading towards the west and their home in the Waning Wood.

When they are home and safe, I shall return to you, brother.

Aye, Gorgoroth.

Endessa limped to where Vyder stood. She grinned at him. "And how do you fair, Vyder?"

"I'm tired, exhausted in fact."

She stepped closer and appraised him. "And terribly sad, I see."

"Aye," he whispered. "I led my Highlanders to their deaths. Hundreds upon hundreds of them."

She shrugged. "And yet any one of them could have turned away and left you at any time. But they didn't. Not a single man or woman. They all followed you here and fought alongside you."

"True, but that does nothing to absolve the bitter taste in my mouth, nor the guilt in my soul."

She chuckled. "That is for you to resolve. You will, or you won't. But at least you brought the weak king's son back to him as promised. You protected Lisfort as best you could and stopped a mad king from destroying the land like some spreading consumption."

"He *is* weak, *and* a coward."

The witch spat on the ground. "I could have told you that at the beginning. Had he been a warrior king, you would have been without a job. Any other king, or queen for that matter, would have gathered their household troops, perhaps even their entire army and marched into enemy lands to retrieve their child." She sneered and gestured at the palace nearby. "Not him, though."

Vyder nodded.

Miriam stepped forward. "Thank you for all your help, Endessa. I'll never forget it," she said, hugging the old woman.

Endessa smiled. "You are welcome, Miriam. It was my pleasure, but I fear I did more damage than good in bringing Gorgoroth into this whole mess. But what is... is."

She released Miriam and stepped back. "It is time for me to take my leave and return to my forest. We must rejuvenate what survives. I shall see you both again one day."

They offered their thanks to the witch as she left, but Endessa ignored them. The old woman limped around a corner and disappeared from sight.

It was near midnight as Vyder lay on his bed staring at the ceiling when he felt suddenly faint and breathless. He and Miriam had searched the entire house for Huronian soldiers before locking every door and cleaning the place up.

I am back.

Took your time.

I am in no rush, my friend.

How is the forest?

In pain, Vyder. She has been greatly damaged but is not beyond repair. Agogathoth, myself and others of our ilk have a lot of work to do. It will take many years.

I'm sorry to hear that.

It is not your concern, little brother. Sleep now, you need it.

Over the following days, the remnants of the Wendurlund army, spearheaded by the King's Own, spread across Lisfort and flushed hiding Huronian soldiers out of every house, alleyway or barn. No quarter was given and no mercy spared. King Fillip's head was placed on a spike at the eastern gate facing out towards the kingdom of Huron – the message blunt and brutal.

The bodies of the dead, both Wendurlund and Huronian, were carried far out of Lisfort on an endless

244

convey of wagons. The Huronian dead were stripped of their weapons and clothes, stacked unceremoniously in a giant pile of rotting flesh and burnt.

The corpses of the Wendurlund people, both civilian and soldier, were treated with more reverence. They were offered a mass funeral led by priests and overseen by Henry, and which many of the survivors of the siege of Lisfort attended.

The stink of burning flesh was still assaulting Henry's nose when he and Ahitika arrived at the entrance to the King's Own barracks. Two mounted warriors stood guard over the gate barring entrance to all but those allowed to attend the funeral of the fallen horse warriors. Each soldier carried an unsheathed musket, buttstock resting on their thigh, barrel pointing to the sky.

They spotted Henry and nodded at him. "Sire," they said in unison. They shifted their focus to Ahitika and offered her a greeting as well.

The regiment's graveyard was a hive of activity as men worked in teams to dig graves. Gone was the armour and weapons. The horses were in their stables where, no doubt, they'd been washed, brushed, watered and fed.

He spotted Commander Tork and made his way over. The officer was stood chest deep in one grave using a pick to break free clumps of dirt. His hair was plastered to his head and face. Sweat drenched his shirt. He glanced up, breathless. "Henry!" he managed. "I need a break." He climbed out of the grave and another soldier leapt in with a spade to clear the dirt Tork had broken free.

Henry shook the hand of the King's Own. "How goes it, Tork?"

The commander took a swig from a leather bladder and wiped his mouth with the back of a hand. "Tired. This is bloody hard work. I'd prefer to fight I think!" he grinned. Tork looked at Ahitika. "And how are you, young lady? Do you still carry the bastard king's scalp?"

She chuckled and patted the pouch at her hip. "I not let it out of sight."

Tork drank again. "Good!" he said after he'd had his fill.

Henry noticed the small number of Huronian cavalrymen who'd fought beside Rone were also present, they seemed to have been taken in as members of the unit. They worked tirelessly alongside their Wendurlund comrades.

"Let us help, Tork," said Henry.

The officer pointed towards a few shovels and picks leaned up against a nearby building. "Of course!"

Henry took a pick and Ahitika a shovel, then they went to the furthest grave where only two soldiers were working as a team to dig the grave. It was hard work, but somehow refreshing to be contributing to assist a unit that had been so instrumental in carrying him to freedom. Henry grunted as he brought the pick down into the earth. *Gods that feels like a lifetime ago now.* The King's Own had also had such an influence on the successful defeat of the Huronian Army. For such a tiny force, they were an immensely powerful unit. They treated him with respect, but not as a royal, more like one of their own.

He felt a tap on the back and a warrior thrust a water bladder at him. "Here, drink."

Henry pulled himself out of the grave and took the offer, drinking deep. Ahitika leapt in, landing lightly at the bottom of the rectangular hole to dig out the spoil. They continued in that way for hour upon dogged hour, moving from one grave to the next until the task was complete. Then tired, covered in sweat, dirt and blisters, they laid their dead to rest.

The remnants of the King's Own stood together in the regiment's graveyard in silence. All but a light breeze moved across them.

Tork stood before the group. "Our brothers are gone, now. Departed for a better place and their duty done forever. Their mission is complete. We'll never forget them. Goodbye, warrior brothers, we'll see you again someday."

A soldier lifted a bugle to his lips and played the last post, the haunting tune echoing around the graveyard, singing one final farewell to the warriors who'd laid down their lives to protect their home and families. The tune drifted to silence and the soft flap of a nearby flag imbued to life by the gentle breeze was the only noise across the area.

The King's Own might have lost the majority of their number in combat and although only a mere three hundred survived to fight another day, Henry could see they were far from broken. He knew those three hundred would ride out into combat again at that moment if required. Defeat hadn't, at any point, entered their thinking.

"Until we meet again!" Tork called.

"Until we meet again," the throng of warriors repeated in quiet, reverent voices.

"Your duty is done, brothers!" Tork's voice broke.

Henry bowed his head and closed his eyes. He swallowed, but the lump in his throat remained.

Later that evening, long after nightfall, he and Ahitika were invited to attend the funeral of the fallen Highlanders. They cantered out the northern gate and travelled the half hour to reach the area allocated for the ceremony to honour the dead. Vyder had requested a northern site so as the deceased were facing the direction of their homes. The Shadolian Highlands.

"Henry!" Vyder turned as they approached. "I wasn't sure whether you'd be coming."

Henry noticed Vyder once again sported a bright, shining blue eye. He hadn't seen the Highland warlord sport that strange eye for a long time and wondered what it meant. The Highlander stared at Ahitika. "And my partner in crime!" he cried. "You might be small, lass, but you've the heart of a lioness."

Ahitika grinned and leapt from the horse's saddle, approached Vyder and hugged him. Henry stepped down from the horse and tied both mounts loosely to a nearby tree. Then he removed their saddles and placed them on the far side of the tree.

He strode to Vyder and shook his hand. Saigh pushed her nose into his thigh then looked up at him. He patted the hound and squatted. "And how have you been, mighty war hound?" he whispered, stroking her face. She wagged her tail and planted a wet tongue on his forehead. Rising, he looked past the Highland warlord. The Shadolian dead had been placed in a neat row where they'd be doused in oil. In the distance, a brazier burned in preparation.

"You look like shit, Henry," Vyder said with a chuckle. "And you stink like burning flesh, sweat and fresh soil. What the hell have you been doing?"

Henry nodded. "Just came from the King's Own funeral."

"Aye," Vyder said. "A more stoic bunch of soldiers I've never seen. They took a heavy loss."

Henry gestured towards where the dead lay. "So did the Highlanders, my friend. But we wouldn't be stood here right now were you and your Great Highland Army not here. We would have failed in our defence of Lisfort."

"Aye," Vyder whispered, following Henry's hand to look upon his deceased people. "I led my people to be butchered."

Henry placed a hand on the giant Highlander's arm. "You led your people to defend a neighbouring kingdom in crisis. And had we fallen, it wouldn't have been long before the Huronians would be looking to the north. Your warriors were fighting to protect our homes and people as much as they were their own."

Vyder looked back at the prince and smiled. "You have a way with words, young prince." He slapped Henry on the back and put an arm around both he and Ahitika. "Come!"

There was one lifeless warrior who'd been placed separate to the others, shield placed over his chest and right hand holding his sword.

"Rafe," he whispered.

Vyder smiled, although his eyes remained sad. "Yes, that is Rafe. He saved my life more times than I care to remember."

The berserker displayed horrific wounds all over his body. It seemed he finally succumbed to them at some point. *Gods he must have been a bloody monster in battle. Near unstoppable.*

Vyder bellowed something in the Highland tongue and a roar went up from the Highlanders standing nearby. They beat weapons on shields in a rhythm. One woman took the torch, held it to the flames licking inside the brazier and waited for the blaze to catch on the oil-soaked head. Once the torch was alight, she approached the far end of the row of Highland dead and held the torch until fire rippled across the bodies of the deceased. She then set to flame Rafe's body.

Each of the fallen warriors, both men and women, held their swords and shields in their hands. He noticed that in some instances where this wasn't possible, the shield and chosen weapon of the individual were tied to their arms. Henry knew enough about the Highland culture to know that the Shadolians believed they'd need them in the afterlife.

The sound of weapon on shield grew in intensity and bagpipes blared into life. Highlanders sung together, their voices deep.

"It is the song of the fallen," Vyder said quietly by way of explanation, his eyes never leaving the flames licking upon the bodies. "This is the old way. We inter the fallen into the keeping of the gods."

Henry nodded his understanding but remained silent. The breath caught in the back of his throat. For one fleeting moment he swore he'd seen a face formed inside one large flame which had flicked up amongst the middle of the fallen bodies. It had looked inhuman yet sad, nevertheless.

Ahitika touched his arm. "That was the flame demon who helped us," she whispered where the face had appeared. *So, she saw it too!*

The fire licked higher, sending flames towering thirty feet into the sky. A deep blast came from the centre of the ceremony and sparks flew in all directions. Then the face was there again. The pitch-black eyes focused on Henry.

"Thank you," he whispered. "Thank you for your help."

You are welcome, little prince. It is my pleasure to be here with these great warriors.

Prickles travelled down his back. Vyder looked at Henry, that blue eye boring into him. The Highlander smiled and looked back at the blaze again.

Miriam stood on makeshift wooden battlements that had been erected especially for the royal ceremony. The multi-tiered constructions were massive, some fifty feet high and hundreds of feet long, allowing many thousands of people to watch the progress of the day below. It seemed impossible that only three weeks had passed since the defeat of the Huronian horde. Palace Green, still a huge patch of dirt from the battle, had been cleared of the cannons which had provided the last bastion of defence for not only the palace, but the city. Gun Commander Humber's face floated in her mind. Sadness lanced her and the view of the palace disappeared as she closed her eyes. *Those men saved my life. I owe them everything.*

She opened her eyes and she admired the neat ranks of soldiers arrayed in front of where King George languished on a large dais. Near him stood Prince Henry and his Kalote woman. The two men were worlds apart. King George wore shining, bright silver armour that had probably never seen a nick or dent. Henry, tall and powerful, stood dressed in a neat white shirt, black pants and a green cloak he wore pinned at his right shoulder. He had his hair tied at the nape, a sword was sheathed at his hip. He looked half Wendurlund prince and half Highland warrior.

The Kalote woman wore her traditional tribal clothes, her black hair hung neatly behind her and her bow was slung over her shoulder, quiver at her hip. Miriam immediately liked her, even though she'd never spent much time with the woman. *She will be good for Prince Henry.*

The Wendurlund soldiers took the lion's share of the Palace Green. They stood eight ranks deep and in perfect lines, their armour and weapons glinting in the sun. At the front right of the formation stood nine cannons evenly spaced, no artillerymen stood with the giant weapons an even more stark reminder that not a single gunner had survived the fighting. They had died to a man beside their weapons. The ramrods lay on the ground, reversed. On the far left of the field were arrayed the King's Own, sat upon their powerful warhorses. At the rear of the formation was a tiny number of soldiers dressed in a uniform foreign to Miriam. *They look almost like Huronian soldiers.*

The square allocated to their formation was monstrous and contained mainly open space. The three hundred warriors sat in perfect, neat lines at the front right of the open square.

"Granddad, who are they?" a boy's voice whispered from nearby.

Miriam turned to see the boy, who was tugging on an old man's shirt.

"Those are the King's Own, my lad. There are only a few hundred left alive."

"Why are they taking up so much space?"

The older man turned to the boy and lifted him into his arms, then sat him upon his shoulders. He pointed at the horse warriors. "That square is the size needed to fill the formation of a full King's Own compliment. The open space surrounding those few soldiers shows how many died in the fighting."

"Did they start the war, Grandad?"

The old man chuckled. "So many questions, my boy. No," his hand dropped to his side. "The King's Own don't start wars. They win them."

At the rear of the lines of Wendurlund soldiers were the Highlanders. They stood in a blob. Miriam searched their number and her eyes finally rested upon the tall figure of Vyder at the centre. Beside him sat the ever-loyal Saigh. Unlike the clean looking soldiers of the Wendurlund Army, the Highlanders were tall, bearded, broad-shouldered and their hair was worn long and ragged. Tartan cloaks of varying colours adorned their shoulders.

She wanted to call out to him, but knew the distance was too great. He'd never be able to hear her.

Vyder idly patted Saigh's head and listened to King George drone on and on about how thankful he was for the courage of the Army and how they had assuaged a great defeat. All around him Highlanders talked softly to one another. One chuckled and another started mimicking the king with subtle gestures of his hands. Vyder smiled. He had no respect for the monarch standing up on the dais before them. He hadn't raised a hand to help defend his kingdom or people. Why then should he be offered respect? Respect was earned, not demanded. Especially where the Highlanders were concerned.

Exhaustion continued to rail his body, he grew weaker by the day and even a small walk now made him short of breath. Soon he would need to sit, but he refused to do so, especially when his countrymen and women stood tall around him. Saigh licked his hand and he glanced down to see her staring up at him, her tail wagging slowly.

King George's voice grew higher pitched as he spoke and Vyder lost concentration on the words. The world dimmed a little.

"Vyder," a woman's distant voice called. "Vyder!"

His heartbeat quickened. "Verone?" He whirled, eyes wide. "Verone!"

The king came back into view and he noticed Highlanders all around staring at him. "What's that you say, lord?" Hyglak appeared beside him and held his arm.

"Nothing, my friend. I thought I heard something."

Hyglak squinted at him. "You look like shit, Vyder. Are you sure you are well?"

He nodded and stared back up at King George who continued to waffle on, although this time Vyder was oblivious to the words.

We must go soon, little brother.

I know, Gorgoroth.

Polite applause from the crowd on the makeshift battlements behind them drifted around the area and Vyder realised the king had finished speaking. Prince Henry stepped forward and a roar exploded from within the Highland ranks. Warriors held swords or spears above their heads and shouted their support of the young warrior. Vyder grinned, unsheathed his blade and thrust it towards the sky, lending his voice to the raucous. Enthusiastic claps and cheers from the crowd joined them. Prince Henry held out his hands and the noise slowly subsided to silence.

The world dimmed and Vyder stumbled, almost losing the grip on his weapon. "Vyder!" Verone called for him. "Come to me, my love."

It is time, Vyder.

Vyder sheathed his sword and then felt his legs give way beneath him. He sat heavily on the floor and groaned.

"Lord!" Hyglak shouted. "Give him room!" the warrior yelled, pushing Highlanders away. He knelt beside

Vyder. "Lord!"

An ice wind whipped his hair away from his face and his ears were frozen. He squinted against the chill wind and stumbled forward on the Frost River. His feet slid from beneath him, but a powerful hand grasped his shoulder and righted his balance. He noticed Gorgoroth strode beside him. The nature spirit was just as huge as he remembered, bright, piercing blue eyes staring down at him from within a face of branches, tendrils and vines.

That was some adventure, brother!

"Aye!" he shouted, the wind whipping the words from his mouth.

We must do it again sometime.

Lord! The word boomed around the heavens, deafening him and warmth flooded his soul. He opened his eyes to stare into the face of Hyglak. The man looked worried.

"Lord! Are you well? What is happening?"

"Everything is fine, my friend." He patted the warrior's arm and then unpinned the multi-tartan cloak depicting the colours of every clan of the Shadolian Highlands and passed it to the man. "You are now Warlord of the Highlands. You have earned it."

"But I have no right to—"

"You have every right!"

"You are our lord, Vyder. You are the Warlord of the Shadolian Highlands."

He pushed the cloak into Hyglak's hand. "Not anymore, my friend. My time," the world dimmed, "is at an end."

Blizzard-like winds assaulted his clothes, skin and bones. He shivered against the bitter cold. His hands were numb, lips stiff and dry. Another step onto the Frost River, then another.

You are in pain, little brother. Let me help you.

A warm cocoon surrounded him and he breathed a sigh of relief.

Miriam smiled as she listened to Henry speak, his powerful voice projected over the area and not a sound was uttered from within the crowd. They were mesmerised by the young prince. Her attention was broken by a commotion amongst the Highlanders. The warriors stood in a large circle staring inward at two men. One knelt beside the other, holding him up in a seated position.

"Vyder!" she screamed as realisation dawned on her. "Vyder!"

She pushed her way through the crowd, ignoring curses and finally made it to the ground. Miriam ducked down a side street, ignored the call to halt by a guard and ran as fast as she was able towards the Palace Green.

"No, Vyder. Not here, not now!" she rasped between breaths.

Several more steps across the river and the bank from which they had departed was no longer visible. It had fallen victim to the freezing ice particles being blown across the icy surface. Neither had the bank to which they advanced made itself known to them. They were surrounded by a sea of ice and freezing wind. The warmth that surrounded Vyder was a welcome relief. Gorgoroth's massive hand, tree trunks for fingers hovered over his head, blasting warmth down around him.

You little ones don't like the cold much.

"Nice of you to notice, Gorgoroth. Thank you for your help, my friend."

"Vyder," Verone's voice pierced the icy winds.

"Verone! I'm here, sweetheart."

"I can hear you. Come to me."

Miriam shot a glance over her shoulder and noticed three guards giving chase. They were gaining on her fast.

"I said halt!" one roared.

She ignored them and pressed on, her legs aching, lungs burning. Palace Green appeared around the next corner and she headed straight towards the throng of Highland warriors.

"Let me through!" she yelled between breaths. "Make way!"

The Highlanders watched her approach with curiosity but stepped aside to let her through. They knew Miriam was a friend to Vyder.

"Please don't let the guards through," she yelled over her shoulder as she passed through the lines.

They closed ranks behind her and locked shields.

Breathless, she skidded to a halt beside Vyder and knelt on the other side of him. The warrior who was supporting the man who had once been her master looked at her and nodded. His eyes sad.

Vyder was pale beyond belief. As pale as he'd been when she had first reached him after he'd been mortally wounded so long ago. She grabbed his shoulder and shook.

The far bank was a dark smudge against the snowstorm. The blurred figure of a person stood at the edge. "Vyder!"

Vyder! A new voice boomed from the heavens and air

exploded into his lungs. He took a deep breath and his eye lids peeled apart. Miriam hovered over him. Beyond her reaching high into the sky were the Shadolian Highlands, their peaks topped white with snow. They looked regal, powerful and dangerous.

He looked back at Miriam and smiled. "You are here," he whispered. Vyder reached into his shirt pocket and took out a piece of paper and pushed it into her hand. "Everything I own is now yours. The house, gold, Storm and Saigh. Everything."

Miriam burst into tears. "It's not about that, Vyder." She pulled him into a hug. "Thank you for everything, I wouldn't be here if not for you." She stroked his face. "Travel safely, Vyder. I'll never forget you."

"Miriam," he said, pulling away. He grinned at her and pointed over her shoulder. "Do you see the Highlands?"

She turned to follow his finger and saw only Highland warriors watching them. They all knelt on one knee shields flat on the ground and weapons too. She wiped her eyes. "Yes," she said.

"Miriam," he continued to point. "The Shadolian Highlands. So beautiful." His hand dropped to the ground and he looked at her. "I'm going home, Miriam."

Vyder's eyes closed with lethargic lack of speed. "I'm going home."

Vyder ran across the Frost River and into Verone's arms. Colour returned to the world and he buried his face into his wife's hair, smelling the peach perfume. It'd been so long since he'd smelt that scent.

"At last," he said holding her close. "I am here."

She pulled him tight and didn't let go.

I shall leave you, brother. I must help Endessa and the others to mend our home. I might see you again one day, little human.

Vyder pulled away from Verone but kept an arm around her. He smiled at the towering nature spirit and smiled. "Perhaps, my friend."

A roar exploded around her from soldiers and crowd alike and she jolted with the sudden noise. She stood, alongside the Highlanders around her. Like her, they were silent. Saddened by the loss of Vyder. She hesitated, looking around to see what had caused the crowd to erupt so. Her eyes came to rest upon the dais. Henry stood with head bowed before his father, who placed his own crown upon Henry's head.

"Long live the king!" the shout was taken up and spread across the Palace Green in a thunderous roar.

The young prince was a prince no longer.

Acknowledgement

Due to the Consent Order as part of our divorce proceedings, I must, by law, acknowledge the help and support of my former wife Simone McArdle.

I'd like to acknowledge the people in my life who have stood with me and offered support and assistance. First and foremost, Deb and Jorge, you both inspire me to be a better man and I am fuller and happier for having you in my life. Mum, Dad, Ian, Ros, Leah and Brianna, after 16 years we have finally come back together again as a family unit and I love it! Woodsy and Sarah, Lisa and Brad, Lee and Lynsey, you have all helped me probably more than you know, and were it not for your kindness and support, Vyder would never have finished his mission.

To the tiny army of avid readers beside me, it's taken far longer than my other books, but without you, it would have taken twice as long to write. So, thanks so much for your patience and waiting with me.

Thanks so much for reading, I hope you enjoyed the adventure! If you'd like to see what else I've written, please scan the QR code below: